Jeffrey Caine is the author c <!-- barcode: KU-178-596 --> *My Boy* and *The Cold Room*. He is married, with two daughters, and lives in Shropshire.

JEFFREY CAINE

Heathcliff

Grafton
An Imprint of HarperCollinsPublishers

Grafton
An Imprint of HarperCollins*Publishers*
77–85 Fulham Palace Road,
Hammersmith, London W6 8JB

Published by Grafton 1993
9 8 7 6 5 4 3 2 1

First published in Great Britain by
W. H. Allen & Co. Ltd 1977

ISBN 0 00 647604 X

Set in Times

Printed and bound in Great Britain by
Cox & Wyman Ltd, Reading, Berkshire

To Fay Caine and Beryl Williams, with love

1

1803. – It is now almost five months since my brief and not signally happy tenancy of Thrushcross Grange in Yorkshire was concluded; nor, I own, was I ever more relieved than when I finally quitted those bleak, moors and their wild, clannish inhabitants for the refined atmosphere of London. I did so without any expectation that I would hear further of Earnshaws or Lintons (those being the predominant family names in that far-flung quarter), whose strange history was told to me during an indisposition by my housekeeper, Mrs Dean. I had taken cold early in my sojourn, after an ill-judged expedition to my landlord's wintry abode, climatic extremities necessitating my return through waist-deep snowdrifts. So I was for a time confined to my bed, where, wanting diversion, I prevailed upon the good Mrs Dean to entertain me with a history. What I got from that excellent woman was a tale that has yet to be published, though literary friends who have read my manuscript assure me that it would not want for readers. The tale's protagonist, however, might cause offence to readers of sensibility for his monstrous nature and lowly origins (he was a gipsy foundling) could be said to detract from his tragic stature; and if Mr Heathcliff is not a tragic hero in the Greek mould, he is nothing. I have been prevented also from publishing by a lack of information concerning the means by which he acquired his wealth and education, since at the heart of the story is a disappearance of some three years by its youthful hero, a caesura which, like the flaw in the gem, renders the whole imperfect.

But whatever its shortcomings as art (and perhaps one-half of it I judge to be fiction), it was Mrs Dean's skilful narrative, combined happily with a kindly manner and the twin gifts of prodigious memory and lively imagination, that saved me from certain death by tedium during my stay in the north. Yet, as one does with entertainments, I had chosen to accommodate Heathcliff's story by modifying his character in my reflections, preferring to exercise the charity of one who has suffered at hands now still and who has been abused by lips now for ever silent; thus I had elected to suppose the man a deal less monstrous than in Mrs Dean's portrayal, and had succeeded in putting him from my mind and from my dreams.

My reader may imagine my feelings, then, upon receiving in my post a few mornings since a weighty packet bearing northern postal markings. Within I discovered a sheaf of papers, closely written on both sides and in an uncouth hand, whose decipherment would have taxed a member of the Antiquarian Society versed in hieroglyphical inscriptions; this together with a scarcely more comprehensible missive from the good matron herself.

For the most part Mrs Dean's letter was such as one might expect a better-educated woman of her class to write, its content being largely an account of domestic affairs at Thrushcross Grange during these last months. Thus I was informed (though I will not trouble my reader with these passages) that events in Gimmerton parish have taken place according to plan, Joseph's Old Testament avenger having elected not to intervene with a timely thunderbolt; and that the impending marriage between the cousins Catherine Heathcliff and Hareton Earnshaw (the oaf whom at my last visit she was in the process of domesticating as one would a colt or dog made savage by excessively harsh training) is at last solemnized. Afterwards the household moved from

Wuthering Heights to the relative comfort of the Grange, where, Mrs Dean informs me, all are contentedly ensconced. A fair change indeed, was my reaction, and one I approve with all my heart. Mrs Dean's *raison d'écrire*, however, concerned not this removal but a discovery attendant upon its upheaval.

As you surmised, Mr Lockwood [she writes], the properties did indeed revert to their lawful owners on Mr Heathcliff's death, my mistress becoming entitled to the Grange and Mr Earnshaw (as I must now call him) to Wuthering Heights. Lawyer Green paid us a visit shortly after your departure and explained the position. As for my late master's personal property, it should have gone forfeit to the Crown, but letters were exchanged and only a token portion was asked for; the rest Mrs Earnshaw was to have, and since her father-in-law died a wealthy man, a fine dowry it made.

The day following the wedding my mistress surprised us all by insisting that we return to the Heights to 'fetch some last things'. All that was rightfully hers had not yet been removed, she claimed, and got into such a state about it that none of our entreaties could prevail on her to change her mind. Mr Earnshaw accompanied us, and after a walk that had the three of us almost starved (it was a bitter day, even for January), we arrived at the house. Joseph gave us for his greeting a snarl and an 'Ah know'd it, yah'd nivir stop a day at yonder hahs, Ah know'd,' before settling himself back in his fireside corner with his Bible.

'Is that Bible mine, Joseph?' Cathy wanted to know at once, approaching to examine the book.

Joseph drew it protectively to his breast, as if prepared to fight a host of demons in its defence. 'Nay,' he answered, 't'maister nivir oppen'd t'Blessed Book in all his wicked lahf. Nay, nur owned one norther. If yah want t'owd maister's, Aw sud think it's in Hathecliff's rahm if yah're noan feard un th' sperrits.'

'That would also have been my mother's Bible,' replied my young lady pensively. Then, 'Give me the key, Joseph,' she said with a determined set to her jaw that I knew of old. 'I will not see my lawful

9

property go by default to the dead, however dreadful their custodianship.'

Joseph morosely produced the key, stirring himself only enough to fish it from some lodging deep in his clothing, and steadfastly refused to leave his place by the fire 'to go poking abaht in Heathcliff's cham'er.' I would gladly have remained there with him, but my mistress had no desire to get herself dusty and required me to go along to do the rummaging. I contrived to hang back on the stair, though, appearing short of breath for the climb. I had no intention of being first in that room. Let its spirits launch their worst fury on those foolhardy enough to disturb their repose.

When I was satisfied that my master and mistress had entered Mr Heathcliff's bedchamber with impunity, I deemed it safe to go in myself. The cold struck me immediately. The room had not been heated since the death of its occupant, having stayed unlocked just long enough for the corpse to be removed. A thick layer of dust covered everything, which perturbed me, I must confess, more than Joseph's talk of 'sperrits'; I'd as soon have had a broom and dustpan with me then as a Bible. Miss Cathy (Mrs Earnshaw, I must call her now) turned up her fine nose at it too, sniffing and running her gloved fingers disdainfully over the surfaces.

'Nelly,' said she, 'see if you can find my mother's Testament. My dress will be ruined if I look.' There was much I could have said to that but I held my tongue, mindful of my mistress's temper, and slid back the sides of Mr Heathcliff's closet-bed. I half expected to be confronted again by his corpse, Mr Lockwood, for it was in this same bed that he died, and there that I discovered him with the rain on his face. But I remembered what you had told me, sir, that you had passed such a dreadful night there after reading Catherine Earnshaw's diary written in the blank spaces of a Testament, and reached across to the window ledge and felt around in its dust (it was too dark to see clearly). 'Bring out whatever you find, Nelly,' came Mrs Earnshaw's voice. I was about to call a tart reply when my fingers touched a pile of books, and, as I reached behind them to get a grip, something else, a thick bundle of papers between them and the window.

'I think I have it, miss,' I called, teasing out the papers. 'There is more than one volume here.' On impulse I tucked the papers under my apron and emerged holding only the books. I had resolved in that moment to enjoy my find at leisure before handing over to my petulant mistress the rest of her inheritance, whatever it might be. I felt sure I had found Heathcliff's will, though it did seem rather bulky for that unless he had God knows what property elsewhere. Will or not, I was determined that Miss Cathy should not have it yet. It would possibly do her character some good to be kept waiting.

Oh, Mr Lockwood, what a strange document it proved to be, as you will see for yourself. I wish I had not found it, or that having found it I had refrained from reading it. For this I did that same night in my room at Thrushcross Grange, where it kept me from my bed until an hour before dawn. Afterwards I was for burning the thing upon the kitchen fire for the torments it contained and the wickedness it described, and perhaps I should have done so. I have been plagued since by fearful dreams at night and in the day by vexation at what course I should take. It was only when I recalled your kind interest in our family's history that it occurred to me to send the letter to you (for a letter it is, though never sent). What you do with it afterwards, let that be your own decision. I am merely glad to be rid of the flaysome thing and have it out of reach of my bairns now that they are at last able to forget that man who so disturbed their lives.

Mrs Dean concluded her letter with a wish that I would visit the new household at Thrushcross Grange to see for myself what bliss follows the death of a tyrant: an expedition I may one day be disposed to undertake.

Now I once more turned my attention to the enclosure, certainly a voluminous set of papers, and one that would need to be interesting indeed to reward the labour of perusal. A letter, Mrs Dean had said. I leafed through a few of the brittle pages, thinking it unlikely that any of the laconic denizens of Wuthering Heights could have been responsible for such a Herculean epistle. Heathcliff least of all. Surely the good woman was in error, for if this was

11

a letter it was one without a date or a salutation. But as page succeeded unparagraphed page, and as my progress was arrested here by a phrase, there by an allusion, I realized that these writings could have had but one author. I had no sooner formed this opinion than it was confirmed by my arrival at the final, half-blank leaf; there, written with a bold flourish that God Almighty Himself might have envied, was the signature 'Heathcliff,' and a date – June, 1781.

A quick calculation told me that here was the missing portion of my housekeeper's story, for the letter must have been composed during the period of her hero's self-imposed exile. In this last assumption I was correct, but my supposition that I had in my hands the whole account was to prove unwarranted.

Mr Heathcliff's letter is given below. In transcribing it I have confined my amendments to those which are permitted an editor, namely grammatical and orthographic corrections – many such being required – and the occasional refashioning of a clumsy or otherwise unhappy expression. I have also added an explanatory note where I deemed it appropriate and have arranged the narrative into paragraphs and chapters to facilitate reading. The sentiments, however, remain those of my erstwhile landlord, though I alone must accept responsibility for their decipherment.

2

I have little time left and much to relate, and so will dispense with niceties. Expect no gentle lover's letter, Cathy, no drawing-room matter, for which I have neither the wit nor the gentility. Edgar Linton may tell you whether your bonnet warrants a ribbon this season – I write with a heart dry as powder only to share my pain with you, for I would not deprive you of what is rightfully yours. Before long I must pay our account in this life, but I ask no pity from you. Save that for yourself when you are required to answer in heaven; there must be one – there is assuredly a hell.

It is now above a year since you saw my face or heard my voice, and in all that time I doubt you have spared me a single thought; while I have thought so often of you, living with your image scorched into my brain, that I have no sense of separation from you. I can see you now, seated close by the fire in the Heights kitchen to read this, your fingers touching the paper I have touched, your brow corrugated with vexed surprise as you push back that wanton lock of hair from your face. Do you care where I am? Are you curious to know how I learned to write? You shall know it all soon. For the present you may picture me with my tongue protruding as I write, the pen gripped as though it were a plough-shaft; and since I would still plough a furrow sooner than write a sentence you must guess at the labour this costs me. Wring what pleasure you can from it. There will be little else here to amuse you.

Betrayers rarely see the consequences of their work. It requires a rare taste for torture. But you will see it all,

Cathy. I'll force you to watch. You were all I had in this world, and whatever kindness or compassion, whatever love I possessed, I gave to you. Others apportion their love, some to their parents, some to their friends, some to their god. I had no family, and you were my only friend and my only god. I gave you so much of my love that I had too little left for self-esteem, needing none as long as you esteemed me. Then, that wet summer's day more than a year since, you at last revealed what I meant to you. We'd quarrelled over Edgar Linton's visits – no other subject had ever divided us – and afterwards I overheard you telling Nelly that Linton had asked you to marry him. I heard you say that you loved him because he was handsome and young and rich, and that as his wife you would be the greatest woman of the neighbourhood. You said it would degrade you to marry me.

If you had fired a ball into my brain you could not have used a more perfect means for my annihilation – a sentence of death would have been kinder. I was more beast than man when I ran from Wuthering Heights that night. There was murder in me, a strange and savage potency for which I could find no expression. It was a cloudy, moonless night and I remember crossing the Blackhorse marsh in total darkness – scarcely a sane man's act – and laughing at my luck when the swamp failed to claim me. I would have drowned with equal joy. A storm was approaching – I had a beast's awareness of it – and in my madness I made for its centre, the wind burning my throat; as if there had been hot coals in my belly and I could, by fanning them, boil the very brain out of my skull.

In this fashion I must have run in a wide arc round Gimmerton, for eventually I found myself at the beck where our moor slopes down to Thrushcross park. I drank from it, not cupping the water in my hand but lying at full stretch to lap it direct, and it was numbing to my lips and tongue, underground cold, death cold. The air was warm, though, with the earthy smell of storm in it. And when, a while later, the first drops of rain fell I fancied that it was your movements I was hearing, the rustle of your skirts, light as rain in the tall grass. Had it been you, come to fetch me back, I would have forgiven you everything in an instant. But then I felt the rain sting my eyes, and I forgave you nothing.

As I lay on that moortop, the storm growing around me, I was suddenly a creature devoid of will. There seemed no course of action I could take, all options being equally fruitless and unattractive. Let the storm wash me away in the beck if it cared, as it washes away the bodies of drowned sheep. That even struck me as fitting: to be nothing, to have come from nowhere and lived as a stranger, finally to die alone, a nameless thing that perished one night in a storm. Lightning was already snatching at the hilltops and heavier drops began to spatter on my skin, warm as blood. It was strangely exhilarating to be contemplating my death, and to command it afforded a spiteful pleasure. Life had cheated me. Well, death would be an honest dealer. And I would rather have died by slow torture than trudge back to the Heights to your scorn and Hindley's. But when I tried to picture myself dead all I saw was the Blackhorse marsh closing over my head and instantly smoothing itself out again – we've seen it swallow a lamb that way. And that angered me, as much because nobody would exult as because nobody would grieve, and I felt there needed to be some response. *Would* you have grieved, Cathy? More than at the death of the lamb? Yet it was not any doubt I had about your grief that forced the notion out of my head, but a sudden strong sense of its wrongness – nothing moral, I assure you – just a feeling that the time was wrong as long as there was still anger and power enough in me to tear up a few acres of life and leave signs of my passage. Better, I thought, an act of pure destruction than no act at all. Better never to have existed than to leave no greater impression than a fly leaves on a pond. And at once I knew what for me was the most irresistible attraction. It was a vision of my enemies, your brother and your lover, lying in their own blood with gaping throats and staring eyes, with myself far removed and folk saying: 'Heathcliff's work' as on the morrow, beholding an uprooted tree, they would say: 'T'storm's work.' Their deaths should be my monument.

Almost lighthearted, I began the descent to the Grange, wet grass squeaking under my boots. And it seemed that my misplaced will flew to me out of the storm, having been there all along, pushing me, unseen.

It must have been close to midnight when I reached Thrushcross Grange. The storm was directly overhead, whipping me with my own saturated shirt as I hugged the glistening stonework of the house for shelter. I knew from experience what savage brutes the Lintons keep to defend their property, and from your descriptions that Skulker and his fellows are shut up in the kitchen at night, as the dogs are at the Heights. I also knew that Edgar Linton's chamber was on the far side of the house, directly above the library. It must have taken me fully half an hour to inch my way past the kitchen windows, anger and hate burning in my gullet like vomit as I took each measured step. Once I thought I heard a low growl from one of the dogs, but he might have made the sound in his sleep, or else the noise of the storm confused him. My prayer, though, was not for the brute's silence, but that I should find Edgar Linton's window unhasped. Let it be so and the puling wretch was as good as dead.

At last I found myself under the library window. I crouched there, awaiting the next flash of lightning, and when it came I used it for a lantern, springing to where its brilliance had shown me a handhold. My fingers fastened on the rough edge of a stone block, where the mortar had weathered away, my legs flailing against the slippery stonework, seeking purchase. Then my right foot found a crack just wide enough to support my weight momentarily, while I reached up and felt for a grip. As I did so my hand brushed, then grasped, a wide projection, which proved to be the ledge of Linton's window itself. It was a task to heave myself up there, but I managed to gain the wet ledge and balanced precariously on it while I set to examining the window. I was not surprised to find it closed – it would be unthinkable for a milk-blooded Linton to sleep with fresh air in his chamber, particularly during a thunderstorm – though in the dark I couldn't tell whether it was latched. I had to support myself entirely with one hand and pull at the thing with the other, the strain proving well-nigh intolerable, but it gave a little, and a few seconds later I was able to reach my hand inside and complete the operation. The hasp had been off.

His curtains were drawn too, and I nearly had a small china figure off the sill as I pulled them aside to crawl through. Otherwise there were no obstacles. A few steps brought me to Edgar Linton's bedside.

I had the strangest sensation, Cathy, standing over that motionless form in the gloom. I could scarcely hear his breathing for the raging storm outside, or see him, save when the lightning revealed him to me. Then I beheld the sleeping face of a child, all soft lines and gently fluttering eyelids. His hair, fine as yours but silver in that weird light, fell as if carefully arranged by a body-servant, half across his pillow and half across his cheek. There was something daunting about his unmanly beauty, which aroused in me feelings of repugnance and envy mixed. Those full, pink girl's lips of his seemed fit objects to be kissed, yet I longed to sink my teeth into them and rip them from his face in a bloody, ragged strip. His throat, too, caught my attention. White and flawless it

17

was, stretched there on the satin of his pillow. I reached into my pocket and drew out my penknife, thinking how easy it would be with one stroke of its blade across his bleached skin to let it all out of him like air from a punctured bladder – his beauty, his rank, his wealth, whatever attraction he held for you – all of it would gush out on the bedclothes in a thick, pulsing stream. You cannot know what a temptation that was for me or how close you came then to losing your precious Linton. In my mind's eye I could already see his startled-fawn's eyes open wide with horror at the prospect of his own pale blood; and I delighted that his last vision, as he ascended to whatever private heaven of silk and cushioned comfort such people inhabit, would be of me, of my grinning dark face, cheering him into oblivion.

Shall I tell you what saved him? No fear of consequences on my part, certainly. I'd gladly have danced a gallows jig for him. Not compassion. I would sooner spare a snared rabbit out of compassion, for at least I'd know the creature had none of your love. And what should have deterred me most, the thought of incurring your displeasure, was no deterrent at all – I wanted you to suffer, as I had suffered, the loss of the person you loved best. No, what saved him was just that which excited my loathing for him: the sight of that opulent setting, where he was heir-apparent to so much luxury, and of Linton himself sleeping snug and contented, with all his book-knowledge and fine speech and elegant manners wrapped protectively around him, his armour against fortune. Far from having too much, he had too little to satisfy me. Why should I settle for a paltry payment from Edgar Linton? He hadn't means enough to recompense me for my degradation. No, I would make his entire genteel world pay, the whole of it – for his offence and yours. That was the promise I made myself, solemnly, there in Linton's private chapel of privilege. To embark on a holy war against them all, all their kind, and in doing so to raise myself beyond their power. It made me proud. I could feel my blood respond with a surge; and the blood knows what the soul requires, the blood always knows. No crusader could have enjoyed the certainty of his rectitude more than I, or doubted the outcome of his expedition less. Only it was myself I would recover, not saintly relics. My enemies had what I valued far more – they had learning and genteel manners; so I would have learning and learn to ape the gentlemen. They had money; I would get money, and buy whatever my low birth had denied me. Perhaps one day I would buy you.

Yet I was conscious that I had nothing with which to accomplish it. A man who knows nothing of his birth finds all possibilities open to him, but all certainties closed. And though I might make of myself anything I chose, like the Israelites I would first have to fashion my own bricks. As for materials: these amounted to the clothes I stood in, which were dripping on Linton's carpet, and the scanty contents of my pockets. I had no money, not a farthing. Your brother saw to it that I was kept the prisoner of his charity. But I had youth, and strength. Besides which I was not witless and thought to make up with eagerness and ferocity what I lacked in accomplishment. And the knowledge that I was at least my own master now that I'd cut myself free from Hindley's tyranny cheered me; I began to consider where I might go. There were a good many places where fortunes could be made – America was one, London another, Leeds a third.

But my reflections were disturbed before long by sounds from Linton. I heard him stir and mouth some incoherent sentence relating to his horse, I think, for he clucked in his sleep. And I reached over suddenly, the knife still in my hand, and carefully, as if I'd come there for no other purpose, trimmed a lock of his fine, light hair. He did not wake. He seemed to feel nothing.

Has he ever spoken of missing that lock? I doubt it was a quarter as precious to him as it was to me. I've kept it about me since and have it still, bound with a loop of twine, in my waistcoat pocket, near my heart. From time to time I take it out and examine it, and smile, reminding myself of the moment when his existence depended on my ambition, and that you have enjoyed him ever since by my grace.

3

There were indeed places where fortunes could be made, but as I quitted Thrushcross Grange and found myself again on the rain-sodden moor, tired almost beyond endurance, it was no easy matter to decide among them.

The storm had abated, though a steady drizzle was still falling, the kind which, not content with penetrating cloth and worming its way into the skin, must seek the bone's marrow. I knew that whichever direction I chose I'd have a hard walk before me on an empty stomach, and this, rather than considerations of opportunity, inclined me not to attempt London, a three hundred miles journey, but to make for Bradford or Leeds. Accordingly, I turned east.

After an hour or two the drizzle ceased, but I had a dree night's walk of it, getting by dawn as far as Heatondale, which I approached in fine, clear air, the sky opening like a bruise from blue-black into red, raw weals after its drubbing from the storm. My spirits lifted. I allowed myself to entertain hopes of a hot breakfast, for I was clammed near to death by this time, having had nothing in my mouth since yesterday's dinner. Hearing church bells, I remembered it was Sunday, and for some reason I cannot fathom, this raised my expectations instead of lowering them – my brains must have been soaked through. At all events, I was so desperately in need of fortifying that I began to knock on cottagers' doors, asking my porridge in exchange for work. I might have spared myself the pains. Heatondale showed its Sunday spirit by slamming its doors in my face, to the accompaniment of glib Sabbath pieties proscribing labour and threats to beat some Christian respect into me if I didn't frame off at once. By God, how I hated their twisted, Bible-warped souls! I damned them roundly, and their Sabbath, and their devilish notion of charity. Tell Joseph he can always count on a willing audience among the Heatondale folk if ever Gimmerton tires of his sermonizing. One woman, throwing out some scraps, saw me eye them and proceeded to grind them into the mud with her heel, muttering that she had 'nowt to sustain gipsies'. I came within an inch of kicking her, but contented myself with as blasphemous a curse as I could muster and went on my way. Now, at least, I had nourishment – I had Heatondale stuck in my throat like half a loaf of unbaked bread. I chewed on that sour lump all day.

You may be sure I'd had my fill of human welcomes too, and for the rest of the day I avoided habitations and turnpikes, keeping to the rough moorland tracks where they existed, striking out across boggy fields where they did not. With the mud never below my ankles, so that I slid and squelched about within my boots, I covered most of the distance to Leeds at the rate of a mile every hour, resting frequently. For company I had the music of my growling guts. At nightfall I stumbled, out of sheer exhaustion, into a half-filled ditch, and there I slept the night through, heedless of the discomfort.

The next morning was bright and warm, the first truly warm day we'd known so far that summer, though it was still only the beginning of June. But it was enough to put fresh heart into me, and, stopping only once to quench my thirst from a river, I walked the last two or three miles to Leeds with a vigorous step.

Even at that early hour – it couldn't have been seven o'clock yet – the streets were crowded with carriages and walkers, as well as with the waggons and pack-horses bringing in woollens from the hill weavers. Leeds was hardly a degree less bewildering to me than Liverpool had been ten years since, when, as a child, I'd wandered its busy streets with my mother – until, depositing me on a corner, she whispered to me I must wait there for her, she wouldn't be long, and kissed me on the cheek; I waited four days and then I went with the stranger – your father. But as I say, I needed all my wits about me now to keep from ending under the wheels of a coach as I marched from street to street – it was all I could do, having no more idea than my boots where to commence making my fortune, and would gladly have settled, then, for Jacob's mess of pottage in exchange for such prospects as I had.

It's far worse to be alone and hungry in a town, Cathy, than on the hills, for in town there are always well-fed men and women all about you, each engaged on his business and knowing just where he'll be this time a fortnight, and what doing, and why. Towns are not repositories of the idle, as hill folk believe, but purposeful places usually, filled with shrewd, knowing people who'll neither do nor say anything unless it will turn a penny for them. And none more so than the poorest. It had been easier on the moors to want food – there were no inns or chop houses there – and easier on the moors to harden my belly. I could have snared a meal there; here I'd first need to snare its proprietor.

I happened to pass a coaching inn at one point and heard from within the sound of beer casks being shifted. It seemed likely work, so I traced the noise to its source and found the landlord moving a great stack of kilderkins from one side of his cellar to the other. He was a broad, hulking fellow, with a face red enough from booze to be hung out as a signboard and as much the figure of a John Bull as you'll see outside a caricature. I hallooed him and asked if he needed help.

'I do,' said he, 'if you know of a strong man with half an hour to spare. I've the London passengers to feed before long, or I'd finish it mysen.'

'I've some time,' I told him, 'and want no wage but a good breakfast.'

'My coach breakfast's the best for fifty mile around,' was his answer. 'Climb down, lad.'

So I took off my coat, climbed down, and set to helping him with the casks. After twenty minutes or so we'd both worked up a fair lather – the work was a good deal heavier than he'd made it look. Each kilderkin held close to twenty gallons of beer and couldn't have weighed less than two hundred pounds, so that to stack them one on another, as the innkeeper was doing, was like stacking John Bull on his brothers. He had a trick, though, of using his knee to help him, and made quicker progress because of it. A further ten or fifteen minutes saw the task completed and both of us out of wind. As for my wages, he told me I must wait until he prepared breakfast for the stage passengers, and with that he disappeared into his kitchen.

While I waited I passed the time with studying the London passengers. There were half a dozen of them, and it didn't take me long to sort out the 'insides' from the conveniency danglers. Two of the men I marked as wool merchants or well-to-do farmers; a third, a pasty-faced, indoor-looking fellow, as a lawyer's clerk or possibly a schoolmaster – he'd ride outside, by the look of him, for want of fare rather than any love of the atmosphere. The remaining two inside riders I couldn't mistake, not if I'd been blind. One was a woman – lady I should say. She sat primly by herself, looking as if she found the greater part of the world offensive and was only waiting for some gallant to come along and remove her to a better one. But the sole candidate for such a role was busy reading a book.

He was a decidedly strange-looking gentleman of about forty, fashionable and not unhandsome in his dress but a little too portly for elegance and with crude, ill-proportioned features at odds with his otherwise genteel appearance. He interested me more than the others. For all his pretended absorption in his book, I never saw him turn a page of it, and he betrayed a natural alertness by darting a glance about the room occasionally, as if to make certain he was missing nothing. Once that glance rested on me, only once, and briefly, but it took in my muddy boots and breeches before moving on; I wished him damned for his summary dismissal. Opposite him sat a tall, sturdily built fellow wearing a brace of pistols in his belt, and though this one was clearly not quality, by his manner and familiarity I judged him to be the gentleman's companion. I was prevented from exercising further curiosity about these two, however, by the sudden arrival of breakfast.

Breakfast was bacon and eggs, served with honeyed havercakes and small beer. The landlord himself brought it and attended first to the bookish gent, and then to the others in strict order of precedence, so that my lady had hers before the rest of the inside passengers, and they before the half-fares. I was last, of course. When it was my turn I was given a wedge of cheese, hard and yellow as an elephant's tooth, and an oatmeal crust. That was to be my meal. All I could do was stare uncomprehendingly at it, while the innkeeper stood over me grinning.

'What d'you call this?' I demanded.

'I call it breakfast,' was his reply.

'We had a bargain,' I reminded him, taking care to moderate my voice so as not to anger him precipitately if the matter could be settled by argument.

But he soon left me in no doubt about that. 'I made a bargain,' he said, 'to feed a strong man my coaching breakfast. You're nobbut a bit of a lad, and this is what I feed beggars. It's a proud dog turns up his nose at scraps.'

I got to my feet and carefully pushed my chair back from the board. My legs were trembling – not from fear, I assure you, but from uncontrollable rage.

'I'll thank you for something fit to eat,' I said, 'or you'll find I've a dog's fangs right enough.'

He indicated the cheese. 'That's fit for your sort. That or nowt.'

By this time we had the attention of everyone in the room, and I noticed that the gentleman with the book was watching the scene with obvious pleasure. Clearly the unexpected diversion delighted him. I'd have found it hard at that moment to decide which of them I hated most – him or the landlord. I heard myself say: 'Then let's settle what's fit as both dogs and men do.'

The oaf of an innkeeper responded with a laugh and turned his back. He would have done better to remain facing me, for this expression of his contempt was more than I could stand. I at once snatched up my chair – a hefty, carved thing – and brought it down with all my strength on the man's head. But at the last moment he must have heard the whistle of it, for he dodged its worst effects and took the blow on his shoulders. Still, it sent him staggering, and I wasted none of my advantage but threw myself upon his back like a terrier on a bear.

The momentum carried us both to the floor, and there we struggled impotently for a time, each becoming entangled in the other's limbs and roaring in the other's ears. At first I had him face down and worked at rubbing his flesh raw on the rough boards, but he soon managed to wrench himself around, snarling, and with a sudden flick of his paw sent me half across the room. I rolled a few times before fetching up against the well-polished top boots of the gentleman with the book. He prodded me with his toe, then called out: 'Fifty guineas says the boy will walk away at the end of it.'

I didn't wait to hear if he had any takers, but there couldn't have been any, for I heard him reduce the bet to twenty as I pulled myself up. My adversary had by now regained his legs and was lumbering towards me with his arms outstretched, as if holding aloft an invisible barrel. I knew that at all costs I must keep from being seized by those murderous-looking hands. I looked around for a weapon, and finding only the gentleman's stone beer jug within reach, snatched that up and flung it into the landlord's sweating face. It struck him on the forehead, a glancing blow, and bounced off leaving a small red mark. But it neither halted him nor deflected him, and his only acknowledgement of the injury was a slight grunt, and some twitching of the left eye where a quantity of beer had run in. I found myself backing away, but a table immediately behind me blocked my retreat and before I could move crabwise around it I felt myself grabbed and lifted in a single swift movement above my opponent's head, then dashed upon the table with great violence.

The affair did not end there, however. Even as I lay fighting for my breath the big ox came after me, with the plain intention of finishing me. I felt thick fingers go around my neck as he leaned over, parodying the surgeon at work on his patient. Then he began to press upon my windpipe, shutting off my air. A shrill sound started up in my ears, like that of a piano tuner's fork, a single ringing note remarkable for its clarity. The devil's calling-bell, I've heard it called. I remember thinking that I'd never walk away from this – yet the ignominy of such an end, the prospect of quitting life on a table in a Leeds public house, made me mad. And in my madness, sensing that my adversary's strength was growing while my own ebbed – as if some mysterious exchange of energy was taking place between us – I resorted to a measure of desperation. I extended the first two fingers of my right hand and, making a dagger of them, plunged that dagger into the fellow's eye socket.

The effect was immediate and salutary. Bellowing like Polyphemus, he let go his fatal grip and staggered back a few paces. He threw his head about and clasped both hands to the injured eye, which must have been severely hurt – I noticed blood trickling between two of his fingers. Meanwhile, it was all I could do to get up from the table, so weak was I, and when I managed to stand my legs threatened not to support me. But the betting man seemed certain the contest was over. He was calling: 'Pay me, sirs, pay me!' He now beckoned me over to him and coolly thanked me for enlivening a dull morning. I told him to go to the devil; that gentleman would surely provide a longer entertainment for him. At which he seemed amused and offered me the little beer I'd left him. But we were both wrong to assume the business was over. The noise of the fight had brought others into the room, and for the first time I became aware of them – cooks with kitchen knives, vintners brandishing bottles, at least one stableman armed with a club. They had stationed themselves around the room and were beginning to close in on me. The landlord, one hand still over his wounded optic, waved them back, however, and with a 'Mine, by God!' made a sudden bull's rush at me, head down.

In the ordinary way I'd have jumped clear. But I was too weakened to have much speed and knew it. So it was almost with the air of a spectator at a fight involving two other men that I watched this human battering-ram aim himself at my midriff. Then, when he was no more than a yard away, I came suddenly to my senses and, stepping forward, brought up my knee sharply into his face. The crunch of bone was distinctly audible as I connected with his nose. But the force of his charge had thrown me on my back again, and while I lay trying to fetch my breath, my knee paining like the deuce, I was unable to tell how the innkeeper had fared or whether the broken bone was his or mine. It was only when I got to my knees – an agonizing effort was required for that – that I saw him lying face down and insensible in a puddle of his own blood. For all I cared, he might drown in it.

His cohort of armed servants was not so careless. They now advanced once more, and their murderous array of weapons left me in no doubt about their intentions.

I must have suffered the beating of my life had not the betting gentleman decided to stir himself. He and his companion now got to their feet, the latter drawing both his pistols, and took a step forward so that they were between me and the armed party. Then, without as much as a glance in my direction, the gent said: 'You've won me twenty pounds. It might have been fifty. I take it you have no business to keep you here.'

'No more,' I answered. 'You've just seen me settle it.'

'Convincingly,' he said with a slight smile. 'What are your plans now?'

'My own,' I told him. I was suspicious of his interest and wanted him to know it.

But he was not put off. 'My chaise is outside,' he said. 'I'm returning to London in a minute or two, and if you've a mind to go there I'll take you.' Seeing me hesitate, he added: 'It's an honest offer. Yes or no?'

'London will do as well as any place,' was my reply.

He nodded, and signing to the other fellow – his driver, as I discovered – he began to walk slowly towards the door. 'Pray don't detain us,' he said over his shoulder to the company. 'The horses will be impatient.'

4

He was plainly a man of considerable wealth – the chaise, comfortably sprung and luxuriously appointed, was his own, though he used post horses – and this as much as anything made me cautious of him. I could not guess at his motives for playing benefactor and companion; I heartily detested his class, and since my feelings have always been plain on my face as a book to a reader, he should have harboured no liking for me. I told him so as soon as we had settled in the conveyance, but he merely smiled, and ignoring my remark, introduced himself as Mr Alexander Durrant of Mayfair and St James's. I said my name was Heathcliff Earnshaw, having determined to call myself by that loved-hated name which defines the scale of my passions, and though both its surviving owners have caused me grief, to aggravate a constant pain wilfully can give satisfaction; we pick at scabs sometimes just to see them bleed.

Mr Durrant made little conversation at first and encouraged none from me, but contented himself with gazing out at Yorkshire as his coach took us south. Then at Doncaster, where our third or fourth change of horses was due, he invited me to have a bit of dinner with him. I was too hungry to decline. I'd eaten nothing for two days. We occupied a small table apart from the other travellers, and the driver did not join us. I assumed he was busy with the horses, but did not concern myself with his whereabouts, being more interested in the food, which I commenced to devour with all the dignity of a starved cur. I swallowed great chunks of beef without chewing them, drained pot after pot of ale, while Durrant watched expressionlessly, waiting for me to finish before he spoke a word.

'You've just told me as much about yourself,' he said then, 'as I have gleaned from four hours of your taciturn company, Mr Earnshaw. Shall I tell you what I know of you?' Taking my silence for assent, he continued: 'Your laconism itself tells me much about your character, though when you have something to say you say it forthrightly, and I like that. I have seen ample evidence also of pride and bellicosity – your face even now says that you'd as soon dash that beer in my face as wipe your own chin, which, by the way, wants the attentions of your sleeve. Yes, you've a quick temper and an eloquent pair of fists to match your eyes. No, let me finish. You have other qualities I prize, Mr Earnshaw – may I call you Heathcliff?'

'You may call me what you like,' I told him. 'I'll choose what I answer to.'

'Exquisite rudeness. I wonder you've stayed alive as long as you have, but perhaps provincial people take offence less readily than some I know in London. You're a strange mixture, you see. Proud, but practical enough to put appetite first, which again pleases me since I'm a collector of practical minds. I'll come to that later. For now, am I right in supposing you a farmer's son with a more independent spirit than rural life can cater for? Extreme hunger together with a robust frame, you see, indicates a fugitive state; the condition is not habitual and of short duration.'

'And am I right,' I said, colouring, 'to suppose that you are a sporting gentleman with a taste for anything that runs? Horse, man or snot-nose.'

He chuckled at this and slapped the table. 'Excellent. A wit too, by God.'

'And if I'm the object of some wager you've made,' I went on, 'you may as well resign yourself to losing your

31

money. I've a mind to do the exact opposite of whatever you may suggest, Mr Durrant.'

'I love a contrary fellow,' he said. 'But calm yourself. I'd bet on nothing as unpredictable as you, except in a brawl. There you show striking originality. A chair, my word. And eye-gouging. Oh, yes. Yes, indeed. You've good stuff in you, Heathcliff, if you'll learn to manage it, and I'm not put off by your manner. As for my interest, say I have a sentimental man's fancy for waifs and runaways. Now tell me, pray, what you intend to do when you get to London.'

'Get lodging,' I said sharply.

'Yes, yes,' impatiently. 'I mean afterwards. When you've settled yourself.'

I shrugged my shoulders. 'Seek employment. If I've a mind to.'

He touched his lip with a finger. 'To what end?' was his next question.

This perplexed me, so I hesitated, examined the ground for traps, and finding none, said: 'To make money.' I felt like a child unsure of his responses, repeating what might even be the wrong lesson. Durrant nodded.

'I assume you have no trade besides farm work,' he said musingly, as if thinking aloud. 'Consequently, until the Strand has to be ploughed up, you may expect employment as a porter or a chairman, at a wage of fifteen shillings a week. Out of that for lodging you'll pay not less than half a crown, and for your week's sustenance a further eight shillings at the least. In addition you will need to clothe yourself and warm yourself in winter; to which add the expense of beer, candles – unless you've a cat's fondness for the dark – soap and laundry – unless you prefer foul linen – and hairdressing. The money remaining you'll be at liberty to save like any miser, and since it is well known that misers prosper, you will assuredly grow rich, if you live long enough. That is the life you should look forward to in London.' After a quite lengthy pause he said: 'Do you trust me, Earnshaw?'

'I'd sooner trust a snake,' I answered promptly.

'Capital. It's a habit of mind you'd do well to foster, mistrust. Don't on any account learn to trust a soul in life. Unless you are paid to, and then first bite the coin.'

We returned to the chaise and found it ready, with a fresh team, in the inn yard. Of Mr Durrant's driver, however, there was no sign.

'Haskell has some business to attend to,' I was offered in the way of explanation. 'Can you handle a team?' And when I said I could, 'Ah, he has left the blunderbuss. I believe I could not hit my own foot with one of those. Are you anything of a shot?'

I declared that I could hit my foot if I aimed at it, but that he needn't expect me to defend his property, and as I had none of my own to defend, all the highwaymen in England might ride down the coach before I'd lift a finger to prevent them. The answer seemed to please him, and reaching into his purse he pulled out five gold guineas and gave them to me. 'Now you have an interest to defend,' he said, and smiled as I tested each coin.

The drive to Newark was uneventful, and it was pleasant to be sitting aloft controlling a quartet of fine post horses, with money jingling in my pocket. I could not remember when I was last so content. But I recognized even as I enjoyed it the trap that such contentment always is, for a sapping benevolence began to invade my spirit on that journey, a readiness to share the world even with Hindley and Linton, which, if I maintained the comfortable life, would soon lead me into idleness and the dissipation of my energies. So when, at Newark, we received our first news of what was happening in London, I welcomed the excitement it caused in me.

The stage-coach going north brought intelligence of riot and destruction in the capital. On Friday a mob led by

Lord Gordon had marched on Westminster and attacked peers outside the House, and there were rumours of mutiny among the militia and of city magistrates in flight for their lives. One report said the King was gone to France, though in the general view that was false. Mr Durrant became very animated at these news and questioned the London people like a lawyer, demanding details and evidence and exact figures of the dead on both sides. But there were few certainties in each bushel of conjecture, so that Mr Durrant couldn't decide whether to be hot or cold about the business.

'If it's as far gone as they say,' he confided to me, 'it means nothing short of revolution, Earnshaw. That would suit you, would it not?'

'But not you,' I said with undisguised pleasure. I would have welcomed anything that might shake this man's detestable self-assurance.

But he gave a sneering grin. 'I would not suffer if the world turned the other way about its axis,' he assured me, 'though nothing very momentous will come of these riots unless they have the arsenal, and I fancy they're too ill-led to have taken that. Besides, unless I miss my guess, the London mob is not aggrieved enough to revolt wholeheartedly, and an unaggrieved mob can as easily be dispersed with bread as with lead shot.'

We discussed the riots no further but resumed our journey in haste, having stayed longer at Newark than we'd intended. Stamford was to be our overnight stopping-place, and since we still had above thirty miles to cover, I drove the next stage somewhat faster, making up time while daylight lasted. It was flatter country now, with few hills to slow us, but the ruts in the road were baked hard by the sun and once or twice our wheels caught, giving us a bad jolt. A chaise, being light, is prone to overturning, but I felt it was worth the risk to get us to Stamford before nightfall, and did not regret having to give my passenger a shaking. Yet we were still an hour from our destination when night began to draw in. I heard Durrant rap sharply on the roof, signalling me to slow down, and this I was obliged to do as it soon became difficult to see more than a few yards ahead. After half an hour at near walking pace we reached a particularly gloomy stretch of road, where an avenue of poplars cut out what little daylight was left, throwing the chaise into deep shadow. It was a likely spot for ambush, and my instinct was to whip the horses on and to the devil with caution. Yet I had hardly formed the intention when a figure, indistinct but perceptibly that of a mounted man, moved into our path. I reined in my team and reached simultaneously for the blunderbuss, determined to send at least one of them to perdition should there prove to be a gang. Those trees might have concealed a small army.

'Why are we stopped?' came Mr Durrant's voice.

Before I could speak the horseman supplied an answer. 'Because I've a barking-iron pointed at your driver's pizzle,' says he, 'and he's only to twitch to make himself a eunuch.'

'Is that so, Earnshaw?' called Durrant.

'He's fully thirty feet away,' I shouted back, judging the distance with difficulty. 'And we're in shadow.' I found it damned odd that the highwayman could see me at all, leave along distinguish that part he claimed to have sighted upon. So I said, loud enough for both him and Durrant to hear: 'Unless he's half owl I doubt he can see more of me than I can of him. And I see no confederates.' Here's a man who doesn't know his business, I thought, for in his place I would have chosen a position that gave me advantage. To the horseman I called out: 'You'd better be a marksman if you're to make that shot, for I've a blunderbuss here will cut you in two at this distance. I've held off so far for fear of hitting your horse.'

35

My speech drew a 'Bravo!' from Durrant but had an unexpected effect on the robber. Far from being outfaced, he seemed emboldened by my threat and began to walk his horse towards the chaise.

My breathing became fast and shallow, my hands slippery around the gun. How I cursed the fool for making a murderer of me, but even as I cursed him I was estimating the range for my shot and tensing my muscles to receive his.

'Now!' cried Durrant, and with no time to think or question or aim properly, I pointed the gun at the approaching rider and fired.

There was a flash in the pan as the flint struck steel, but no explosion. Before I had time to brace myself for the shock of a bullet in my vitals I heard the horseman give a low chuckle and Durrant's voice call heartily: 'Will he do, Haskell?'

'Aye,' answered the other, who was now close enough to be recognized as Durrant's man. 'He will.'

I was so maddened by their low trick that I would not listen to Durrant's explanation, and maintained a sullen silence throughout the evening. That night in Stamford I couldn't sleep for excitement at the thought of hundreds of Lintons and Durrants being whipped through the streets of London, and when at last I did close my eyes, the hundreds became thousands in my dreams, and I exhausted myself with scourging every one of them as they stumbled through my feverish brain.

The next day, Tuesday, was a far hotter one. I found the chaise interior insufferably stuffy and rode most of the way to London on the box beside Haskell.

'He has a use for you,' the driver told me. 'But that damned pride of yours is an unlooked-for quality. Mark me, lad.'

'I've no use for him,' I replied, 'or for this conversation.'

He shrugged. 'Please yourself. Proud beggars starve soonest.'

At Highgate, however, Durrant prevailed upon me to join him inside, and as we rode into the metropolis by way of Tottenham Court Road and High Street St Giles he showed a side of his character I'd not guessed at.

'Iniquitous, is it not?' he said. 'Here is a great city of three-quarters of a million souls and capital of the most civilized nation on earth, yet in the quarter we are now entering and others like it children are to be seen starving in the streets. Scald-headed, bandy-legged wretches, Earnshaw, often abandoned by their mothers or sold for a pint of gin, or worse. How could any man drive through these streets and remain unmoved by the thought of it?' Here he gave a precious wave of his hand and I wondered that he did not dab at his eyes with a handkerchief. 'I would not blame the populace of this city,' he continued, 'for rising in anger against such injustices, except that I see no sign of it here.' And it was true enough. I'd expected to find the entire town in flames or being demolished stone by stone, but the streets we passed along were undamaged and quiet. The only sign of disturbance was some dark smoke over the rooftops to the south, and this could have been a fire begun by accident. 'You must pardon me,' said Mr Durrant. 'I am always so affected when I enter the more miserable parts of London. You, of course, will have a much closer view of them before long, for it is in these insalubrious quarters that you will necessarily make your way.'

'I'm no stranger to such places,' I said.

'Then why repeat the experience? Let me speak plainly, Heathcliff. There is too much good stuff in you to be wasted, and I deplore waste. You have qualities I not only admire but can put to use – I need not enumerate them, though I will say that they are not always conventional virtues; indeed, that is what I like best about them. True, I rate you low for loyalty and think you have an excess of pride, but you've a healthy respect for money and once you commit yourself to me that pride of yours, which has the disadvantage of making you explosive, will bind you to continued good service. In return I am able to offer you handsome remuneration and a clean bed at night. Come, will you work for me?'

I had been anticipating this and had my answer ready. 'Mr Durrant,' I said, 'I would not have you for my employer if the alternative were a noose about my neck.'

'Hard, hard,' said he, shaking his head. 'What a pity it is that so little trust is possible between men. Otherwise we might have a Christian society. You've saddened me, Heathcliff. I believe you intend to join the mob, in which event Tyburn probably is your alternative to me.' He seemed to dismiss the subject from his mind then, and sat whistling to himself as Haskell drove us into Broad St Giles's. 'Why,' he commented with startling suddenness, 'this must be the genteelest revolution that ever was.'

But he spoke too soon. For ahead of us, just around the bend where the Watch House stands, the way had been blocked by a roughly erected barricade of furniture and paving slabs. A score or more ill-dressed fellows sporting blue ribbands or cockades in their hats and wielding cudgels lounged against it. They had stopped a carriage in front of us and were crying: 'Turnpike, Protestant turnpike! Pay your toll!' through its windows. A short, stocky man had stuck his head inside the carriage, and a shrill female scream resulted. Haskell, meanwhile, had brought us to a halt and was now attempting to turn the chaise about.

'Do you recognize any of them, Haskell?' Durrant called. The driver said he could not be sure at that distance. 'No matter,' said Durrant. 'Turn the horses.' He looked at me then. 'Well, Heathcliff, there they are.

Ugly, are they not? A proper attitude towards them is that of the surgeon to disease – he works with it but does not make his home too close. Where, pray, is your kinship with those brutes?'

I made no reply but opened the door. He placed his hand restrainingly on my shoulder, then quickly removed it, and I jumped down into the road. The mob had let the carriage through and now a small detachment was advancing towards the chaise, as if anxious not to let it get away.

'Make haste, Haskell,' Durrant called. 'I've no wish to be seen by these fellows.' To me he said: 'My offer will not remain open indefinitely, Mr Earnshaw. When you change your opinions call on me at my house in Hill Street. Do not leave it too late.'

With that the whip flicked out and the chaise completed its turn and began rattling back the way it had come.

'And you,' I shouted after Durrant, 'may go post-haste to hell!'

5

Cathy, I could not have approached long-lost brothers with greater warmth than I evinced towards that crowd, yet my first encounter with it made me aware how narrow was my experience of human nature, how limited my understanding of the way men think. I had expected the welcome due to a recruit. What I received was the scorn and rough handling appropriate to a captured enemy. I was pushed from one grinning fool to another like a shuttlecock, while their talk was of whipping me around town and of delivering me piecemeal in a sack to the justices. And the determination on their faces left me in no doubt that they were in earnest. I was punched about the head and body and only with great difficulty avoided being forced to the ground and trampled upon. Since it did not occur to me at first why I was being subjected to this treatment, I had no idea how to prevent it but spat curses and threats at them and kicked out when my arms were pinned behind my back. But before very long I realized what must have been in their minds, their talk of magistrates providing the clue. They had seen me arrive in a gentleman's private chaise and had concluded, by a process of reasoning that would disgrace a half-witted child, that I belonged to the quality camp and was sent to spy on them.

God, the beauty of that piece of logic brought me close to laughter. But, recognizing that to laugh would scarcely endear me to my captors, I scowled instead and addressed myself to that same squat fellow I'd noticed earlier, supposing him to be their leader. He was an ugly brute right enough, his nose and upper lip all but eaten away by the pox, and, as I soon learned, he had a disposition to match his looks.

I hadn't uttered three words before he cut me off with a stinging blow to the cheek and a snarled 'Shut your mouth, before you dig your grave with it.'

'If I stay quiet you'll dig it for me,' I managed to get out before a second, harder blow caught me on the mouth. I tasted blood that time.

'Name,' said he. I gave it. 'Protestant or papist?' was his next question.

'Neither,' I answered. 'No Christian of any kind.'

'Jew?' I shook my head. 'What then?'

'I've no religion,' I told him, 'unless it be gentry-hating. You'll find none more pious in the service of that doctrine.'

This seemed to perplex him. He was silent for a moment. Then he asked where I was from. I said I was just come from Yorkshire and, hearing of their activities on the road, had resolved to join them at the first opportunity. You would have thought from their response that I'd told the mother and father of all jokes. They began bowing to one another and sweeping off their hats, and saying: 'He's heard of our *activities*. They know of our *activities* in Yorkshire.' The word went around like an echo in a cave, until my interlocutor silenced them and demanded to know what activities I meant.

I said, 'Tearing down buildings and the like. I'm sorry you should be so amused by it.'

'Oh, this is a rare one,' said the pox-faced fellow. 'And whose rattler was that you was in?'

'Mr Durrant's,' said I.

'And who might he be?'

'A gent I met in Yorkshire.' I marvelled at the simple-mindedness of his interrogation, for if I had been a spy I would hardly have admitted it or have arrived in a manner calculated to arouse suspicion. But to have said

41

so would have been forward, and forwardness was not appreciated in this company. Nor could I tell him how I'd met Durrant, since that was an implausible truth. So a careful answer was needed to a guileless question. After a moment's hesitation I added, 'A gent whose purse I stole in Yorkshire, if you want the whole truth. Though he doesn't know it, and engaged me to ride to London with him as guard.'

This earned me a few gaumless grins. But the poxy one wasn't so easily satisfied. He screwed up his face at me, which action gave him the look of a death's head too long with the worms, and asked in a sly voice how long I'd been a diver. Or was I an eriff? And seeing that I had no idea how to begin answering him, he then fired off a charge of canting terms that had me nicely peppered, concluding with: 'Don't stam flash, do you?' He seemed to derive great satisfaction from my ignorance of his language. Yet I could sell him at Bradford market, thought I, without his knowing.

'We cant differently in the north,' I answered, and proceeded to give him back a stream of gibberish of my own – I'm damned if I know whence I got it. 'I've been a sleezer these two years,' I said, 'mooning it with a nab or two, though lately I've taken to tweaking the libbies, or that frill would have pinned me sure for a darper.' I'd have been hard put to translate this sentence if he'd insisted upon it, but fortunately he swallowed the nonsense with a knowing nod, and my story with it.

'Still got the purse?' he wanted to know.

I replied that I'd thrown it away in Leeds lest it incriminate me, but that I still had its contents, which I was ready to show and as ready to fight for, since they were mine now. Here the poxy fellow smiled for the first time, revealing black and broken teeth in putrefied gums.

'Keep it,' he said. 'We're no cloyers.'

So volatile are these people in their affections, so capricious, that though a moment ago they had been prepared to flay me alive, now they accepted me as one of them, without reservation, and took me along with them through St Giles. My inquisitor – Tom Burns, he said his name was – had me march alongside him at the head of his troop and explained to me the mode of living there.

The place itself is not pretty. We passed through wretched alleys and passageways so narrow that two couldn't walk abreast, and I saw into yards where the sunlight never penetrates, so that in the perpetual dampness and obscurity the walls drip with slime, which turns the brickwork green and then forms teeming green puddles on the ground. There are rats in these yards as big as cats. They have no need to wait for night, but mass in the middle of the day to forage and bite out the eyes of sleeping babes – I witnessed one huge brute beaten from an infant's face, the child's outcry having alarmed the mother. The stench everywhere is indescribable, and such noxious air must carry diseases of all kinds, the effects of which are probably aggravated by the living conditions. For as many as twenty will lodge together in a space no larger than the Heights pantry, and often half that number may be found sleeping in a single bed. Yet if this is how you are accustomed to live you see nothing extraordinary in it, and their way of life affords them a unique security. Cathy, it is a separate State! Not a hundred yards from the Newton Street Watch House. They are a perfect sovereign nation, these denizens of the St Giles alleyways, permanently at war with England, permanently in rebellion against its laws, yet magnificently inviolable. The thief-takers will not pursue them into their fortress, except in strength, and then only when they have a Sheppard or a Wild to apprehend – they'll venture inside for nothing less.

Would you have imagined that such places could exist? To me it seemed as improbable as El Dorado. I found my entire body trembling with the excitement of the discovery, and believed I wanted nothing more than to earn my citizenship.

We came at last into the large enclosed area called Lincoln's Inn Fields. Here a sizeable crowd was assembled – I would put it at between two and three thousand, though in volume and martial fervour it could have rivalled many a larger army – and as mixed a crew as you'd find anywhere. Besides tradesmen and labourers were many of that class the justices call vagabonds and rogues, being persons of every race and hue: gipsies, mulattoes, lascars, negroes, Jews and Irish, and as like as not Turks also – women and boys as well as men and all variously armed with cutlasses, bludgeons, knives and axes and an assortment of other weapons. I even saw a musket here and there and several bayonets, taken, I presumed, from soldiers sent against them earlier.

I cannot easily describe the effect that crowd had upon me, for as we entered the square their chant reached our ears: 'No Popery!' issuing in strict rhythm from hundreds of lusty throats, the expression of a monstrous will that sang in my blood, though the sentiment meant nothing to me. Our St Giles detachment took up the cry at once, and before I was aware of it I found my own voice added – 'No Popery! No Popery! No Popery!' – until my throat burned with the strain of yelling and tears formed in my eyes. It is impossible to explain, but I expect *you* to understand it. The sensation endured only a moment, yet in that moment I *belonged*, Cathy, as I had never belonged before in any human company except yours. Suddenly my dark skin and low birth and penniless condition were of no account and nothing mattered but my presence there, in that place, among that tumultuous throng. Perhaps the damned know such fellowship in the antechamber of hell, in the seconds before the furnaces obliterate them. If I'd been asked then, I'd have avowed it was worth dying for at the very least.

On the far side of the Fields someone – not Gordon himself but a lesser leader – was addressing the multitude. I was too far from him to hear what he was saying, but I observed that from time to time he struck the ground with his stave or shook his fist, whereupon those who could hear him would let out a great roar and brandish their own weapons in response. And often a phrase of his they thought particularly rousing would be passed in relays back through the crowd, the listeners setting each other alight like clumps of furze in a moorland conflagration. Once a mighty shout of 'No!' went up, followed hard by an equally emphatic 'Yes!' that had Burns almost splitting his lungs, though he could not have known what he was affirming. Not long afterwards, however, a phalanx broke away from the rest and began marching determinedly towards the north-west side of the Fields, carrying torches and buckets of pitch and crying: 'To Newgate! On to Newgate!' Others began to stir, then to follow. And soon, as if we were a great serpent uncoiling itself after sleep, the body and tail of us was set in motion, until we stretched from Holbourn Row the entire length of Little Queen Street. We squeezed through into High Holbourn, a wide thoroughfare now deserted, its shops barred and shuttered, and then spread ourselves out to fill the road, closing up into a compact body some hundred yards long. In this formation we commenced the march towards Newgate.

It was a queer introduction to a great city – I've seen Gimmerton fairly bustling by comparison with Holbourn that June day. We might already have taken over Government, so completely was that part of the city in our hands, and it had about it an air less of mere quietude than of hasty abandonment, as if the inhabitants had fled before a sudden plague or an invading army. We all sensed it, and knew *we* were the plague, the invading horde, and relished it. Those with torches lighted them and waved them about in the gloom (the light was going by this time) to make themselves appear more fearsome, and once again the anti-papist chant was taken up – 'No property!' would have been a more appropriate cry, considering our purpose. Between bouts of chanting there was talk of what course we should take if we encountered troops – though none seemed to think we'd be troubled by them, as the magistrates were too much in confusion to call them out – and of how those same magistrates would manage once the King's Head Inn (so they call the gaol) was demolished.

I heard one fellow say, 'If we're snabbled the beaks won't have a place to put us up. Shame, that is.' But I thought it ominous that he took such a narrow view, for we had only to succeed to be able to change the laws to suit ourselves and provide our own justices to uphold them. But when I pointed this out I was hooted at, and the same man said, 'Hey, lads, when we've ripped up Bow Street who wants to be Fielding?'

There was general laughter from the St Giles men. A few of them promptly bound kerchiefs over their eyes and, adopting magisterial attitudes, sentenced each other to hang; this being enacted on the march by two of them holding up a third by his arms, who stuck out his tongue and kicked his legs in pantomime death throes. Their hilarity perplexed me, for one of these clowns had told me he had a brother in Newgate under sentence of death and was along in the hope of getting him out. I remained silent after that, not trusting my tongue.

Eventually St Sepulchre's came into view, and we extended our line of march to take us through the

46

narrows of Hart-Row Street. Facing us was Newgate Prison.

I had expected the crowd to go wild at the sight of that grim fortress, as men do upon coming eye to eye with an inveterate foe or hunters when they sight their quarry; but I did not count upon the prey petrifying the snake. Yet so terrible is that place to those who live within its shadow, so forbidding its aspect, that it had on them the effect of a Gorgon, bringing them to a sudden halt and striking them dumb. They were in awe of it. The Keeper and a handful of constables might have routed them. I cannot say how long they would have remained immobile had not a single harridan among them broken the spell; this she accomplished by snatching a firebrand from one of the men, running forward with it, and screaming at the top of her lungs: 'Burn it down!'

Immediately the cry was repeated by others, and the scene rapidly became one of frenzied confusion. One party set about smearing pitch over the prison doors, while another attempted simultaneously to batter them down – they used axes and iron bars, but wooden spoons would have served them as well, the doors being half a foot thick and iron-plated. Meanwhile, a third party, ignoring the efforts of the other two, got ladders from somewhere (I noticed none on the march) and tried to scale the walls.

But participants rarely see much of the battle and often must be told afterwards who has won, and from my position with the crowd in Newgate Street I could not witness the decisive events of that afternoon. If it is true that Ackerman (that's the Keeper) refused to release his prisoners and had his house fired in consequence, I saw nothing of it, though his house did burn and set off the prison. Very soon after the assault began, the gaol was ringed with fire, and we had to step back as far as the kennel for the heat. Glass and stonework cracked like

47

musket fire, so that more than once we believed troops were attacking and prepared to defend ourselves. We might have spared ourselves concern, for falling masonry constituted the only hazard, and the few constables who showed themselves were in flight for their lives and no threat to us.

I have told you all I know of the storming of Newgate, and it is as much as anyone knows who did not enter the prison. I believe the storming party got in by the roof, for they came out that way, choking with the smoke and leading the inmates they had released, still in their chains. I have never heard such exultation as the onlookers expressed when the first chained figures appeared on the roof and began their awkward descent of the ladders. Christ Himself would return tomorrow to establish His Kingdom if He could count on half as spirited a reception. Hats were thrown into the air, flags waved, children held aloft for the scene to be burned into their memories for life: Newgate in flames, giving up its sons. My own image of it will endure as long as I do.

There was no order to break off, such as armies receive after an engagement. We had no commander to give it. Instead, without reforming, our force quitted Newgate in companies, and not at the same time. A good many went along Old Bailey, and these, I later found out, made their way by Fleet Street and the Strand to Bow Street, where they attacked Fielding's house and tore it down.

I returned through Holbourn with the St Giles men and some others, including two who were fresh out of the gaol. We found a blacksmith near Gray's Inn who struck off their chains and was glad to do it.

'Where now?' asked one, rubbing his wrists, which were badly chafed.

Tom Burns grinned. 'Want to get back for that?' he said. And when the fellow nodded: 'Right. Lord

Mansfield's house, then. He's a Pope-licker too, so he can have double measure.' He turned to me then, and said: 'This'll be to your liking, eriff. You said you wanted houses to tear down. My Lord Chief Justice has one of the finest in Bloomsbury.'

6

It was almost dark by the time we reached Bloomsbury Square. The street lamps had been lighted and those above the porches provided additional illumination as we gathered before Lord Mansfield's town house. From within came sounds of some defensive activity, of servants shifting furniture to barricade doors and windows; hearing which, and knowing the house to be occupied, we took turns to wear out the knocker and call upon the owner to show himself. We saw no sign of him, however, and at length, impatience proving the best locksmith, we broke in the door with bar and mattocks.

Entering the hallway, we found ourselves confronted by a trio of footmen who, having supplied themselves with muskets, seemed determined to offer a Roman defence of the stairs. I could not help admiring their spirit, if not their sense, for two of them were grandfathers while the third was devilish young and had the build of a whittled fence-post. All three were plainly out of their wits with fear and looked as if they had no idea which way up to hold their weapons. But when ordered to stand aside they gamely held their ground, declaring that as His Lordship had already quitted the house by the back way (much laughter), we might as well leave too, since we could not have what we'd come for.

'If we can't have His Lordship,' says one of the freed prisoners, 'we'll make do with his things. So stand aside unless you wish your heads caved in.'

This speech got no result, save to set the young footman trembling – he was in a muck sweat and would doubtless have capitulated if he'd been alone.

'You've more than earned your wages already,' I told him. 'Your swine of an employer has left you to take his beating. I'd be damned before I'd let loyalty extend to wood and cloth.'

One of the older servants curled his lip at this. 'What would you know about it?' said he. 'We've a duty to protect his property also, with our lives if necessary.'

He meant it, too. And I've since found the same warped notion of honour in every servant I have ever met. They will defend objects sooner than lives, particularly their own lives, which their station has taught them to regard as next to worthless. Society runs on such unthinking devotion, and I can think of no attitude which disgusts me more. Finding it there, in a beleaguered camp deserted by its commander, angered me beyond reason. In my rage I turned to the nearest object at hand – it happened to be a vase – and hurled it into the panelling, where it shattered beautifully, showering us with fragments.

'Item,' I commented. 'One vase, property of Lord Mansfield. Come, will you blow a hole in me for that?' I expected no reply and got none. 'Not precious enough, I suppose,' I said then. And I gave a tremendous kick at the little table on which the vase had been standing. It was a flimsy, delicate thing of satinwood with spindly carved legs, one of which snapped off like a dry twig under the weight of my boot, sending the whole affair crashing to the floor. There was some hard breathing from the servants and some chuckling from the St Giles men, a few of whom had been working their way steadily along the far wall in order to get behind the footmen. 'How many make a pile of sticks?' I asked. 'You've been duped. Your master's somewhere safe, laughing up his sleeve at you. Yet you stand here, solemnly deciding whether your lives are worth a sideboard or a secretary.'

The boy shifted nervously, but the old retainer who had spoken up earlier stiffened and was about to make some reply when all three servants were simultaneously grabbed from behind and disarmed.

The old man found his voice a minute later, as I passed him on my way upstairs. He hissed at me: 'You'll hang for that vase alone.'

I could cheerfully have broken *his* neck for that, but contented myself with saying: 'Under your master's bloody system, perhaps. Not under ours.'

'I'll remember you,' I heard him call after me. 'That table was made by Mr Hepplewhite.'

'Then return it to its maker in a box,' said I. 'I'd do as much for you.'

I thought no more about the fellow but joined the others, who were ravaging the house, stripping it of its furnishings with the single-minded dedication of locusts. We prised loose what was fastened down, smashed what was too large, and threw everything out of the windows. My Lord's possessions were then piled up in the street below according as they were judged burnable or not, which depended not only on their combustibility but on how easily they might be fenced.* Thus, his plate went on one pile, whereas his paintings and papers were consigned with his tables and chairs, curtains and bedsheets, to the other; which, once it was ignited, we used as a beacon to direct our aim.

It was intoxicating work and I soon warmed to it. The bedrooms yielded some fine porcelain jars, the study a selection of snuff-boxes and an etui in the palest blue with little cupids dancing hand in hand around it. This I saw Tom Burns crush gleefully under his heel into blue powder, whitened here and there by the mutilated

*Mr Heathcliff occasionally employs cant terms, most of which require no explanation, though the interested reader is recommended to refer to Grose's *Dictionary of the Vulgar Tongue* (1785). This expression signifies the disposal of stolen goods through an agent, whose profession it is to receive them. – W.L.

cupids. From another chamber came the crash of glass, a set of crystal goblets being flung against a wall, then stamped upon. A number of china figures in a pastoral setting met the same rude end, as did a dinner service depicting the labours of Hercules, two enamelled coffee pots, three cut-glass chandeliers and several clocks. We threw marbles out and bronzes down the stairs, cut up the carpets, struck the noses off busts, lit fires with manuscripts, and would have carved our wishes in the walls – NO POPERY from Burns, DAMN ALL GENTLEMEN from me – if we'd known how. It was an orgy, Cathy, made more exciting by our awareness that we warranted the gallows for the least of these offences. We were cheating the hangman. I longed to cross the square and start on Bedford House, then begin elsewhere, until I had demolished every great house in London; after which I'd unleash myself on the provinces and not quit till I had the razing of all such dwellings from Land's End to Carlisle. And maybe Scotland, too.

At one point I found myself alone in the library. Burns and the others were happily breaking coffee cups downstairs, having devastated the study and bedchambers. For some reason they'd neglected Lord Mansfield's library, and I had it all to myself. God, it was magnificent. I have never seen – before or since – such a collection of fine books, all beautifully calf-bound and gold-lettered, in great pedimented bookcases with glass fronts, elaborately carved and gilded. For a long while I just stood and looked at them, trying to estimate how many books he had. Above five thousand, I'm certain. And he had them arranged according to subject, for I made out the word 'Law' on one cabinet, the largest, and assumed the longer words on other cabinets denoted different classifications.

I pulled out one of the law volumes, the handsomest in binding but small in compass, and leafed through it idly. Words. Thousands and thousands of black smudges on smooth white paper, but annotated here and there in the margins in a tiny, careful hand which I presumed was Lord Mansfield's own. Of his notes I could make nothing. The text itself was verbal treacle, viscous, opaque, incomprehensible. I could manage some simple words and knew my letters (you taught them to me), but islands of 'the' and 'it' in an ocean of print were as much use to me as pennies are to an imprisoned debtor. The sight of so many books was an affront to me. I put the first one down and took another, and searched through it in such a frenzy for a sentence I might understand that several of the pages came away in my fingers, and still I went on looking, weeping now with the frustration of that exercise, breathless with exertion and expended passion as I commenced to rip out the offending scraps of paper in handfuls. Cathy, I was insane. I wept like a child while I did it, while I wrenched the bindings off books, tore away their spines, twisted their covers into tormented shapes and shredded their leaves into black-flecked flakes of white paper. Twice I cut my finger on the binding twine and bled over some great judge's commentaries on English or Roman Law.

But the going was too slow for me. So I turned out the bookcases on to the floor, piling up the volumes into pyramids of learning as high as the reading desk, mountains of erudition, each bookcase another peak, until the library floor was an undulating encyclopaedic range and I had no clear space in which to place my feet. And I raged and kicked at the things, and saw their mottled bellies flash in the lamplight as they fluttered, like broken-winged birds, from end to end of that damnably superior room.

Then I set the lamp to them.

They blackened and curled and shrivelled as fiends are supposed to do in hell, and if I'd stayed long enough

I might have mistaken the hiss of melting glue for reproaches and fancied I heard them shriek at me as the fire consumed them. For they were as real to me as their proud owner, as real as Linton is. He might be made of boards and paper since he shows no evidence of flesh-and-blood existence. He is dry, dry. And pitiful. And without soul, Cathy. You could as readily love a book as that man, yet you do love him and I burn like those books at the memory of it.

I said I burned Lord Mansfield's library. Not all of it. That first book, the one I took down first because it was so handsome – that I had left lying on the desk while I destroyed the others. When I had set them all alight and turned to go, I saw it there, and instead of casting it into the flames I tucked it under my shirt and took it away with me. I cannot say why I did so.

I was suddenly very weary. In some strange fashion the destruction had drained me of energy – creative acts can scarcely be more exhausting – with the result that I desired no more of it. Now I felt none of the elation that had filled me a short while since, only disgust where anger had been and a profound emptiness through my whole being. I wandered from room to ruined room, wading through the glass and china debris, and then made my way downstairs.

Those below, having dismantled even the banisters, were gone outside to stoke the bonfire with them. Sparks drifted across the square, threatening to set off whatever they touched. I was in time to see, by the fire's light, a troop of foot soldiers arriving from the direction of Bedford House. They halted ten or fifteen yards from us and arranged themselves line abreast to block the entire roadway from the outer railings to the inner. Otherwise they did nothing, but leaned on their muskets. Their bayonets made them appear so much like a fence of railings themselves, that we called out to warn them against rust should they remain too long in the night air. They ignored our taunts, however, and seemed to be waiting for something.

'Don't mind them,' Burns told me. 'They've no power to fire on us without they're ordered by a beak, and they'll take root waiting till one comes within spitting distance of us.' I inquired if there was a chance of subverting the troops. He laughed at that and said, 'Not with cherry-ripes. Can't buy redbreasts.'

'*Would* they fire on us?' I persisted. 'Half of them must be pressed men. Why should they fire on their fellows?'

He sucked thoughtfully at a broken tooth. 'They know their place,' he said. 'Same as we know ours.'

You can imagine how this perplexed me. He had lately laid waste Newgate and was fresh from demolishing the house of the Lord Chief Justice of England – yet he knew his place. But I was prevented from questioning him further by a sudden commotion in the crowd. A carriage had drawn up, from which a bewigged gentleman emerged, flanked by officers.

'Beak,' was whispered in my ear.

An uneasy silence descended on the crowd as the magistrate stationed himself behind the rank of soldiers and, producing a paper, began to read something aloud to us. Had not Burns muttered, 'Riot Act,' I would not have known what was being read, for the fellow had a thin, low-pitched voice which did not carry even in those windless conditions. The effect of that mumbler addressing us from behind his human palisade was almost comic, and relieved some of the tension.

'Speak up,' called one wag. 'Can't hear you.' At which we all placed our hands to our ears and leaned forward as one man, shouting, 'Louder, louder!' and 'Take your thumb out of your mouth!'

Undeterred, the magistrate read on. Then, finishing, he hastily rolled up his paper and nodded to the troop's captain, who shouted an order. And a score of muskets were shouldered and levelled at us.

It had all happened so quickly that we were caught unprepared. One moment we were enjoying a comedy that would not have disgraced Sheridan, the next in peril of our lives. I felt the crowd press back upon me, lost my footing and went down. It was all I could do to keep from being trampled as that mob surged over me in its panic, feet flying like horses' hooves so that I was obliged to cover my head with both hands or have it split open. As the last of them went by I managed to regain my feet, intending to follow them, but I had hardly done so when a savage shove from behind sent me sprawling. At that precise moment I heard the volley fired.

Thoughts succeeded each other with lightning rapidity in my brain. My first impulse had been to turn upon the coward who had pushed me and knock *him* down, but I realized at once that whoever was responsible had saved my life. So I was then inclined to thank the fellow, if only I could manage to move. For it began to dawn upon me that all was not right with my body. My limbs would not obey me and I had become aware of a fierce burning pain in my left shoulder, front and back. Furthermore, as if I had been doused with icy water, I felt suddenly deuced cold – I was trembling all over – and nauseous. It was exactly like the ague. I shook my head in an attempt to clear it, but the effect was to increase my dizziness and to aggravate that infernal pain.

I must have become insensible for a few moments, because my next recollection is of being rolled over on to my back. More than one pair of hands fumbled at my clothing, and I heard a familiar voice say: 'Try his boots.'

'Damn you, Burns,' I said. 'Help me.' But if it came out at all it must have emerged as a whisper. I heard him chuckle as he tugged off my boots and shook them.

'Aha!' said he. 'Who's the sly one?' For I had stowed Mr Durrant's guineas in my boots, and there he had found them. I know not what threats I uttered, but the least of them would have made a coal-heaver blush. His response, however, was to prod me with his toe and advise me to crawl back north before the patrols found me. 'They read a musket ball in the back as a confession,' he said, then flung my boots down beside me and departed without another word.

I wasted none of my strength on curses. I would need all of it to get myself to safety, and Tom Burns would wait as Hindley waited, and Linton. My most urgent requirement was to get my boots back on, which was more difficult and more tiring than I imagined, since by the time it was done I was nearly out. Somehow I struggled to my feet – I think I used the railings for support – and received my first view of Bloomsbury Square since the events I've described. Soldiers and rioters were gone, and I shared the square with two corpses – a woman shot in the head and a man with a gaping wound in his chest. Otherwise the place was deserted. A little smoke trickled from an upper window of Lord Mansfield's house, but plainly the dwelling was saved – no doubt that was due to the conscientiousness of his servants. Nor would it be long before curiosity overcame caution and people emerged from their houses to gape at the cadavers and flatter their own bravery by arresting the survivor. I had to make sure of disappointing them. But how? I was weak as an infant with loss of blood, and still the stuff insisted upon dripping down my side, whence it spattered the paving in large drops like summer rain. Within half an hour, unless I could stanch it, I would be bled white as a fish. Using my right hand, I pulled out my shirt-tail and, tearing off a strip of the linen, wadded it over the wound in front – I knew that where the ball had entered my back it would have left a far smaller hole, and the most profuse bleeding seemed to be in front.

Thus patched like a leaking boat, I launched myself into the night.

You could place me in total darkness on any nab of heath in England, and, as you well know, I would find my way. But London has no natural geography, and even those who know it intimately are constantly surprised by it. To wander in that vast city at night is like nothing so much as being lost in an immense black forest, where the paths are always crossing each other and turning back on themselves; so that the careless traveller can trudge ten miles through an ever-changing landscape of squares and courts and alleys and at the end of it find he has not put himself ten yards from his starting point. The London I saw that night I have not seen since and never will again. Fires had been started in every part of it, then left to burn. The West End was dotted with them. They made the sky glow like sunrise, fully three hours before dawn, and from the highest buildings the city must have looked like the encampment of some gigantic army. Detachments of troops moved about the streets, seeking rioters, and these were my greatest danger. Luckily the ring of their boots on the cobbles announced them well in advance, so I was able to conceal myself in doorways when I heard them approach.

My other problems were not so easily overcome. One was that I not only had no knowledge of London, but had no destination. I soon learned what a hunted fox feels whose earth has been stopped up, for, weak and cold as I was – I have never been so cold in my life, notwithstanding the mildness of the night and the contribution of warmth made by all those fires – I say, weak and cold as I was, it could not be long before I fell into the hands of a patrol. From there it would be a short step to Tyburn. Had I been unhurt I would have gone directly west, gone to ground on Hounslow Heath – I'd have felt at home there.

Perhaps this was in my mind, because the direction I took was westerly; though in city streets a true course is impossible. I remember making my way along Piccadilly and passing a signpost, and my fury at being unable to read it. Then I had a park on my left for some way (Green Park it was, I now know), and before long another on my right, which gave me heart, for I assumed I must soon be out of town. There were some houses here, and a Lodge with a milestone in front of it, and a little way beyond that a Turnpike. But I never reached there. Of a sudden my legs collapsed under me and the world began to revolve at a rate, and I felt the road cold against my cheek.

And I remember a watchman standing over me and the light of his lantern dazzling my eyes, and his voice reaching me from a very great distance, demanding to know who I was and where I resided, and how I'd come to be hurt.

If I answered, I have no memory of it.

7

It seemed that sick with fever and already tried and
sentenced, I lay in the condemned hold of Newgate on
a pile of sweet straw. My universe was a moist, stifling
place filled with pain. You visited me often – though your
presence was blighted by your detestable association with
Linton – as did one other: a tall, genteel lady in velvet,
who was admitted to my cell to attend me. Even in my
delirium I thought her a strange figure to be found in a
gaol, so cool and elegant was she, so obviously a person
of refinement. She came every day to dress my shoulder
and feed me broth in little spoonfuls – I hardly remember
swallowing any – and often I fancied I was a child again, ill
with the measles and ministered to by Nelly Dean; though
Nelly had not her patience and gentleness. I had little
awareness of time. Once a surgeon came and bled me,
and once – that first night, I think – another gentleman,
but they were not regular inhabitants of my world as she
was. The room went from dark to light, from light back
to dark, as the days passed; I hadn't the wit to keep count
of the changes.

Then, quite suddenly, I found myself troubled by the
light. It streamed in through a large window – too large
for a prison cell – and as I began to revive I grew confused
by what I saw of my surroundings. It was no cell I was
in. I was occupying a spacious, opulent bedroom, not
unlike Lord Mansfield's, furnished and decorated with
the exquisite taste that only those who have bottomless
purses can afford. The floor was richly carpeted in deep
blue, the curtains were of damask, the furniture inlaid
with marquetry and lustrous with fresh beeswax; and my

straw mattress proved to be a comfortable down-filled bed with satin pillows. By comparison, Thrushcross Grange would have seemed a hovel.

I cudgelled my brains to recollect how I'd come there, but no amount of reflection would give it me, and, finding a small bell beside the bed, I rang it vigorously to see what it would bring. The effort required for so simple a task exhausted me and set my shoulder throbbing, and this reminded me to investigate what I might have supposed an ideal wound; but I found it to be real enough and healing nicely under the bandages – the upper portion of my chest had been expertly bound, my shirt having been removed for the purpose. So had my breeches – a development which must make escape, should it prove necessary, an immodest business.

The bell brought a maid-servant, who poked her head into the room, giggled once, then retired. Two or three minutes later I heard footsteps outside. There was a cursory tap on the door, and it opened to admit a woman of about thirty dressed in a gown of sea-green silk. It did not take me long to recognize her as the nurse of my feverish dreams. As she approached the bed her gown clung to her body and showed a very handsome figure.

She now seated herself carefully at the end of the bed, arranging her skirts, and I had my first opportunity to observe her properly. Her face was rather long for perfect beauty, but I could fault it in no other particular, and I'm no flatterer of women's looks. Her complexion was most striking, being entirely unmarked by natural blemish or cosmetic artifice (I was later to learn that she had a horror of paint, though all ladies of fashion invariably use it in London), and her teeth were small and even and hardly worn away at all by pumice. She wore a light perfume – very agreeable – and had her hair fastened in a knot instead of heaped a foot high on top of the head in the

French manner. In all, she was as far as you are, Cathy, from being one of those stupid, fussing, empty-headed creatures who enslave themselves to modishness, ruining their health and looks in the process.

'Well,' said she, curling her lip so that only the tips of her little teeth were revealed in what was more of a sneer than a smile, 'you lived.'

'Apparently,' I said. 'Was the outcome doubted?'

'Oh, no. Never. You have the constitution of a rat.' The comparison did not flatter me and I was quick to say so. Her reply was, 'Pray, do not mind it. Rats have the most fortitude of any creatures I know. Besides, you required a deal of nursing.'

'By you?' was my next question.

'That was my unpleasant duty,' she replied. 'Some acquaintance on your part with soap and water would have rendered it less onerous.' Again that sneering smile – it was a favourite trick of hers, I was to discover. 'Are you in the habit of sleeping in your clothes? Or do all persons of your class do it?'

Her impertinence astounded me. And since I could not believe that she was too much of a fool to appreciate how unwelcome were her remarks, I concluded that it was her intention to provoke me, which made me wonder how this could be the same tender person who had nursed me so devotedly through my sickness.

'Do not colour up so,' she said. 'It makes you look like boiled lobster.'

'Then,' I replied calmly, 'I'd advise you not to goad me. Persons of my class do not scruple to pay back a lady's insults, and you'll find me readier than most to answer you in kind.'

'Aha!' she exclaimed. 'I see I was not misinformed about you.'

'That would depend,' said I, 'on what you were told and who told it you.'

63

'Oh, I can tell you that. You were described as a surly, ill-bred ingrate, entirely lacking grace or finer feelings; a rude, boorish provincial person who is used to the company of pigs and would sooner grunt swinishly than utter a civil word. There. What, has that heated the water? I declare you've gone quite into the purple. It must be untrue, then.'

'Who are you to speak so to me?' I demanded, almost beside myself. 'And I insist upon knowing who has been slandering me.'

At this she threw back her head and laughed freely, her mouth wide open and a cruel temptation to my fist. 'How its hackles rise,' she teased. 'Elizabeth Durrant speaks so to you, Earnshaw, and being your mistress gives her the right. As for the other, truth is no slander, the less so when your master has uttered it. And he is no mean judge of boors. Yes, you may open your mouth like a landed fish. You owe me your life, I fancy, and your continued freedom depends on the hospitality of this house. A little respect, therefore, if you please.' Here she touched me lightly, playfully, on the arm. 'There are those who would dearly love to question you concerning your part in last week's disturbances.'

I contained myself sufficiently to inquire where I was, since my last memory was of wandering about London in a wretched condition.

'You are in Hill Street,' Mrs Durrant told me. 'The watch brought you here three parts dead on the night Newgate and some other places were burned by the mob. It seems you had wit enough to say you were my husband's servant.'

I said, 'I am nobody's servant.'

She shook her head firmly. 'You are what you have made yourself, as my husband will no doubt delight to tell you. As soon as you're recovered you'll commence earning your bread, and I doubt you'll prove a degree less objectionable than poor Haskell. I do not always share my husband's judgement of men.'

She got up and crossed the room to the door, leaving me in such confusion that I could not get a sentence together with which to detain her. At the door she turned, however, saying: 'If you would like to read your book I'll send the girl up with it.'

'Book?' I said foolishly.

'A volume of bound, printed pages,' she replied with heavy sarcasm – I noticed she inclined to it. 'In this case a pocket edition of Blackstone's *Commentaries*. You had it with you when you were brought here, so naturally I asked if you would care to read it.'

I could think of no other evasive answer than that I was too tired to read, but she seized on it at once and offered to return later. I said I thought her husband might object to that, at which she sniffed. 'He is frequently away,' she said. 'And he would hardly object to my being in *your* company.'

'Is he away now?' I asked, puzzled by her last remark.

'I expect him back this evening. No doubt he will want to speak to you when he returns, so our tryst must be deferred.' And with a sneering grin, she left me to my thoughts. Crowded and curious they were, as you may guess, and they occupied me until evening.

Just as I heard a clock strike nine somewhere in the house, a carriage drew up outside my window, and about half an hour after, Mr Durrant came into my room.

'You are much better, I see,' he said, pulling a chair up to the bed. 'My business took me out of London for a few days quite unexpectedly, or I would have visited you before this.' He paused. I began to speak, but he held up his hand to halt me, then continued: 'I hear you made the acquaintance of my wife today, Heathcliff. I am interested to know what you thought of her. Is she not

65

the sweetest, the loveliest, the most enchanting creature in the world? Are you not already in love with her?'

'I am not,' I said.

'Not?' with raised brows.

'Decidedly not,' I confirmed. 'Mrs Durrant seems to have formed a hearty dislike for me, and I am not in the habit of entrusting my affections to enemies.'

If I expected this to displease him I was no judge of character, for his response was a delighted chuckle. 'So she tells me,' he said. 'And I own I am not entirely surprised. On the contrary, it would have astonished me if your unaffected manner had endeared itself to her, for she has a marked preference for the bowing, hat-waving, hand-kissing kind of macaroni she invites to her drums. No, this suits me excellently, Heathcliff, I assure you; and benefits you more than you can know. Oh, yes. I had intended using you elsewhere, but that is now changed.' He chuckled again and moistened his lips with his tongue. 'The thought of you as her constant companion will in every way make my absences endurable.' His face became serious again. 'But though I cannot make you two mutually agreeable and would not dream of attempting it, I will take it very unkindly if you do not always show her the utmost respect and courtesy. I dote on her, you see. I am a fool about it. If you have experienced the affliction, Heathcliff – for that is what it is – you will understand how the thing works. To invest love in such a woman is like investing money in the South Sea Company – the more you pour in, the more is demanded, swallowed up; and with small hope of a return. Yet I do not mind it as long as I can justify my folly, and I justify it like the beast in the fable – what I cannot have myself I take pleasure in denying others.'

This last remark of his brought a faint smile to my own face. I knew more about it than he imagined, though it was difficult for me to recognize love from his description – I would not deny *you* to any man on earth if I truly believed he could make you happier than I could. 'I understand that impulse, certainly,' I told him. He offered me his hand and I took it, warming to the fellow. Nothing endears us more to another than hearing our own opinions from his mouth.

'I think you will prosper in my service, Heathcliff,' he remarked, pumping my arm until my shoulder ached. 'You may even improve yourself by it.'

For the next half hour we conversed on a number of topics, and I found him a capital fellow to talk to. I told him something of my part in the rioting, but took the precaution of speaking only in general terms and omitted to mention Bloomsbury Square – I said I was shot in error by a patrol, while walking the streets in search of his house. He complimented me on my wisdom in giving his name to the watch – it was a respectable one, he said, and the hue and cry after the rioters would be unlikely to reach Hill Street. 'Besides,' he assured me, 'you are not named on any warrant.'

With some bitterness, I said, 'I assume from all this that the revolution was not accomplished.'

It drew a laugh from him. 'No, not accomplished. It was neither intended nor desired, Heathcliff. The sum of the mob's achievements in a week was four prisons and a gin distillery broke open – labours of love, if ever there were any – a few private houses sacked, and a miserable attempt on the Bank of England which was beaten off single-handed, if one credits the accounts, by Mr Wilkes. Mr Wilkes is the author of the accounts. No, London is again the inequitable sink it has ever been, a condition your low companions of last week are anxious to maintain. If you doubt it, take a louse from your body and place it in a glass jar, then observe its conduct. You'll find it will not survive long away from its source of nourishment. No parasite can.'

'Indeed,' I said, remembering Tom Burns. 'They have no wish to tear down society while they can profit from it.'

'It is a myth,' he affirmed. 'And, like the Christian myth, which extols meekness and subservience, it is spread by the strong to discourage opposition. That the weak swallow it is a fair measure of their folly. Forgive me, my dear fellow, if you are a Christian.'

'As much of one as you are,' was my reply, at which he nodded approvingly.

'Then all that remains to be seen,' he said, 'is whether you are a hypocrite.'

I asked what he meant by that, but he seemed not to hear and went on to a different subject – something about the soul's enslavement to the body, I think it was; at any rate, a doctrine he expounded with considerable passion. By the time he rose to go I had got to like him well enough to accept his offer of employment. He appeared perplexed when I said this, as if my refusal had been unimaginable, and when I said I had no clear notion of what were to be my duties he answered a little snappishly: 'Plain as your face. Be her companion as Haskell is mine. Drive her, escort her, protect her about town and at home. You will lodge here, taking your meals with Mrs Durrant when I am away from the house, in the servants' hall when I am in residence. There, it is simple, undemanding work.'

'Is that all?' I said.

'Ah, your wage. From me you will receive two pounds each week, but you are never, for any reason, to take money from her. You are in my employ, not hers. Is that enough? Or must I also tell you what is obvious?' He sighed. 'I see I must. Very well, then. Never be her messenger – she has others for that – and see to it that she entertains no male visitors, save with my approval, and is alone with no man other than yourself at any time. In this regard you have my permission to use whatever means you consider appropriate to convince any gentleman who shows more than a polite interest in Mrs Durrant that his attentions are unwelcome. And of course you must report any such occurrences directly to me.'

'I'm to be her guard and your spy, it seems,' I commented.

'There,' he said. 'You did know my requirements. Don't frown, my dear fellow. From time to time I'll relieve you of these responsibilities for a short while, in favour of other work that should be more to your taste.'

I pressed him, but he would not be more explicit, and soon after quitted the room.

8

Within a few days I was sufficiently recovered to be out of bed for several hours together, and though I had not yet the strength to take up my duties, I was provided with a more serviceable suit of clothes than my own, fresh linen and some other necessaries, including a somewhat rusted sword. This last Mr Durrant gave me, with the assurance that he did not expect me ever to draw it from its scabbard, as almost any gentleman in England would be more skilful with it than I and to do so might prove fatal; but it looked well and he might one day arrange to have me instructed in its use. At Mrs Durrant's insistence I was made presentable by being taught to wear a tye wig and encouraged to bathe and change my linen with uncommon regularity – all of which made me feel disgustingly like a molly (as effeminate men are called). But I left off bathing after I heard Mr Durrant accuse his wife, one day, of attempting to 'mollify' me; which she seemed to consider a huge joke.

I soon discovered what an odd creature she was: a wilful, pettish, unpredictable woman, given to fits of sulking and ungovernable tempers; but capable of being the next minute sweet as a moorland breeze. Anything would set her off – it wasn't necessary for her to be thwarted; a misplaced fan might do it – and an equally trifling occurrence would suffice to put her right. She was contrary as summer frost, and her husband showed himself a poor farmer: the more accommodating he was, the more she raged at him and found fault. Witnessing a good many such scenes during my first weeks in that household, I realized he'd spoken the truth when he declared himself a fool about her; and I determined that I'd drown her in her own bathing tub if ever she showed that shrewish humour to me.

But through the month of June I saw surprisingly little of her. The London season was at its height and Mr Durrant was on hand to escort her to the succession of balls, masquerades, theatre parties and expeditions to Ranelagh that filled her evenings. Her custom was to spend her mornings in bed, her afternoons shopping for silk and lace fal-lals at the New Exchange (I accompanied her once or twice and was much embarrassed by it), and her evenings, when there was no entertainment to attend, twittering or playing at loo with her fashionable friends in the drawing-room at Hill Street.

One afternoon, however, I received a summons to her drawing-room and found her alone in there, reclining on a sofa. She was reading a book.

'I want company,' she said in that imperious way of hers, and waved me to a seat, a low stool she'd placed at her feet.

Deliberately taking a chair on the other side of the room, I said: 'Your husband's in the library, I think. I'll call him.'

'I don't desire his company,' was her reply. 'He has an uncultured disregard for reading, and I want to be read to.' I said that was not my impression of Mr Durrant, but, 'Pray, don't contradict me, Earnshaw,' she snapped. 'And sit here if you please.'

'I'm not your lap-dog, Mrs Durrant,' I told her, 'so don't expect me to sit at your feet like one.'

'Lap-dogs sit upon laps,' she laughed, 'and that's a privilege I haven't extended to you. Come, don't be such a baby, Heathcliff – that is your name, isn't it?' I affirmed that it was. 'Such a peculiar name,' she mused. 'It has the sound of a natural name, a geographical region perhaps, or a mountain. Heathcliff. It could be a country

71

seat, though. "I trust you'll stay a few days with me at Heathcliff, for the shooting, My Lord." Yes, now that I think of it, you look like something fashioned out of stone or rock, Heathcliff. Are you a statue come to life? Hardly a Galatea, though, I think.'

I had no idea what she was prattling about and said so, drawing from her a look of amazement. I was half-way to the door when she called out: 'Who gave you leave to go?'

'My legs,' I answered.

'By God, you're an impertinent rogue.' But she did not say it in an ill-natured way. Then, 'Come back, Heathcliff.' I had the door open by now and gave no sign that I'd even heard her. 'Please, Heathcliff,' she whined. 'I'm vexed with loneliness.'

'If I'm to sit with you,' I said, returning, 'you'd better first understand this, Mrs Durrant: I'm no servant and haven't the disposition of one. Peremptory commands will get you nothing from me but a view of my back.'

'I've already had the pleasure of seeing it,' she replied. 'It seems able to support more weight than you show inclination to bear. I am surprised that you consider it manly to display such sensibilities to a woman.'

I mumbled some answer, but evidently she thought she'd won a victory over me, for, appeased by it, she made room for me beside her on the sofa. I seated myself there with great reluctance.

'Now,' she said in a sweeter tone, 'our quarrel is finished. You mustn't brood over it. Would you rather read or tell me how you got your fine name?'

And so, by degrees, she wheedled it out of me – not everything, but more of my history than I'd given her husband and more than I wanted known by anybody in London. I told her how your father had found me and named me after his own dead son, how since his death Hindley had treated me abominably; and how I'd finally run away, thinking to make my fortune before returning to Yorkshire. As soon as I'd said all this I regretted it. It made me feel vulnerable to have confided so much to her, yet it was oddly comforting too.

'So you're a foundling,' she said at length. 'How interesting. Though you are not the first nameless person I've encountered in my life. Am I to keep it secret?' I scowled at her, which made her say: 'Of course I am.' Then she gave a little sigh and said: 'Now tell me about Cathy.'

I could not have been more confounded if she'd declared herself a witch and claimed to have plucked your name from my skull. I stared at her like an idiot and, playfully, she gave me back what I took to be a fair copy of my own gaumless, open-eyed gaze, then dissolved it in a hearty laugh.

'You spoke her name in your fever,' she explained. 'It was I who nursed you and she who got the thanks. I've been mildly curious about her since. What is she like, Heathcliff? Some little country wench, I imagine, fresh-cheeked as an apple. Did you play country games together? Do tell me.'

'I've no desire to discuss her with you,' I said.

'Aha!' was her response. 'The lobster's on the boil again. How charming your coyness is, and quite unexpected. Come, don't be a silly boy. My interest is harmless enough.'

'The more so if you keep it to yourself,' I snarled.

'Very well,' said she. 'Who is Linton, then? No friend of yours by the sound of him, so you needn't be protective about him.'

'I have things to do,' I said, shifting on my seat.

'Nonsense. You have nothing to do but what you've been engaged to do – which is to amuse me when I require it. And I require it now, Heathcliff. Tell me about this Linton person, therefore.'

'I'll be damned if I will,' I growled, for she was putting me dangerously out of patience with her frivolous questions.

'How boorish of you,' she said lightly, tossing her head. 'I assure you it really does not matter whether you tell me about your dull provincial life or no. I simply thought it would provide an easy topic of conversation for you. Perhaps you would prefer to talk about classical authors, or the opera, or Doctor Johnson's opinions of Shakespeare, or Reynolds' style of painting, or Gainsborough's, or the progress of the American war, or Monsieur Rousseau's philosophy compared with Mr Hume's. No, your interest is law, is it not? We'll discuss Locke, then, or Fielding, or Barrington, or Blackstone – have you only that one volume of the *Commentaries*? He is most enlightening on Inheritance, don't you find? Ah, me. What a stimulating conversation this is. I do not remember when I last enjoyed the company of such a well-informed man.'

By now she had me almost choked on my own bile, and she knew it, for out came that sneering smile once more, as if she knew how well it suited her to play the superior bitch. I believe I would have throttled her if she hadn't ceased then, of her own accord. But she was a clever one. She sensed how far I'd let her go before being compelled to place my hands around her slender white neck and squeeze her into silence.

'I shall read to you from Blackstone,' she announced then, and produced the volume from beneath a cushion. 'My, what a neat hand you write,' she said, leafing through. 'Such learned comments, too. Ah, this passage will do nicely.'

And she began to read about estates of freehold and inheritances fee-simple, going on to heirs and successors and estates tail – none of it comprehensible to me, all of it dull, dry, tiresomely repetitious stuff that had me near to yawning. Her proximity was distracting also, for I was close enough to smell her perfume and to observe the undulations of her bosom as she drew breath for each new sentence. Suddenly she broke off to say: 'Heathcliff, I believe you are not attending. Surely my reading cannot be so spiritless. You shall read, then. Here, take it.' And she thrust the book into my hands.

Imagine my torment as she leaned back expectantly into the cushions and closed her eyes. I was in hell at that moment.

'I prefer to listen to you,' I said, but it emerged with little feeling. I felt myself growing hot and began to fidget, and ran my fingers around the inside of my collar. But she would not have it. It was my turn, she said, and she was already quite hoarse. I must continue in her stead.

When I still did not make a start she said: 'Why, your response is enough to make me think you cannot read, Heathcliff.'

'I can read as well as –' I commenced, then quickly halted myself.

'As well as . . .?' she probed.

'As well as I wish to,' I supplied. 'And since I do nothing to order, I've no wish to read to you.'

She sat up now. 'I gave no order, Heathcliff. But let me be more polite. Please read to me, Heathcliff. I should be most grateful if you would, Heathcliff. There, you cannot complain at that.'

'Damn you – no!' I cried.

'Because you cannot. So admit it.'

'Why should it matter to you,' I demanded, 'if I can or cannot read?'

'Because it matters to you,' she said coolly, 'or you would not lie about it.'

I jumped up then. The book fell to the floor and I kicked it across the room. 'You are a damned bitch, Mrs Durrant,' I thundered, my mortification complete.

75

'I have been called worse,' she replied calmly, adding: 'by sedan-chairmen. You have missed your proper vocation.'

Then she held up her hands in mock-terror to ward off the oaths I vociferated, but she was proof against them, and we both knew I had nothing in my armoury that could even scratch her shell. My humiliation was such that I had no choice but to run from the room like a scolded child, my brain teeming with phantasies of what I should enjoy doing to that infernal bitch, if ever I had the chance.

That evening I decided to quit Mr Durrant's service, and had arrived at his study door to tell him so when I heard raised voices from within. Uncertain whether to announce myself just then, I hesitated, and could not avoid witnessing a pretty conversation between Mr Durrant and his wife.

'I intend to go to it,' said she, 'with or without you.'

'I think not, madam,' came his heated reply. 'You've flirted with enough of your foppish friends this season. Here's one ball you'll miss.'

'It's a masque,' she corrected, adding petulantly: 'and I'll not miss it. Everybody who counts will be there. You may be low, but I have a certain rank to maintain. Why cannot you postpone your expedition? Surely the fruit will be that much riper for being left a few more days on the tree.'

'That fruit, as you call it, keeps you in luxury, Elizabeth. Pray, remember it. If you must go, go. Heathcliff will accompany you.'

She gave a brittle laugh. 'Heathcliff! I should be mortified to death with him alongside me in that company. My God, it's bad enough with you. They snigger at you behind your back. They would laugh at him to his face. I declare you excelled yourself, Alex, when you chose that one. I'd rather the company of a monkey.'

'Monkeys bite,' said Mr Durrant. I heard him snort, but whether in amusement or derision I couldn't tell. 'And this one has a quick temper.'

'Ha!' was her response. 'I can manage him. But, dearest Alex, why put me to the trouble? Be a good boy and send him away.'

'You would like that, would you? Well, *there's* an excellent reason to keep him. It will give you an opportunity to discover what a low-bred person really is.'

'I despise you,' she said. 'You are utterly contemptible.'

'More so for loving you as I do,' he answered. 'Pray excuse me, Elizabeth. I have work to do.'

A moment later the door was thrown violently open and Mrs Durrant stormed through. 'Eavesdroppers should learn not to colour up, for they're spared nothing,' she flung at me as she passed, pausing only to hoist up her skirts for the stairs.

Before I could respond, Mr Durrant called from his study: 'Who is there? Is that you, Heathcliff?' When I said it was he bid me enter and take a seat. Then, 'How much of it did you hear?' he inquired.

'Enough,' I said, 'to let me know I'm unwelcome here.'

'Nonsense,' he retorted. 'It would be extremely naïve of you to suppose I meant my remarks, and a sign of weak character to let my wife's drive you out of doors. She loathes you, certainly; but she despises me, and reviles us both with the same breath. You must take it as a challenge, as I do – a sport, even. We'd be poor foxes to flee while the brach only slavers.'

'You are a gentleman,' I reminded him. 'I am not fitted for field sports.'

'Tush. Then why be chivalrous and quit the field when a lady offers you combat? Besides, you have a certain natural nobility and lack only the other prerequisite for gentility – pounds sterling. They are become as great a leveller with us as death. Hundreds will make you a gentleman, whatever your breeding; thousands will elevate you to the peerage; and with hundreds of thousands you may command like any emperor. So let me start you up the ladder of ennoblement with five of the things, which I'll give you in exchange for an evening's work.'

My suspicion must have been apparent, because he hastily assured me it was not intended as a bribe. I was free to take or refuse it, stay or go.

'What am I to do for the money?' I asked.

'Good fellow,' he said. 'Enjoy this, for it's undoubtedly the easiest commission I will ever give you.' Then he explained to me what he required. He was very particular about one or two puzzling points, but the short of it was that I was to call at several houses in Covent Garden, collect from each a packet for him, and bring these back, unopened, to Hill Street. 'You are perplexed now,' he said, 'but it will be plain to you later. And the experience may teach you a thing. Now be good enough to go directly, and do not neglect to arm yourself.' He appeared amused by something, but did not explain the joke and, waving me away, busied himself at his desk.

9

My first instruction had been to walk as far as Piccadilly, then hire a hackney-coach – he'd given me some coins for fare. It was a cool, fresh evening for late June and I was glad of the opportunity for a walk, having been out of the house little during my convalescence, and then rarely on foot. As I made my way along Piccadilly I could not help comparing its appearance on the night I wrote of with its aspect in the normal conditions now prevailing. There was no longer a hellish glow to the sky, only the even brilliance of the street lighting – all the West End of town is illuminated after sunset – and the road and pavement, far from being empty at that latish hour, fairly bustled with coaches, chairs, chariots and groups on foot. It might have been broad day.

I got a coach at Coventry Street, though the driver would have been happier to go in another direction and had to be sweetened with a florin. There was a gloomy patch around Leicester Fields, which he treated like the course at Newmarket – footpads are as numerous here as squirrels in woodland – but we arrived without mishap at the Piazza, and since the fellow would not wait I had to pay him off.

All the houses I was to call at were in this vicinity, the first of them in the Piazza itself. This is a singular, vaulted street – more like some Italian cathedral than a London thoroughfare – partly in shadow from the great arches which line it, and on the other side splendidly illuminated by the light-filled windows of a terrace of grand houses. Each seemed to vie with its neighbour in the magnificence of its chandeliers. But the house I sought proved the most luxurious of them all. It had marble staircases and everywhere was marble and gilt, plush and glass. The curtains were velvet and silky paper covered the walls, while one entire wall, from floor to ceiling, was a gigantic rose-coloured mirror, in which all that opulence was not merely reflected but enhanced. A fairy-tale palace it was, such as Nelly used to describe to us, and which my childish imagination would provide with a hundred servants, there expressly to guard against any intrusion of mine.

Yet I not only walked into this place unchallenged, but was warmly welcomed by a pretty little lass of twelve or thirteen, who had been sitting with some older girls in the window. I inquired, as Mr Durrant had told me to, for Mother Makepeace. Without a word the child went to fetch her.

She returned presently with a stout matron dressed in a purple gown – I took her for the child's mother. This person greeted me with a simpering smile that threatened to crack open her face – it was a mask of white paint I know not how many inches thick – and asked what was my pleasure.

'I'm come for the rent,' I said, faithful to my instructions, 'for Mr Sherall.'

Her response was to take my hand in one of her own, which was white and puffy and loathsomely moist – like a skinned rabbit-foot – and draw me aside. Then she studied me closely before saying: 'You're new. Green, too. Describe your master to me.' When I had done so she nodded and grinned at me. 'Sour-looking, but not badly put together,' was her next comment. 'Never seen a *bagnio* before, have you, my sweet?'

'I wouldn't know one if it kicked me,' I answered.

'Ha,' said she. 'Not from hereabouts either, and greener than Fleet Ditch. Well, you can be kicked if that's your pleasure, though I doubt it is, from the look of you. I fancy you more for a kicker. The rent, as you call it, is ready. But tell your master it's short because I'm short three, and will he kindly provide three fresh as soon as convenient? No notion, have you, what I'm talking about?' I said I had none and was not paid to. 'Bit weak in the loft, my sweet?' said she. 'But I dare say you keep your wit in your breeches for warmth.' She seemed to think for a moment, then announced in a loud voice: 'Girls, this is Mr Sherall's new boy.'

To my embarrassment the young women in the window came over and set to scrutinizing me like so many wives at a market stall. Thinking to be polite, I remarked to Mother Makepeace that she had a handsome family, at which all of them burst simultaneously into giggles, and without the least sign of apology for their rudeness.

I determined to say nothing more if their humour took that turn, so did not reply when Mother Makepeace asked me which of the girls I liked best. But my obstinate silence, it seemed, or the set of my countenance, was fuel also; for their amusement was instantly rekindled, the little one having to pound two of her sisters on the back to keep them from choking.

'I like none of them too well,' I said with feeling. 'They are too silly and ill-mannered.'

If they'd judged my last remark comical, this they greeted with such clamorous merriment that the tears ran – I'd have fain boxed their ears for a farthing. 'Tush,' says Mother Makepeace, her face now streaked, 'they're among the finest ladies of the town.' Then, seeing I was out of all patience and ready to go with or without the rents, 'Louisa,' says she, 'will attend to you,' stroking the hair of the young lass I'd met first. 'She's the best little milkmaid in the Garden.' To the girl she said: 'Go upstairs and give him what he wants, my sweet.'

Mindful of my errand, I followed the child upstairs, relieved to be out of that cackling company at last. I had the sense of being badly used, though just how I could not have said. Louisa ran pertly ahead up several flights of stairs and conducted me at last into a small bedchamber near the top of the house, where, stopping only long enough to kick the door shut behind us, she commenced unfastening her dress with practised swiftness, damning this hook and cursing that lace as she did so. So sudden and so striking was her transformation from saucy child to coarse-mouthed slut that before I could untie my tongue she'd managed to shed every stitch of her clothing, and, leaving them where they'd fallen on the floor, she now hopped naked as a nestling on to the bed.

'Got your own armour?' says she. 'Or shall I provide?' I articulated some perplexed sound, I think. This was all so unpredicted I hadn't quite got myself together yet. 'Mrs Phillips' best,' the little minx went on, not minding me. 'Unless you've some more out-of-the-way fancy.'

'You're a whore,' I managed to get out, finding my voice. 'A child-whore.'

'There's a quick wit,' said she. 'What did you take me for? Duchess's grandmother?' She sat up suddenly and put her head on one side. 'We're all game girls. Didn't you know?'

I said it was only just become clear to me, and told her to get her clothes on directly. But my mistake was to regard her as a wayward child, for in doing so I forgot to take account of the harlot's pride she'd developed in the Piazza. Instead of leaping up to cover herself, she twisted her small face into as malevolent a mask as I've seen on man, woman or child in my life, and set to cursing me up hill and down dale with such black imprecations that if oaths were wings my soul would have flown straight to the devil. Then she started mincing around the room, and flaunting, and mocking me, and teasing – Didn't I want her? and was I man or eunuch? – so that it was like being tempted by she-devils in hell.

By God, I was tempted right enough. She heated my blood, that one; but to rage, not to amorous passion – I'd none of that to waste on such a pitiful, degenerate creature as she was. Aye, I pitied her. It was not all her doing. Others had a hand in it – Mother Makepeace, for one, and Mr Durrant or Sherall, as he would have himself called there. Undoubtedly he was not blameless.

'Cover yourself, damn you,' I snarled, flinging one of her petticoats in her face. 'You'd be better served by a sound spanking.'

'Birch twigs are under the bed if that's your pleasure,' answered the wretch, dodging the cuff I aimed at her. If I'd caught her in that moment she'd have answered for more than herself. But she was a wick slip of a lass – I could have chased her till morning without catching her.

My only recourse was to quit the room, which I did without saying another word or giving her another glance. She was shameless enough, too, to stand in the doorway and send her harlot's taunts after me, crying in her shrill child's tones: 'Prefer a boy, would you? We can get you boys, that being your fancy.'

Below, I collected Mr Durrant's packet with such a murderous look in my eyes that neither the Mother nor any of her whorish tribe dared smile or say a word to me, and I said none to them, fearing to do execution in that place if provoked by an exchange.

The other whorehouses being close by, I soon completed my business – my indignation would not have been diminished a jot by the loss of five pounds – and found a hackney-coach to take me back to Mayfair.

I brooded on the way over that experience. Durrant had made a fool of me, and for that he would pay as soon as I could settle how to extract the price from him – five pounds were scarcely sufficient to recompense me for such humiliation. I had decided, by the time the coach turned into Bear Street, that he must pay in kind; but my thinking got no further because suddenly the coach came to a halt, to the accompaniment of cries and scuffling sounds. It rocked as the driver was pulled or pushed from his perch. I heard him grunt as he fell.

In an instant I had both pistols in my hands. It was an instinctive move, not a reasoned one, for I was in two minds about what I should do – fight or let the robbers have Durrant's money. The latter had some appeal for me just then. I cannot say what my course would have been had not a masked face appeared at my window and a voice I had cause to remember snarled: 'Out, damn your eyes, or I'll send you to hell!'

Tom Burns. There could be no mistake about it – we were close enough to the holy land (as they call their quarter) to be within his hunting grounds – and even in the poor light I could make out enough of his features, notwithstanding the mask, to identify him. So here was a fine dilemma: if I moved closer to the window to hand him Durrant's rents, he'd recognize me sure, and having once already left me for dead he'd leave nothing to chance a second time – I was too dangerous to him. Yet if I offered fight the conclusion was as certain, for judging by the sounds they were making, there could not be under five of the devils; and I had lead for two. Edging carefully towards the other window, on the side away from Burns, I peered out into Bear Street. One of the footpads had stationed himself by that door, and beyond him, in the gloom, any number of his confederates might be lurking. Or none at all. It was a risk I had to take.

In as shrill a tone as I could manage, both to disguise my voice and to suggest an innocent traveller's terror, I called: 'I've money. You can have it all, but pray, let me hand it out to you and be on my way.'

'If you're not out of there by the count of three,' came back the reply, 'I'll come in and take what I want off your damned corpse.'

Ah, he was so close. It would have been an easy matter then to have put a bullet in his brain, and for as long as it took to think it I was tempted. What prevented me was the likelihood that I'd need both charges to make my escape, and I had no intention of trading my life for his worthless one – that would have been grander larceny than anything Burns aspired to. I'd not be his accomplice in it. So regretfully, while he counted, I grasped the handle of the opposite door and braced myself, crouching as low as I could get.

'Three,' he said grimly.

In the same moment I twisted the handle and threw all my weight against the coach door. The fool outside had placed himself imprudently close, with the result that the door, having every ounce of my twelve stone behind it, caught him full in the face. He went down like an axed steer, without even a grunt, and I was out and running, iron in both hands and a scream in my throat calculated to freeze the blood of anyone who stood in my path. And there was one, a reckless fellow who launched himself at me from the shadows before I could take aim. His fist grazed my cheek, but mine was weightier, having the pistol in it. I brought up my left arm and fetched him such a mighty clout on the head with the barrel of the weapon that I swear I felt it sink into the depression it made.

This action had lost me time, however, and my pursuers were already uncomfortably close. A hand clutched at my collar. I shrugged it off easily and swung around in time to catch another man diving for my legs to bring me down. I kicked him in the mouth, rattling his teeth nicely, like dice in a cup.

But now I had them all around me, at least four of them – discounting those I'd already settled – and armed with bludgeons. I could see no guns, though. It was a narrow street, with not much light in it, and in the darkness they seemed like rats – dark, wicked shapes, swarming in doorways, gathering for the killing leap at the throat. It was unnerving, I'll own it.

'You'd better keep your distance, scum,' I called in my natural voice. The walls bounced my words back at me, so 'scum' sounded twice.

A moment's complete silence followed. Then I heard Burns say, 'I know you. What was your blasted name, now?'

'Heathcliff Earnshaw,' I said boldly. 'And it's a name you'd do well not to forget again, Burns, for we've a score to settle.'

'We'll settle it presently,' said he. 'Don't be in a hurry. First I want to know where you got the slap. The shiners in the rattler.'

'That money isn't mine,' I answered, and at once remembered what Mr Durrant had instructed me to say to any inquirer. 'It belongs to Mr Sherall.'

'*Does* it?' I got in return. 'And what would a cove like Prince Prig Sherall want with the likes of you? No, I won't swallow that one.'

During this exchange I found I had to keep turning in slow circles, to forestall any attack from behind, and in doing so I had brought myself gradually nearer the edge of the street. A shade further and I'd have a brick wall at my back, in which position I'd have a fair chance of holding the pack at bay. 'You've got the money, haven't you?' I said now. 'You'll get nothing more from me tonight but a leaden bullet. I've two loaded and cocked pistols here, Burns.'

A scornful laugh greeted this piece of intelligence, and, 'Damme if you have, boy, or you'd have used 'em by now. And only two, you say? Take more than two to stop us.'

'I'll need but one to put you underground, Burns,' I roared. 'So be sure you come at me first.' As I said this I felt the touch of cold brick at my back. I permitted myself a slight smile then, for that wall was worth two allies, and with my pistols hot in my grip as two more, I outnumbered the scum.

But I had no time to feel complacent, for just then Burns yelled, 'Get him!' and all of them rushed me together.

I wasted no precious seconds with aiming but fired at the first man in line. The report was shockingly loud in the quiet street, so loud that I'm convinced I gained more from the noise of the shot than from its effect – it hit one of the thieves in the chest, I think, for he fell to his knees with a curse and clutched at his coat buttons. The rest of the swine turned to stone at the sound.

'Now I've only one,' I said steadily in the silence that ensued. 'Who will have it? You, Burns? You?' pointing the loaded weapon at the nearest rogue.

'Another day, Earnshaw,' came Tom Burns' voice from the shadows. 'All right, lads. Before the redbreasts get here.'

I derived grim satisfaction from their departure. Leaving their wounded where they lay, the whole pack of them scuttled away along Bear Street towards Seven Dials and their nest.

Returning to the coach, I found the driver reviving and sound enough, though he had a duck's egg on the side of his skull that would hold up his hat. I helped him up to his box and, desiring no business with the watch, bid him deliver the injured rogues to Bow Street direct and keep the reward himself.

I took a brisk walk back to Hill Street, enjoying the night air and pondering what I should say to Mr Alexander Durrant when I got there.

10

It was some time after midnight when I arrived back at Mr Durrant's house. I found him still in his study at work on his papers; a half-empty brandy bottle stood on the desk.

He glanced up when I entered and seemed in that single glance to read my evening's history in my aspect, for his eyes narrowed only momentarily before returning to whatever it was he was writing. He scratched at it with a show of intense concentration, and when he spoke it was in the tones a preoccupied gentleman uses to a footman leaving a tray.

'You appear not to have my rents,' he said.

'I had them,' I answered, 'but was robbed of them on the way here.'

'Help yourself to brandy,' was his only comment, 'while I finish this.'

I poured myself a generous amount and drank it off in a single gulp, relishing the feel of the fiery stuff in my gullet. 'Have another,' he said, absently. I poured a second glass, which I took more slowly.

In a few minutes he laid down his pen and stretched himself. 'Robbed where and when?' he demanded with a suddenness that startled me. I told him that half a dozen footpads had attacked me in Bear Street not an hour since, at which information he nodded, then said: 'I trust you gave a good account of yourself.'

'I shot one and gave two more headaches,' I told him.

'Splendid,' was his response. 'Did you remember to tell your attackers whose property they were taking?'

'I said it was Mr Sherall's. They knew the name, but took your money notwithstanding. One of them called you Prince Prig. Am I to assume,' I went on, 'that these rogues are in your employ too, and that this was another of your damned tests, Mr Durrant?'

'Quite wrong,' he replied, picking up his pen and touching his lips with it.

'I ask,' I said, 'because I'm heartily sick of your tests and damnably unhappy about your business, which is that of a common whoremaster.'

He tapped his teeth with the pen. 'Not common, Heathcliff. Most uncommon, I assure you. And I confess this moral outrage of yours surprises me. It seems you have more to learn than I supposed.'

'If I'm to learn,' I replied with some warmth, 'how to profit from the moral degradation of children, I think I have education enough already.'

'Degradation?' He smiled. 'I suppose next you will speak of Honesty, or Integrity, or Decency, or Duty – the currency of moralists usually.'

'I'm no moralist,' I said.

'But you feel that my business – what you know of it – lacks integrity. A fair estimate of your opinion?' He did not permit me to answer, but continued: 'Let me inform you about that moral commodity, Integrity. It is undoubtedly the dearest in a very dear market, Heathcliff. The poorest fellows – like yourself – can afford none of it, the richest enough of it to place them above any dealings that might sully their conscience (itself a costly commodity). As with other forms of wealth, the richer one becomes, the more Integrity he can afford; so I no more expect a pauper to possess a scrap of it than I would expect him to possess a castle, for a pauper with Integrity is a man living above his means: what he flaunts so proudly ill suits him and points him out among his fellows for a plain fool.'

I smarted at this. 'I don't take kindly to being called a fool,' I said.

He opened a drawer in his desk and pulled out a purse, from which he drew five gold pieces. Throwing them on the desk, he said: 'I promised you these. Do they salve your wounded pride? Will you demonstrate your Integrity by refusing them?'

'I worked for them and earned every farthing,' I muttered. 'And I don't give a damn how you make your money, Mr Durrant or Sherall, or whatever your name really is. But I won't be your dupe, not for any sum.'

'Well said, Heathcliff,' he replied earnestly. 'That was not my intention, I promise you. I merely thought you would, being young and lusty, enjoy sampling the goods. I guess from your reaction that you did not, and am sorry for it. But there are a good many who do enjoy the service I provide, men of rank among them, and if I did not profit from their needs others would. Yet I suspect you were so outraged for a different reason – because your ideas of what a gentleman's occupation should be were not satisfied by what you discovered about me this evening. Am I wrong? You would have been happier to learn that I was a banker, I think, or a landowner (which I am, as it happens). Instead, you find that I own whorehouses – *bagnios* is the preferred term – and am known to cut-throats; in short, that I have dirty hands. Well, you would be wrong to think it. I let others dirty theirs on my behalf. Shall I acquaint you with the extent of my mischief, so that you'll harbour no more boyish illusions concerning me?'

I said I had no desire to know how he made his money, only to make some of my own. 'As much,' I added, 'as will make me the first gentleman in Yorkshire.'

He sighed deeply at this. 'Ah, Heathcliff,' said he, 'you remind me uncannily of a person I knew a quarter of a century since. It is why I care for you, I think. The chief difference between you is that he had patience and was master of his passions, while you rely on violence, which will never get you what any two coal-heavers have a mind to withhold from you. You should not be content with so little. And do not make the mistake of shunning patience, regarding it as a virtue, for I have observed the most vicious have it in greatest abundance.'

'He didn't begin as low as I am,' I said bitterly.

'You know nothing of where he began,' was his sharp reply. 'But since there are only four ways to fortune – honest toil won't get it – it scarcely matters where you begin.'

'Tell me them,' I said eagerly. 'Tell me them now.'

He smiled. 'I fear you'll find them disappointing, Heathcliff. Two are closed to you, I fancy. The first is to conjure up money by judicious investment, by speculation, manipulation and half a hundred more commercial -ations you know nothing of.'

'The second,' I urged.

'The second is to marry your fortune. To achieve this you must gain admittance to the best society, and for that – if you have no social position – you require money, the desideratum itself. Ergo, the logic is tail-chasing – I dare say that pun* is lost on you. And if you are thinking that servants sometimes marry their mistresses, remember that yours is already married. That road is closed.' He paused, but I did not react. 'The third, then,' he continued. 'The third way is to win your fortune at the tables, but it's a confoundedly uncertain method. It

---

*Mr Durrant's pun is on 'estates tail', a legal concept which in later years Mr Heathcliff was to employ to his advantage. It may be supposed, therefore, that the pun was not lost on him. – W.L.

requires luck and bottom in prodigious quantities, both of which, if you possess them, will serve you better outside a gaming hell than in it. Unless you sharp, of course, though sharping is but a degree less hazardous than method the fourth.'

'Which is?' I put in.

'Which is to steal your fortune from those – dare I say? – "fortunate" enough to have theirs already. But it may lead you to the gallows, where, of all places, gold has no value.'

I had expected a more brilliant analysis from him and found it impossible to conceal my disappointment. I asked, sarcastically, if he expected me to take to the highways.

'You have the requisite talents,' said he, 'and could do worse.'

Thinking he meant it lightly, I cautioned: 'Then take care you don't become one of my victims, Mr Durrant.'

'No,' he replied coolly, 'you take care you do not become mine. I would insist upon a share of your takings. That is the meaning of "Sherall" if you'll think on it. I enjoy puns, Heathcliff.'

'You should explain your pun to Tom Burns, then,' I told him, still unsure if he was in earnest. 'He intends to share your money with nobody.'

His brow became instantly corrugated as he inquired: 'Tom Burns?'

'One of the scoundrels who robbed me,' I supplied. 'A delightful fellow whose acquaintance I made during the riots. He left me for dead once, and tonight tried to complete the work.'

Mr Durrant began to show lively interest in Burns, asking if I knew where he could be found, and who were the members of his gang, and what he looked like. I gave a description, which Mr Durrant wrote down. 'Don't expect to see your money again,' I warned him. 'Fielding's people won't enter that rats' nest they inhabit.'

'No,' he said thoughtfully, 'they won't. But you have a personal score to settle, you say?' I confirmed it. 'Then nurture your grievance,' said he. 'Your appetite will be the keener for it.'

I carried that bit of odd-sounding advice to bed with me, deeming it half prophecy, half promise.

About a week later – it would have been at the beginning of July – Mr Durrant departed on another of his trips, this time into Essex. He was to be gone four days. In a moment of idle curiosity I found myself wondering whether the purpose of these expeditions was to procure country lasses for his *bagnios;* but when I examined my interest closely it proved to be shallow. Why should I care what he did? I had my own aims and was clear about them, and had a single-minded determination to achieve them. Let others, who could afford the luxury of philanthropy, wax sentimental about the destitute, degraded wretches who lacked the gumption to keep out of his clutches. I had first claim on my own charity. Do you blame me for that, Cathy? It was a lesson I learned from you.

If I hadn't also cherished the conviction that my association with Durrant would help me towards achieving my ends, I would not have remained ten minutes in that house. But if it was difficult to tolerate my situation when Durrant was home, it became quickly insufferable in his absence. *She* seemed to take a malicious delight in having me constantly in attendance, as if I were some pup of a footman, and more than once I came close to exchanging my hopes for the short-lived pleasure of snapping her pretty white neck. She would send for me a hundred times in a day, bidding me fetch her this or do that thing for her, or just to bide with her an hour or two, as she felt lonely and miserable with her husband away.

On the second evening of his absence she called me into her bedroom to have me close a window. I found her seated, half dressed, in front of her glass, stretching the skin of her face with her fingers. She did not glance up when I entered but spoke into her mirror, as if addressing my reflection.

'Am I not wrinkled as a sow?' she said, pulling her cheek.

'I've closed your window,' I said. 'Don't call me for that again.'

'Don't be tiresome, Heathcliff,' was her reply. 'Am I hideously wrinkled?' I said I was no judge and advised her to seek her husband's view when he got back. She sighed, then turned to face me, revealing even more of herself in that act than I'd seen on any previous occasion. 'I ask you,' she said, 'because I desire an impartial opinion. You are a man. Men observe such things. Am I ugly, Heathcliff?'

'If you suspected I'd affirm it you wouldn't ask me,' I told her.

'How percipient you are,' she said. 'You find me handsome, then?'

'Bonny enough,' I answered. 'More than that if your character matched your looks.'

'Why must you always be the oaf?' she said in a vexed way. 'Whenever I try to be nice to you I am insulted for my pains. Ah, well. I suppose you cannot help yourself. We must behave according to our nature and our breeding. But tell me, do you never wish you were a fine gentleman instead of a lout? That you did not have broken, dirty fingernails?' Here my hands went involuntarily behind my back. 'That you could turn a compliment to a lady without blushing or stammering? Not that you have ever complimented me. Don't you wish you could be introduced in good company and attract admiring looks from girls, Heathcliff? You would not be unhandsome yourself if you took a little care about your appearance – learned to smile and hold yourself up with dignity. You slouch, you know.'

'I don't care to know what you think of me,' I said.

'Ah,' she teased, 'but I believe you do.'

'I'm damned if I do,' I gave her back.

'There, that proves the case. You invariably curse when you're bested. It is your only defence, and a paltry one. Curse me all you will.'

'Hold your whisht,' I blurted out.

She clapped her hands delightedly. 'Oh, dialect! I adore dialect. More, please, Heathcliff.' I was about to put an end to this one-sided conversation by getting myself out of her range and the door between us, when she flung at me: 'You are fond of gold, I hear. There is a subject we can talk about.'

'Your husband pays me,' I said.

She sniffed. 'I have money of my own and can pay you twice as much, in return for a small favour now and then. Are you willing?'

This smacked of one of her husband's tests, so I was cautious. I said: 'It costs naught to listen.'

She hemmed a moment, then said: 'It's quite foolish really, but Mr Durrant disapproves of some of my friends. All I would require of you is that you sometimes deliver a note for me to a gentleman.'

'The same gentleman each time?' I inquired. 'Or various gentlemen at different times?'

'I don't see that it matters,' she answered curtly. 'Will you do it or not?'

'Would it stop at notes?' was my next question – I asked it with some relish. 'Or would the notes lead to meetings? And would I be expected to busy myself elsewhere when the meetings took place?'

'How clever you must think yourself, Heathcliff,' she sneered. 'What a pity you are not clever enough to disguise your wit but must demonstrate it at every opportunity. It makes you a pitifully inexpert spy.'

'Expert enough to keep you in your place,' I responded.

'As he will keep you in yours,' she snapped back. 'If you are satisfied to remain a servant and a boor all your life, that is your affair. Expect no assistance from me.'

'And you would help me raise myself, would you?' I said. 'Precisely how would you achieve that, Mrs Durrant?'

'With money,' she answered, 'and in other ways. I know a good many influential people. I could introduce you to some of them and you might get preferment that way.'

'Preferment!' I scoffed. 'And who's going to prefer a boor like me, and to what? To a cur on a dunghill? No, I've more experience of the world than to suppose anyone would willingly patronize me. Try again.'

'You may be certain of one thing,' she hissed. 'You'll get nothing but crumbs from my husband's table. He intends to keep you just this side of brutishness, and if you deny me I'll encourage him. Don't imagine you can get the better of him without my help, Heathcliff. He's not the man he seems. I've been trying alone for too many years to be in doubt about his strength of character, and my own is far from weak. Despite my independent exterior, I am as much his chattel as a mediaeval lady would have been her knight's. And you are my chastity belt. Give me the key and we can defeat him together. Withhold it and I'm capable of destroying you. You see, one thing he has taught me is how to be ruthless.'

'I've had a lesson or two from him in that subject,' I replied.

She laughed scornfully and shook her head so that a lock of hair fell loose. 'You can't match my experience,' she said, 'or his depravity. Oh, you'll learn all about him in time, but by then it will be too late for you.'

I said, 'I already know what his business is.'

'Ha,' she scoffed. 'I know what you know, and that is nothing. He sent you to his brothels. He told me that. We enjoyed that joke together, you may be sure. There's much, much more. Do you know where he is gone now?'

'To fetch more whores,' I said.

'Only incidentally. He's gone to scour the rural parishes for foundlings. He's a great humanitarian and benefactor, my husband – Coram was a beginner next to him. A charitable Leviathan, a candidate for sainthood. Has he not mentioned his hospital in Moorfields – near Bedlam, amusingly enough? He lodges them there, his pretty foundling charges, and you've guessed what the girls are destined for. But ask him about the boys. And ask him, if you dare, what became of that boy – I've forgot his name – that boy who threatened to peach on him a year or two since. "Peach" is the correct term, I believe. And ask why he keeps the warehouse in Thames Street, and how Scranton came to Tyburn, and why Haskell is sometimes paid fifty guineas for a night's work, and who receives those mysterious boxes of his from time to time, and who are the people he sees in Bristol and Liverpool and Leeds and Bath. And much more even I know nothing of. "Who sees with equal eye, as God of all,/A hero perish or a sparrow fall," as Pope put it. That is your employer, Heathcliff, and my husband.'

I didn't know what to make of all this, so I said: 'Why don't you inform against him yourself if you want to be rid of him?'

She gave that sneering smile of hers. 'Because I could not prove anything – he's far too cautious – and because I love his money more than I detest him. He must be one of the richest men in London, but if he went to the gallows I'd see none of his money, you may be

sure. I married him for his money, naturally. I believed
he'd got it from his properties – he has them, too, in
abundance – but had I known the rest it would have
made no difference. My mistake was to suppose he was
marrying me for social advantage. I imagined we'd come
to an arrangement, each giving the other total freedom to
bestow our affections where we chose. I did not bargain
for what he terms his "love," for this dungeon to which he
has consigned me, for my succession of human chastity
belts – oh, you are not the first; nor will you be the last.
He dismissed the others after I'd made them useless to
him, and I'll subvert you yet, Heathcliff, when I discover
your Achilles' heel – you must have one. I'll find it,
depend on that. But if, when I have found it, you
co-operate, we may deceive him together indefinitely.
And then I'll be able to hurt him. I'm living for that day.
I'd gladly give my life to repay him for his treatment of
me. But it must be done with subtlety, and that part you
must leave to me.'

Her outburst had taken me by surprise. 'How can you
be sure I won't tell your husband what you've said?' I
asked her.

'I expect you to,' was her reply. 'And so will he. I
shall not deny it. But if I tell him and you do not, you
will have cause to worry. So unless you trust me you
must relate this entire conversation to him as soon as he
returns.'

I said: 'You are a scheming bitch, Mrs Durrant. I
have more pity for your husband than I have for you,
and God knows I've little enough for him.'

Her response was to part her legs very slightly. Softly
she said, 'Do you want me, Heathcliff?'

'You are utterly repugnant to me, Mrs Durrant,' I
told her feelingly.

'Ah,' said she with a short laugh, 'then that is not
the way to win you. My husband said it was not.' I

was a yard or two along the hall when I heard her call through the door: 'Heathcliff! You must make yourself trim for tomorrow evening. You'll be escorting me to Lady Blakely's ridotto, and I insist you look the gentleman.'

11

Several times the next day Mrs Durrant sought me out
to remind me how she wanted me to look. I was to
wear the sword – nobody would observe the rust, she
assured me – and make myself fragrant, and dress my
hair, and generally make myself fit to be her companion
at a gathering of the *beau monde*. In short, I was to ape
the gentleman.

Her insistence was enough for me. It convinced me
that she intended making sport of me with her friends,
and since I'd see her damned before I'd give her that
satisfaction, I determined to be myself and confound her.
Consequently, that evening I neither shaved my face nor
washed it, neglected to put on fresh linen, left off the
sword and dressed myself in the same torn and muddied
suit of fustian I'd worn throughout the riots. Thus I
presented myself to my lady at eleven o'clock, when she
emerged from her dressing room having made her own
toilet – a more elaborate affair, seemingly, since she'd
been two hours at it; though it was hard to tell how she'd
spent the time; her hair was carelessly pinned up and she
had on a long cloak, crossed before, which concealed her
from the neck downwards.

She stood quite still on seeing me in the hall, then
curled her lip and narrowed her cat's eyes at me,
declaring: 'Oh, handsome! Princely, Heathcliff! You
have excelled yourself tonight. I wonder that you suppose
I'd let you accompany me to the stables in that attire,
much less among people of *ton*.'

'I've no intention of providing amusement for your
high-born friends,' I answered. 'Being low, I've dressed

100

low. And you've the simple choice of being seen with me as I am or not being seen at all, for you don't step outside this house without me.'

'Well, if you are not abashed at your ridiculous appearance,' said she haughtily, 'why should I consider your feelings?'

'*My* feelings?' I said in amazement.

'Do as you please,' said she, 'but do not say you weren't warned.'

It was a warm night, and though Lady Blakely's was in Berkeley Square, not three hundred yards distant, a coach was sent for to convey us in grand style – Mrs Durrant alone within, myself aloft with the driver. Only the movement of the air kept me awake, I fancy – these modish London folk keep a brock's hours and emerge at night with polished pelts and sharpened claws for hunting; though what they hunt is each other. And as I hadn't acquired the habit of sleeping away my forenoons, I'd have preferred my bed just then to any entertainment, even that of witnessing my lady's mortification at being seen in my company.

Other coaches were there before us, so we had to be set down a few yards from the entrance steps. I made some sarcastic comment about how stone paving tended to blister genteel feet, but Mrs Durrant was too preoccupied with rummaging beneath her cloak to heed me.

'I've just remembered, Heathcliff,' she said suddenly. 'It was not to be a ridotto at all, but a masque. Isn't that to the good, since it means I will not be recognized?' And handing me a narrow mask of black cloth, she bid me put it on. She produced its twin for herself, saying: 'The rule is to be yourself but never to identify yourself.' Then she started up the steps.

I was left in utter confusion. Her instincts had been uncannily sound, and the sly vixen had tricked me beautifully, and in such a way that I could do nothing about it. She had already walked in. If I was to keep faith with her husband's instructions, I had no choice but to put on the mask and walk in after her.

The hallway swarmed with liveried footmen, who sucked obsequiously at the guests like bees at flowers, taking coats and cloaks, bowing and sniffing out vails. To my unspeakable amazement they fawned on me too. One even conducted me to the entrance of the ballroom – a vast pillared place hung with coloured lamps and decorated all around with fresh-cut roses – and asked in what character I'd come so that he could announce it.

Before I could open my mouth an answer was supplied from behind us. Mrs Durrant's voice it was, saying: 'We are come as a gipsy couple.' I turned and saw the result of her two hours' labour in her dressing room. She'd shed her cloak and under it was wearing a shabby, ill-fashioned gown of some darkish, coarse stuff – dimity perhaps, or serge – with little frills around the sleeves and hem, and low enough in front to identify her sex to a blind man. Her hair was unpinned and hung loose over her face like a weeping willow, and she'd fixed gold rings to her ears by some means, and darkened her cheeks with soot. 'It's rude to stare, Heathcliff,' she reproved. 'I look no odder than you, so cast no stones.'

I was given no chance to reply or withdraw. Mrs Durrant took me by the arm and fairly pulled me into that confusion of noise and harlequin colour. There was music being played, and that was in rivalry with the shrieks and shrill laughter of shepherdesses and slave-girls and Cleopatras, and no doubt with the piping merriment of the sultans and the Cupids too – they all seemed to be frolicking about together regardless of their sex, actual or assumed, to the accompaniment of much high-pitched giggling. The entire scene resembled some fantastic brainsick dream, being rather grotesque than merely

102

whimsical. And I felt myself shrink from it as from the portals of hell.

Yet though my instinct was to shun the company of these bizarre, petted creatures, they seemed unaccountably anxious for mine. We had not advanced a dozen steps into the room when a flight of fan-waving nymphs and mincing satyrs and simpering goddesses descended on us with fluttering hands and precious exclamations of delight and wonder. And were we not enchanting! And what absolute perfection was our costume! And how exquisitely dusky the gentleman – that was myself – had contrived to make himself! One obese creature – an Aphrodite, if you'll credit it – actually tapped me on the chin with her fan and demanded to know who I was and where I'd been acquired – as though I were some toy or pet animal that had been bought cheap in a market.

'I'm not her damned possession,' I cried, but before I could get out another word Mrs Durrant interrupted with:

'Take care how you speak to us gipsies, my lady. We've rough tongues. And this one has a thoroughly bad nature too. I'm no better, of course, being his doxy.'

'How remarkably clever of you to master their frightful cant,' said Aphrodite, clapping her hands with glee. Then she gave out some affected superlative – such as that we were the cow's ears or something like it – and insisted on showing us off to Lord Somebody-or-other. Mrs Durrant promised she should do it later, however, and the pack of them went away satisfied.

'I'll not forget this trick you've played on me tonight, Mrs Durrant,' I said when we were alone again.

'Don't be such a silly boy,' said she. 'You've seen how safe you are in that costume. You may say and do what you will, and the result will be that everyone will think you a consummate actor.'

'You are amused by it, are you?'

'Yes, but that was not my purpose. My purpose was to demonstrate to you the refinement and manners you lack. Were this not a masque, Heathcliff, you could not utter two consecutive words here without disclosing your inferiority.'

'Inferiority to what?' I returned. 'Do you suppose there's anything here I covet? God, I'd rather be an ape all my life than one of those sneaking ninnies yonder that call themselves men.'

'They are not all sneaking ninnies,' she said calmly. 'And to prove it I will show you one who is not. Now you will meet a real gentleman, Heathcliff, and if you have any good sense you will take him for a model. He also has what you want – red blood in his veins. He knows how to appreciate a lady. Now, I intend to dance all evening with him, and you are at liberty to dance with whichever of the Cupids you think handsomest.'

Knowing she'd drawn blood, she tripped lightly across the room to where a tall, well-formed gentleman was standing by one of the marble pillars. He was dressed in Roman costume and wore a laurel wreath on his head, his natural hair being cropped quite short. I could not make out much of his face under the mask, but he had what is called a patrician nose and a fair complexion, so that I formed an instant dislike for him, being reminded of Edgar Linton – though he had a better build than Linton and a more upright carriage. I saw Mrs Durrant touch her fingers first to her own lips, then to his, saw him catch her hand before she could withdraw it and incline his head to give it a proper kiss. This elaborate genteel ritual being concluded, he took her arm and led her into the dance.

Why their behaviour should have enraged me I have no idea, but it did, and I was in a black mood as I stationed myself by the same pillar and waited for the dance to be concluded. When it was they returned hand in hand, laughing together.

'Ah,' was Mrs Durrant's first comment, 'His Majesty has condescended to join us. My Lord Caesar, allow me to present to you the King of the Gipsies.'

'A most effective disguise, sir,' said he. 'And who is he really, Elizabeth? Another of your husband's blackguards? He looks like one.'

'His name is Heathcliff, Charles,' said she, 'and he is likely to puff himself up like a snake and spit venom in your eye if you insult him.'

'Is he, egad? Then I must take care to be civil to the fellow. I dare say he has the wit to distinguish jest from insult.'

'Don't risk your teeth on it,' I snarled.

'My dear sir, forgive me,' was his reply to this. 'I meant only that to find the pearl one must first open the oyster. Are you in town for the season or do you reside in London permanently, Mr Heathcliff?'

'Heathcliff is his first name,' supplied Mrs Durrant with evident amusement. 'He is originally from Yorkshire, where he has estates.'

'My apologies again, sir,' said the gentleman. 'Elizabeth is overfond of teasing, so I never know how to take her. I believe the shooting is excellent in the north, is it not?'

'The shooting is good,' I replied, 'wherever there is something worth the lead.' I wished I could decide if the man was being polite or mocking, for until I knew which it was I was uncertain how to respond to him. His conversation vexed me.

'I have been remiss,' said Mrs Durrant. 'I realize I have not introduced you properly. These masquerades have idiotic rules about it. Heathcliff, this is Colonel Charles Bassett of His Majesty's Life Guards. Charles, you are in the exalted company of Mr Heathcliff Earnshaw, gentleman. Pray continue your conversation, sirs.'

'I'm not much at conversation,' I muttered.

'Nor I, sir,' said Bassett to my surprise. 'Perhaps like myself you prefer action. Where do you hunt, Mr Earnshaw?'

I mumbled something about Gimmerton Moor having its share of foxes – he might take that any way he pleased.

'Colonel Bassett's other passions should appeal to you better, Heathcliff,' remarked Mrs Durrant, clearly relishing my discomfort. 'They are pugilism and duelling, and he bets on the outcome of both. Did you not once kill a man and collect two thousand pounds from his executors?'

'You exaggerate, ma'am,' said the other. 'It was a paltry five hundred.'

'And now,' said she, 'it is Mr Earnshaw's turn to dance with me, I fancy. Will you take my arm, Heathcliff?'

'No,' I said, cursing her under my breath for this latest attempt to make a fool of me.

'But it's a minuet,' she persisted. 'I love to dance a minuet. Will you refuse me such a trifling request?'

'I don't dance,' I said, scarcely audibly.

'Pray repeat what you said, Heathcliff. I did not catch it.'

'Confound you, woman,' I cried. 'I do not dance.'

'He don't dance either,' said Mrs Durrant in apparent amazement. 'Charles, did you ever hear of a gentleman who neither conversed nor danced?'

'Not in my life,' returned Bassett. 'And frankly, Elizabeth, had I not your assurance otherwise, I'd doubt he was a gentleman at all. I've never heard one talk so in public to a lady.'

'Perhaps I meant he was a gentleman of the road, then,' said she, biting her finger. 'Some species of gentleman it was, I'm sure. Will you dance with me, Charles?'

'Gladly, madam,' said he, and with a black glance in my direction, led her away.

I saw nothing of them for the next hour, but kicked my heels in a corner, meditating plans for paying them back; but each plan I conceived was more impracticable than the last and more preposterous, and in the end I gave it up and confined myself to sulking aimlessly.

At one o'clock a supper was served. Scores of dishes were laid out on a massive table, with various sauces and wines, and different kinds of knives and forks. We were seated in what is termed the promiscuous style – that is, men next to women. Mrs Durrant sat beside her colonel at the far end of the table, and I was placed between a wizened Cleopatra and some unidentifiable character – a female one, I assume; it was impossible to be certain.

That supper was sheer torment. More than three-quarters of the dishes were foreign to me (French, most of them, I don't doubt), and I knew not how to eat them or in what order, but got along as best I could by adapting my pace to that of my neighbours and eating only what they ate and when they ate it. But I several times saw them simper when I leaned my elbows on the board or sniffed at the meat on my fork before entrusting it to my mouth. I contrived always to have my mouth filled to limit my capacity for talk, but since others were speaking with stuffed mouths this contrivance availed me little, and I was obliged to give my opinions on a range of subjects about which I knew nothing or next to nothing. My remedy was to drink more and more wine and snap my answers to discourage my interlocutors. Yet I was not to be spared. The androgynous person on my left asked me what I thought of General Cornwallis, to which I answered that I did not know the man, and was he at table with us? This reply provoked so much laughter that the creature would not afterwards leave me be, seeking further examples of my brilliance until I was reduced to grunting and swilling more liquor as an excuse for my incoherence. I was never so glad of anything in my life as when that accursed meal was ended.

The drink and the lateness of the hour combined against me, so that when at half-past two or thereabouts the party broke up it was all I could manage to stay on my feet.

I was alert enough, though, to observe Mrs Durrant attempting to sneak out with Bassett among a crowd of drunken nymphs and Romans.

'Make your own way home, Heathcliff,' she said, catching sight of me. 'Colonel Bassett will escort me.'

'I'll take you back,' I told her.

She gave me a frown and said: 'It will be all right, Heathcliff.'

Despite my intoxicated state, my tone was as firm as hers as I replied: 'My instructions are not to let you out of my sight, especially if you're in a man's company. Nor will I.'

'Does this puppy know what he is saying?' demanded the Colonel.

'No more than any simple-minded watchdog knows the import of his bark,' said Mrs Durrant. 'And I'm afraid, dear Charles, that once he has his doggy teeth in, nothing will prise them loose.'

'It might be managed with a well-placed boot,' said he. 'If he had a pedigree, a sword would be a much better instrument.'

I was not too far out of my senses to bristle at this, and only Mrs Durrant's swift intervention prevented me from striking him. She stepped nimbly between us, however, saying: 'No matter, Charles. He would only tell tales on us. Would you not, Heathcliff?' When I made no reply she said: 'He hates me, don't you know? Prefers his master to his mistress like any man's dog, and we should not blame him for following his brute nature.'

108

'Watchdogs can be silenced,' scowled Bassett.

'Not by whippets,' was my answer.

Mrs Durrant was attempting to push me towards the door, but her small strength was not equal to the task. 'Good night, Charles,' she said firmly.

Bassett stood his ground a moment longer. Then, 'We'll test that bold assertion of yours another day,' he told me, and disappeared into the pack of departing guests.

12

I slept late the following day and breakfasted alone, Mrs Durrant taking her chocolate and toast in bed. So I did not see her till dinner, which in that household was served at the fashionable hour of five o'clock. Mr Durrant was not expected home for another two or three hours yet, and his wife had given instructions that the meal was not to be held off on his account.

I dare say we made an odd pair, for we sat at opposite ends of the dining table and ate through the first course in silence. Mine was a brooding silence, though, and hers – hers was pained, as if *she* had been wronged and held me responsible. What I regarded as the injustice of her attitude made me even more sullen, so that by the time the joint was brought in I was on the point of leaving her to her own lovely company and making a solitary meal in the kitchen; at least there I shouldn't have my appetite spoiled by the sight of her wretched countenance and tear-brimming eyes.

As I shifted my chair, however, she said in a hurt voice: 'Oh, Heathcliff, why must you hate me so bitterly?'

'If I hate you,' I answered, picking up my plate, 'it's your own doing.'

'I won't deny it,' she said, artfully introducing a sob into her voice. 'All I know is that I haven't a true friend in the world and wish you could know how it feels. Go away, then. Loneliness is a condition I must accustom myself to.'

'I know well enough what friendlessness is like,' said I, 'and loneliness. And they are not the situation you enjoy, Mrs Durrant.' Then, recalling one of Nelly's favourite expressions, I added: 'Cold tears won't melt icy hearts.'

'Won't you just bring your plate and sit here a moment?' she asked. 'Please, dear Heathcliff. Just for a moment?'

'You needn't think,' I said, taking a seat beside her, 'that you can win me over with six drops of salt water and an endearment.'

'I know that,' was her reply. 'I know how strong your character must be to have withstood what I've subjected you to since you came into this house. And last night. I am not going to make you an apology for it – I deemed it necessary; but I do understand how you must have felt. And I required to know something.'

'What did you require to know?' I demanded.

'You may go now if you wish, Heathcliff.'

'Damn you, you're at it again,' I cried. 'What did you learn from yesternight?'

She placed her hand on mine, but I flung it off like a hot brick from the fire and in doing so dropped my fork into my plate. That made her laugh.

'Here, take mine,' she said. 'I'm not hungry.' I said my own would do, but she insisted I use her fork. 'My mouth doesn't offend you, does it?'

'No,' I mumbled.

'You cannot eat with a fork that has a greasy handle,' said she. 'That will be your first lesson. Now, shall I show you how a gentleman holds his fork?'

'I don't care to know how a gentleman does anything,' I told her. 'I'm a better man than any gentleman I ever met.'

'That is quite possible,' she said. 'So with a little education you might be a better gentleman than any gentleman you ever met. Wouldn't you like that?'

111

'Happen I would, happen I wouldn't,' I replied. But if I expected a sarcastic rebuke from Mrs Durrant, all I got was a teasing tap on the wrist with the disputed fork, so that a drop of gravy was deposited among the hairs there. Like a cat she was. Her head darted down and her tongue came out, and before I could draw my hand back she'd licked off that spot of gravy, leaving a warm, moist patch on my skin.

'Bad boy,' was all she said. 'No dialect.'

I was at a loss how to respond. The confounded woman was as changeable and as unpredictable as October weather, as you can be; but I can usually sense which direction you'll take in a given humour, and I had no instinct at all for her moods. 'Shall I tell your husband that?' I asked her. 'What you did then?'

'Do, and it's you he'll punish,' she retorted. 'Report any fault of mine to him and he will turn on you and blame you for it. Unjust, is it not, Heathcliff? And don't make the error of supposing his bad nature responsible – the whole human world is like it.' She gave a mirthless laugh. 'If we are made in God's image, He must give His angels a wretched time.'

'I may decide to risk it,' I told her.

'Think about it first,' she replied. 'You have two hours. Set what little pleasure you can derive from talebearing against the benefits of an education. I can give you that, Heathcliff. I was well tutored as a girl and have added to my store of knowledge since. And I've observed you. You've a keen mind and long for learning as a starving man longs for nourishment. I'm an excellent cook, Heathcliff, whereas all you will get from my husband is scraps. If you wish me to teach you, you must quit his table and sit at mine.'

Her talk of food must have reminded her that dinner was unfinished, for she took back her fork and speared a piece of beef with it. Then, putting this in her mouth, she skewered another morsel and offered it to me. I accepted it, and for the remainder of the meal she continued to feed me tit-bits off her plate.

Mr Durrant returned late, greeted me jovially, then said he desired to be alone with his wife and would speak with me on the morrow.

The next day was Sunday. And as dreary a day it proved for me as any I'd passed at the Heights – except that here I had no Joseph to preach at me or whip Christian humility into my hide. But I hadn't your company either to compensate. The Durrants were out all day, gone to church, as I learned from the kitchen-maid, thence to Hyde Park in the 'chay,' as she called the chaise. It made me smile to think of those two on their knees for an hour, then perched for the rest of the day in that superior conveyance of theirs.

I took a walk about town in the afternoon, seeing some parts that were new to me, and stayed a short while in a coffee-house in the Haymarket, but as the talk there was of politics and plays, I did not linger.

For the first time since my arrival in London I was completely stalled. I found myself yearning for a thousand things associated with my past – for the moors, for Nelly's homely company, for your companionship above all. Anything that would raise my spirits. London was suddenly become a massive cage hemming me in, every one of its buildings another stone bar. You will understand the feeling. Only you *could* understand it. By four o'clock I fancied I was on the edge of madness and became strangely convinced, more so by the minute, that if I did not at once escape the confines of the town I would perforce turn on myself and begin to rend my own flesh.

Accordingly, out of desperation, I persuaded the groom to saddle me one of Mr Durrant's riding horses (he took some persuading) and set off at the gallop

113

towards Hounslow, where I was assured of some open heathland.

It was a two hours' ride, even over good roads – this is the main turnpike to the west and heavily travelled in the season – but I have rarely enjoyed a jaunt as much. I relished everything about it. A breeze was blowing across me from the south, compensating for the heat of the afternoon sun in my face, and the smell of a sweated horse and the fragrance of July blossom combined to dispel the stench of London from my nostrils. The noise and stink of a great city are never sensible save in reminiscence, when their absence points them up, and my lungs seemed burned clean by the freshness of the air once I got beyond Knightsbridge.

Eventually I found myself riding across an unenclosed tract of land overgrown with whin and heather, but remarkably featureless and low-lying. This was undoubtedly Hounslow Heath, and it bitterly disappointed me. It has nothing of our northern grandeur in it, nothing sublime. It is merely a wretched snatch of common land which, set next to our own wild moorlands, would seem like an untended garden.

Yet my spirits had risen too high to be easily depressed, and, dismounting, I tied Durrant's horse to a bush and stretched myself out in a patch of sickly bluebells. A poor pretence it was, but I imagined I was lying above the crossroads on Gimmerton Moor, where the signpost tells the way to Heights and Grange; the London highway assisted, for that was only a few yards distant and at a slightly lower level. I could see along it for quite a way in both directions, too, though any traveller on the road would have needed sharp eyes to perceive me.

Thus it occurred to me that highway robbers must conceal themselves in a similar fashion, Hounslow being a notorious haunt of theirs. I toyed with the thought for a spell. I watched a coach and four approach from the west

114

and come rattling past, and considered what difficulties there might be in riding it down. It might be managed, I thought. My pistols were tucked into my belt as usual, and I chanced to be wearing my fustian coat again, with Mrs Durrant's black cloth mask still in the pocket – she'd forgot to ask me for it and I'd discovered the thing only that morning. A *gentleman's master* – such is the term I favour – requires no further equipment.

I chuckled to myself, thinking what sweet reciprocation it would be if I should just once command others to deliver to *me*. And why should I not? The question, once formed, began to pick at my mind with such pertinacity that I felt obliged to attempt an answer. My considerations proved interesting, for try as I would, nothing remotely resembling a good reason to forbear suggested itself to me – only abstractions, nothings, moral vacuities such as Probity or Honesty or Conscience – pulpit words, Sunday mouthings. And I'd be damned before I'd permit Sunday terms to rule my conduct. Oh, this was no high-toned moral discourse I gave myself, Cathy, rest assured. The entire process took less than a second, I'll be bound.

So I waited. I made sure my pistols were charged and put on that idiotic mask, and I waited for a coach. And when one came along – a chaise, and without a postilion – I mounted and urged my beast into the road directly in its path.

It was amazingly simple; laughably so. I did not *feel* like a highwayman, Cathy, but like an impostor, a character at a masque, as I pointed my pistols into that chaise and demanded to be paid. Aye, those were my words – I wasn't sure of the proper ones – 'Pay me or I'll blow out your brains!' I had no intention of blowing out anybody's brains, though if pressed I might produce a little blood, just a scratch to demonstrate my sincerity. But I was not pressed. The fellow within paid me promptly, as if his purse was a debt of honour he owed me.

As if I cared a jot for his purse! Nay, it was something quite different I required from this fine specimen of genteel manhood, and I got an abundance of it when I saw his pale eyes strain at their stalks, then quickly avert themselves. His abject terror was payment enough. It demonstrated that I was undoubtedly *this* gentleman's master. He delighted me, Cathy. His miserable, cringing carcase filled me with such extreme joy that in sheer gratitude I flung the damned purse back in his face in an instant, and had the unspeakable pleasure of seeing him freshly startled by my magnanimity. Then with a scornful laugh I turned my beast's head and rode off, leaving him happy, no doubt, in his supposition that he'd been almost robbed on the Bristol road by a fugitive from Bedlam and that only his own judicious compliance had saved him from death.

Mr Durrant at least had returned by the time I reached the house – his wife had too, I imagine, but I did not see her. I had stopped to unsaddle and rub down the horse, being unable to find the groom, and it must have been past nine o'clock when I met Mr Durrant in the hall. He rang for one of the maid-servants and had her bring a cold supper to the dining room for me, and sat with me while I ate.

'You availed yourself of my mare in my absence,' said he as soon as I'd taken a bite of pie.

There was a delay as I chewed and swallowed the food. Then I answered: 'She seemed glad of the exercise.'

'Did she? Then am I to take it that you covet the groom's position?'

'I didn't steal your damned horse,' I objected. 'She's back in her stall.'

'That is not what matters, Heathcliff,' he said calmly. 'What matters is that you understand the nature of property, for until you do you will acquire little and keep little of what you acquire. People are rightfully jealous of their possessions and cling tenaciously to them. All people. But a gentleman's possessions are the man himself – in the world's eyes, at least. The world judges him by them, not, as you might imagine, by his character. So whether he be saint or reprobate, wise man or fool, he *is* what he owns. Try the ale – you'll find it excellent. I have it specially brewed to my receipt. If you read your Blackstone, Heathcliff, you will discover also that property may be either real or personal, immoveable or moveable. My mare is personal; so is my silver. What does that suggest to you?'

I shrugged. 'That it counts for less,' I hazarded.

'That it is more easily filched,' he corrected, 'and must be more carefully guarded. Nobody can remove my house or my land on his back, and cannot deprive me of either without the connivance of the law. But anyone may mount my horse and ride it away. And if you take what is mine you diminish me by that amount.'

'I cannot see,' I replied, 'how you are diminished by my use of your mare for one afternoon.'

'Then the principle is beyond you,' he said curtly. 'But touching this subject of guardianship, I believe your duties took you to a masked ball two nights since. Have you anything to report in consequence?'

I'd expected the question and replied that I had seen Mrs Durrant dance with only one man all evening – Colonel Bassett of the Life Guards. 'But they were never out of my sight,' I added, 'and nothing improper took place between them.'

He laughed unpleasantly. 'Did you expect it to in a ballroom? No matter. That gentleman is known to me. My wife affirms that you were faithful to my instructions – indeed, she was something more than merely acrimonious in praise of your assiduity. She'd

117

see you dead for a brass guinea, I'll be bound.' Pouring me more ale, he continued: 'You've proved yourself, Heathcliff. Now for your reward. Tomorrow is Monday, when I collect my dues – I told you I had properties, did I not? Well, the properties are tenanted, and tenants pay rents, whether they wish to or no. That some of them are often reluctant to part with their pennies, however, is my reason for sending Haskell and one or two other persuasive fellows to collect on my behalf. Tomorrow you shall be one of them. Does the work appeal to you?'

I answered that I did not enjoy bullying for sport.

'Nor will it be sport,' he returned. 'It pays at two *per centum* – that is a florin for every five pounds you collect. There are shops as well as lodging-houses, and since the weekly total is generally some five hundred, your share I compute at ten.' He paused, then said, 'Pounds, Heathcliff. Every Monday. In a year that will bring you five hundred, a gentleman's income. Be satisfied with it, for by your own admission it is all you require. Become greedy and you'll be making a far costlier error than you can imagine.'

The sum astounded me, though I did not much care for his threatening tone.

'You needn't look so alarmed, Heathcliff,' said he with a grin. 'You'll have no writing to read or computations to perform. Haskell will identify my tenants and let you know where to find them. He also counts the money.' He added softly: 'You cannot read or calculate, can you?'

'That bitch has told you!' I blurted.

'Nobody has told me a thing concerning your abilities in that sphere,' he assured me. 'Your countenance was my informer – that and some divination of my own. I guessed from the beginning. Indeed, you might say your employment depended on it. Scholars usually die poor, however – take comfort from it – and some die

118

prematurely; for their learning often leads them into inquiries that were better left unmade.'

He said no more but left me to finish my supper. And I began to realize, as I consumed the last of the ale, how well my dependence suited him; and that my mind would have taken natural leave of its proprietor long before Mr Alexander Durrant bestirred himself to improve it.

13

On the morrow I armed myself and accompanied Haskell
on what he called the Round. This was to be a tour
of parts of Westminster and some outlying parishes to
the north and east, and a small portion of the City by
Aldgate. The extent of the area and the considerable
weight of coin we would have amassed by the day's
end made it necessary for us to travel by coach, and a
private stage-coach was kept exclusively for the purpose
in a yard near Golden Square. Here I met the two men
who habitually drove the Round with Haskell, a pair of
muscular, villainous-looking bravoes marked about the
face with white and yellow scars. These were Durrant's
'persuasive fellows', and I had little doubt about their
capacity for persuasion.

Both were bullies by profession – they were employed
on other days in the Covent Garden whorehouses, and
one of them had done a spell as crimp for the press gangs
in Limehouse. The driver, Richards, wore a drab surtout
which must have swelted him in July but made provision,
by means of six deep pockets around the waist, for him
to carry half a dozen pistols. The other, who sat beside
Richards as guard, was named Twiss. The chief feature
of his dress was a cap made of double-thick leather and
lined with cork. He wore it, he said, because Perrins,
the Midland giant, had weakened his head during their
forty-round prizefight; and I had no reason, from the
look of him, to doubt either the fight or the injury.

The Round was a sizeable area within which lay some
three score of Durrant's lodging-houses and shops, so
Richards had to drive like Jehu to get us from one to

another in good time. We began with the Soho tenements – there were three of these, each with forty or fifty two-shilling rents. The tenants had paid their dues in advance to a landlord's agent living on the ground floor, and we had no more to do than collect the bag from him – the work took less than a minute, the agent being held responsible for the correctness of the amount. It was the rule, Haskell informed me, for all the lodging-houses to be dealt with in this fashion, save where there were tenants in default and persuasion was required. On a bad day it was impossible to complete the Round before nightfall. This might be a good one.

From Soho we drove through London's northern environs as far as Hockley-in-the-Hole, where Twiss and Richards insisted we call at the bear garden in case there should be a prizefight between women. There was not, but we stayed twenty minutes to watch three dogs bait a bull. I had never seen this sport and found it most instructive. The dogs worked in concert, appearing to convey instructions to each other by their barking as they assailed the bull from different sides. Their plan was for the two flanking beasts to distract it so that the brute appointed assassin might fasten his teeth into the victim's jugular and bleed it to death. The combat I witnessed was a lively one, though it ended miserably with the bull mauled past saving and two of the dogs trampled to a bloody mash. The third saved itself by clinging to the bull's right ear, which was all but wrenched off in the struggle – I don't doubt the wretched creature, if he could have managed it, would fain have sacrificed the ear for the pleasure of getting at his tormentor. Twiss said he was a game bull and pity he was spoiled, but won half a guinea on him nevertheless.

Thence to houses in Clerkenwell and to an unspeakably wretched place in Turnmill Street. I was permitted by Haskell to go no further than the hallway, but that was enough. It was a swamp of filth – a well-bottom would be a cosier habitation, I fancy – and the apartments themselves, I learned from Richards, extended from putrid, airless garrets at the top of the house to gloomy and fetid cellars below street level. I wondered, at first, why Durrant should interest himself in the twopenny rents such a place would bring, but when Haskell emerged with bags that bulged and jingled not with coin but with plate and silverware, our purpose there became apparent. These bags were stowed separately from the rest in the coach and disappeared later into a warehouse in Thames Street.

By that time, however, we'd been as far east as Mile End, and back through the City. And I had discovered that there was more to the Round than mere rent-collecting.

I was puzzled as we began to call at shop after shop in the eastern part of the City – saddlers, watchmakers, sailmakers and weavers, cabinetmakers and poulterers, shoemakers, mantuamakers, smiths of various kinds, butchers and chocolate houses; without discrimination apparently. At each one Haskell would be no more than a few minutes, and from each he collected a payment. He offered me no explanation and I asked for none, but at a tallow-chandler's close to the river he was gone longer than usual, with the result that Twiss and Richards began to show signs of impatience. When Haskell did return his face wore a grim expression.

'Says he'll pay no more funk-money,' he informed the two on the box. 'Earnshaw had better stay with the coach. You two come with me.'

Then each of them provided himself with a stout cudgel and thus they entered the chandler's. The coach was in a yard some way from the shop, but even so I soon heard the unmistakable sounds of battle – cries and grunts – followed closely by those of demolition – wood

122

splintering, heavy objects being flung against walls, the ring of metal on metal. Minutes later the three of them emerged, flushed from their exertions, Richards with a slight cut above his eye. The nauseous stench and vapour of boiling tallow followed them through the doorway and they reeked of it themselves. I perceived, too, that one of the cudgels was bloody at the tip.

'You'll get your chance another day,' Haskell said to me as he climbed into the coach. 'Always one or two like him to warm you.' There was a look of relish on his face that I didn't much care for, so I displayed no curiosity and contented myself with a nod and a private resolve never to turn my back on Haskell or the other two. Such questions as I had could wait; Durrant should answer them later.

Our last calls were at several middling houses in and near Jermyn Street. Haskell took me in with him to one of them, where we received a payment in notes of hand from a nervous gentleman who moistened his lips with his tongue all the while we were in his company.

'Er – could Mr Sherall not be persuaded,' said he as we were departing, 'to reduce the amount of interest in – er – consideration of prompt payment?' Haskell merely stared at him. His tongue became immediately busy at his lips again. 'Er – doubtless he has computed the interest at a fair and reasonable sum,' said the fellow quickly, 'and pray do not trouble Mr Sherall after all, sirs, though – er – next week may be a difficult time for me.'

'If you can't pay it will be,' Haskell said in a menacing tone.

The other appeared to shrink several degrees. 'I am sure I shall manage it,' said he. 'Indeed, you may rest assured that I will.'

'We're assured,' replied Haskell with a laugh. 'I'd sooner doubt sunrise.'

The Round was concluded by five o'clock, but I got no opportunity to question Mr Durrant until the Wednesday.

He sought me out after dinner, with an apology for not having seen me earlier, and asked if I'd found the Round an interesting experience.

I hemmed and said it had been, but that one or two things puzzled me, such as how he could derive sufficient income from a poor tallow-chandler to justify wrecking his shop for default of payment.

He smiled to hear me say it. 'You are right,' said he, 'in supposing that my receipts from him and others like him are pitifully meagre; but they pay me a pittance to protect them against the mischief of local gangs of robbers and wreckers. London is a lamentably lawless town, as you've discovered, and wants efficient police. Mine do more to prevent crime than those officers the City employs; but if they are held in contempt by those it is their duty to protect, what hopes can they have of gaining the respect of rogues? There was the purpose of Haskell's lesson. It will be learned, I assure you, by all who hear of it.'

'I wonder,' I said with ill-concealed sarcasm, 'that you feel moved to provide such a service when there is greater profit in money-lending and renting.'

'Don't mistake my motive for magnanimity,' he replied. 'It is something else, something you will recognize, Heathcliff – a profound desire to extend my own will to others. Great lords do it all the time, and, like you, I despise their system, which rewards a fortunate pedigree with privilege and respect, regardless of worth. The notion is absurd – as absurd as it would be for the grandson of an eminent surgeon to expect society to esteem him though he knew nothing of surgery himself. Birth is surely the poorest criterion of honour ever devised by a race that has never distinguished itself by honouring its most worthy members. And if it is to be another criterion, let it be power or low cunning as well as merit. Do you share my belief that we are imperfectible? In a moral sense. No, you would not have the means to answer that. Well I firmly believe it. And since we are born base we must measure our superiority one over another by degrees of baseness – paradoxical, is it not? Yet nature teaches the doctrine. The superior brute in a pack of wolves is the most savage, the most brutish. Do you begin to comprehend my nature?'

'I begin to,' I answered. 'Yet you pity foundlings seemingly.'

'Certainly. It is not inconsistent I pity those whom nature has cruelly deprived of the means to improve or defend themselves. I pity them as the wolf must pity the lamb as he devours it. Yet he does not spare his dinner on that account. Nor, though he respects them, does he spare his fellow wolves if they dispute that dinner with him. Which do you fancy you are, Heathcliff?'

'Nobody's dinner, assuredly,' I returned.

'Agreed,' said he readily. 'You are also a meat-eater; but so are jackals, though they do not hunt themselves but steal the prey of other hunters.'

'Then which are you, Mr Sherall?' I asked. 'Hunter or scavenger?'

'Both,' said he, without hesitation. 'And never complain that you were not advised of it. Haskell will give you your share of last Monday's kill if you will ask him for it. Remember that you are not yet grown enough to make one of your own.'

That was all the explanation I ever got from Durrant of how he conducted his business, but it was enough to convince me that what his wife had told me of him was substantially true. That being so, I determined to take advantage of her offer and, accordingly, broached

125

the subject of my education as soon as an opportunity presented itself.

On the Saturday of the same week Mr Durrant quitted the house early to see to some affairs on his Middlesex estates. His wife was in her drawing-room, where she'd taken herself after breakfast to read a new magazine that had arrived that morning.

I knocked and heard her call from within: 'Go away!' At my second, louder knock, she cried: 'Who *is* that?'

'Heathcliff,' I shouted.

'Ecod!' came through the door. 'I declare you're developing manners. You may enter, Heathcliff.' As I did so I saw her straighten herself into a sitting position – she'd been sprawled gracelessly on the sofa – and lower the magazine to her lap. 'A fortnight since, you would have burst in without announcing yourself,' said she. 'But I thought you were avoiding me, Heathcliff.'

I mumbled a denial, suddenly uncomfortable now that I was in her presence.

'Well, I've seen nothing of you since Saturday,' she said. 'However, you would hardly seek me out for the pleasure of my company, feeling about me as you do, so your visit must have a definite purpose.'

Her bluntness disconcerted me further. When I made no reply she beckoned to me with her finger, and as I approached said: 'You've decided to turn your coat, I think. Am I right?'

'You said –' I began, then faltered.

'I said I would help you to an education,' she supplied, 'if you changed sides. Evidently something has occurred to persuade you. No matter what it was – it has shown you my husband's true colours, and we'll profit mutually from the revelation. Now. Come and sit beside me.' I showed my usual hesitation about complying with this request, but she frowned and said: 'Heathcliff, you needn't fear me. I shall neither humiliate you nor endanger your

126

virtue. Now that I've won you over, those tricks would serve no useful purpose. Our relationship is on a new footing, and besides, if you must know the truth, I find you too unattractive to attempt that kind of seduction.'

I must have bridled up, for she laughed and said I was not to take offence, and that she'd meant nothing hurtful. 'I'm sure you could make quite a stir among country girls of your own age if you modified your appearance a little and your manner. Cathy, for instance. Does she not love you?'

'No, she does not,' was out of my mouth before I could check it.

'But you love her still,' Mrs Durrant said quickly. 'Then you must sympathize with my husband's unrequited adoration for me.'

'If he loved you he would not cage you,' I ventured.

She looked surprised. 'You think him wrong, then, to treat me as he does?'

I answered: 'I have no use for "right" and "wrong," Mrs Durrant. All I mean is that I would not treat you so if I loved you.'

'Which you do not?' she asked coyly.

'Which I do not,' I echoed.

'Do you like me a little?' was her next question.

'A little,' I lied.

'How grudging. I cannot teach you unless we are friends, Heathcliff. Can we not be friends at least?'

I said I did not regard her as my enemy; and as to the teaching, I'd seen no sign of it yet.

'What a hard person you are,' said she. 'But I refuse to be defeated by your armour. You shall call me Elizabeth in future, when we are alone together at our lessons, and that will promote friendship. And though education will not change your nature, it may modify it so that you will be less willing to reveal your unpleasant side to others and better able to conceal it

127

when you choose to. Now let me hear you call me Elizabeth.'

I said I saw no point in it and refused to be familiar, but she pressed me, repeating the name as if to a parrot she was training, until I was compelled to say it back to her.

'Good boy,' I got from her then. 'Do you know any letters, Heathcliff?'

'Yes,' was my answer.

'Yes, what?'

'Yes, I know them all,' I mumbled.

' "Yes, I know them all, *Elizabeth*," ' said the damned woman, and made me repeat it. When I had satisfied her she asked who had taught them to me.

'I know them,' was all I would say. 'Elizabeth.'

'You need not use my name at the end of every sentence. Have you been shown how letters are put together to form words?'

'Yes, but I've forgot,' I said. 'It confuses me when I see too many of the damnable things together in a line.'

She nodded, then pointed to her magazine. 'What is this word?'

' "The," ' I supplied, recognizing that configuration of letters.

'Very good. And this?'

'I can't read that,' I said. She asked me to spell out the letters to her, which I did. *L-a-d-y-'s* it was. 'I don't know that mark above, between the last two,' I told her, and remembered to add, 'Elizabeth.'

'I like the way you sound my name,' said she, and attempted to sound it as I had. It was not mocking, though, or I wouldn't have stood for it. 'That is an apostrophe,' she said then, recalling herself. 'It is a grammatical mark. Marks such as that one tell us how a word is to be pronounced or understood.'

'It tells *me* nowt,' I complained, and saw her hand go to her mouth to cover a laugh.

'Dear Heathcliff, you must not make a joke of reading.'

I scowled and said I'd seen nothing funny.

'Your face when it's being fierce is funny,' she replied teasingly. 'It quite distracts me. Now, the word is "Lady's," and the whole reads "The Lady's Magazine." Look at it as you repeat it.' And she had me repeat the phrase to her several times. Afterwards she turned the cover and began to point at various words, making me say them first with her, then by myself, and indicated how certain letters went together to form sounds in combination that neither made alone. And always she would be correcting my pronunciation, which, when it was not northern and boorish, was vulgar or old-fashioned; but always wrong, and the new way of saying the word was such, or such. Thus, half the letters I read were not to be pronounced at all, and for the other half there were idiotic rules she seemed to invent as we progressed. I must remember, said she, to pronounce 'leisure' short and 'daughter' long, 'dutter' being an affectation. Nor must I say 'spirit' as if it were 'sperit,' and it was 'fort*night*,' not 'fortnit,' in fashionable circles; and the wind blows, but 'wind' with the sound of 'wined' was used only for the verb and had to do rather with clocks than with weather.

These and a thousand other examples of what was prescribed or proscribed rattled about in my head that first day like dice in a cup, until it seemed that whenever I spoke or read a word I had one chance in six of being correct.

After an hour of it I'd had enough and told her so.

'I'm aware that you find the matter dull,' she answered, 'and next time I'll try to provide something better suited. Don't you feel yourself improving already?'

'I'm more perplexed than I ever was,' I said.

'That's an excellent sign,' said she. 'It must get worse before it can get better, Heathcliff. If you haven't the courage to stick at it, please say so.'

I stumbled and stammered and faltered through a further hour of it before she said I'd done sufficient for my first lesson. Then she kissed her fingers and touched them to my forehead, promising another session on the morrow if her husband remained absent.

14

He was not so obliging, however, and the lesson had to be postponed. On Monday the Round intervened, on the Tuesday an infernal rout for which Mrs Durrant spent the entire day preparing; and then it was her husband's stubborn presence in the house that kept us apart. I felt a strange impatience, a strange resentment – I attempted to will the fellow out, but he seemed disinclined to absent himself even for two hours together, until the sight of him was enough to put me into a silent rage. I've rarely known a few days pass so slowly.

I remembered that day not long after you returned from your stay with the Lintons, when I threw your grammar book into the horse trough, declaring that you might display your book-learning to your superior friends and that I'd be better served by a pair of breeches than one of parentheses. You laughed and thought it an excellent jest. Well, I'd have given half my life willingly to have back the opportunity I lost then of learning alongside you. I was vexed almost beyond endurance by the delay, and began to convince myself that having at last tasted the nectar I'd never be permitted to consume it; that Mrs Durrant would lose interest or forget her promise; that when I next saw her she would laugh and scorn me and ask how I could have dared to presume her tutorage more than an idle whim she'd indulged one dreary afternoon. Yet I craved her company in the oddest sort of way – I assure you it was no simple infatuation; I did not even like the woman much – as I have in the past craved yours and do now.

One evening I overheard the Durrants quarrelling, as they often did, and I listened in the earnest hope of hearing her say some spiteful thing that would drive him out of doors. They were acrimonious enough with each other to justify such an expectation, their subject being Colonel Bassett.

'I know you have been sending him notes,' said he, 'and I demand that you tell me who is your messenger.'

'You may entertain yourself,' came her sneering reply, 'with whatever phantasies you choose.'

'If I did not know him better,' he said in lowered tones, 'I would suspect you of having subverted Heathcliff. I don't doubt that you've tried.'

'Has he not told you?' I heard his wife say. 'Possibly he thought in that faithful-puppy way of his not to make mischief between us. But yes, I have tried, to my shame. I believe you might cut his throat, Alexander, and he would crawl outside to die rather than bleed over your carpets. I cannot think how you have earned his loyalty, but the dolt worships the very mud on your boots. You are not content, though, are you? You must have my worship too. Well, all you can hope for is my gratitude, and to earn that you must give me a settlement and my freedom.'

He must have mumbled his reply, for it was Mrs Durrant's voice I heard next, saying: 'Oh, am I? And I suppose my sex is without physical longings? You get all the satisfaction you require from your Covent Garden whores and you expect me to read novels for mine.'

'I believe,' said he in a trembling voice, 'that it is possible to vituperate without being vulgar, and –'

Before he could go further she interrupted him with: 'Vulgar! You dare to speak to me of vulgarity!' Her laugh would have shrunk the devil in his skin. 'Then I should tell you, Alex, that quite apart from other considerations – such as that I abominate you and fear

132

to catch the pox from you – what has kept me from your bed these two years is my insupportable disgust at your vulgarity both as a man and as a lover. Why, I fancy Heathcliff, for all his boorishness, would have more notion of what is proper gentlemanly behaviour in the bedchamber than you have. And on the same scale Colonel Bassett could hardly be less than an exemplar of courtly love, a Petrarch or a Dante. Nothing betrays a man's origins more certainly than the way he sheds his breeches, Alex. And you take off yours à la mode de Temple Bar.'

There followed an interval without speech and in which I fancied I could make out Mr Durrant's fast breathing. I expected to hear the sound of a slap, but evidently he exercised greater control of himself than I would have managed in the circumstances – I'd have beaten her sick for half as much – for when he spoke next it was with cool deliberateness. 'If you are telling me,' he said, 'that you speak from experience, Elizabeth, I will make it my earnest task to learn the names of every one of your paramours, and I promise you they will pay dearly for their association with you. Depend upon it.'

'Are you mad!' she exclaimed. 'Does the gaoler dare accuse his prisoner of dalliance? With whom, pray? The dungeon rats or the turnkey? In the latter case – do you seriously suppose I would be desperate enough to take that dirty gipsy boy to my bed? Alex, I swear you will suspect my stallion before long – if the thought is not too vulgar to be voiced.'

'Since you persist in bringing Heathcliff into this – this *conversation*,' was his reply, 'let me say I will not have you humiliating him merely because he has enjoyed none of your advantages in life, Elizabeth.'

'None of *yours*, you mean,' she retorted fiercely. 'There is a greater similarity there. You enjoyed the advantages of an ill-gotten fortune and a woman's skirts by which to drag yourself out of the kennels. And were I in your position I should ask myself why I kept a degraded youth in my house without attempting to improve him, if not for the cruel pleasure of observing his oafishness daily, and of gloating over it. You keep him as a memento of what you once were and would be still had you not escaped. Surely he is humiliated more by your condescension than by any sharp words I might occasionally throw at him.'

I did not stay to hear more and wished I had heard less. Keyholes must be the ears' mirrors, the prerogative of the incurably vain; and God knows, vanity was never one of my sins. Nevertheless, I could not help being grieved, for Mrs Durrant had lately given me cause to think better of her.

The experience moderated my excitement wonderfully, so that when at last Mr Durrant did go abroad for a morning it was almost with reluctance that I presented myself to his wife for my lesson. Yet she seemed genuinely glad to see me and displayed nothing but patience and good humour, answering the questions I'd stored up for her with an eagerness and an intensity I found it difficult to believe were counterfeit.

She gave me rules for spelling and for punctuation, and some lists I was to get by heart – lists of vowels and diphthongs, prefixes and suffixes, and of the commonest words. Then we practised writing simple sentences. She placed her small, warm hand on my own hand to guide it as I formed my letters, but finding it distracting, I threw it off.

'Why did you do that?' she wanted to know. 'I thought you'd begun to conquer your ill nature at last, Heathcliff.'

I said I didn't like to be touched, that it made me uncomfortable.

She responded by turning down the corners of her mouth in a caricature of my frown. Then, 'I like you better with your lips in a right line,' she said, 'than in the shape of the Northern Hemisphere. I've given up hope of ever seeing them form the Southern.' I scowled all the more and said I had no idea what she meant by that. So she took one of the lists and the pencil, and on the reverse side drew three crude circles, which she made into faces by the addition of dots for eyes, a vertical stroke for each nose, and two curved marks and a straight one for the mouths. 'This on the left is me and the world in general,' said she, labelling the drawing 'World,' and the other two are Heathcliff. I am writing your name on them. Note how I spell it, and note also how my mouth curves upwards in a smile while your Sunday face is at one hundred and eighty degrees and your weekday face points to the ground. There, I've shown you something of Euclid's Geometry at the same time. It has to do with chords and arcs, and once you have mastered Euclid's axioms you will know how to smile and be cheerful always.'

I averted my face, for I was finding it deuced difficult not to smile then.

'Aha!' she exclaimed. 'Euclid is working already, I suspect. Now tell me why you find my touch so disagreeable.'

'Not nearly as disagreeable as you must find mine,' I replied with some warmth.

Her eyes narrowed as she said: 'Heathcliff, you've been listening at doors again.'

'If you shout loud enough,' I told her, 'you must expect folk to hear.'

'Hm,' said she. 'I should scold you, but I will not. I cannot fault your last remark except grammatically, in that you used an adjective for an adverb, and in its style – "folk" is a provincialism. As for what I said, however – it was intended for my husband's ears alone. If you imagine that I express my true feelings to *him*, you are more of a fool than you appear. Now I am vexed, Heathcliff. Your mistrust has vexed me.'

'Well, how am I to know what to believe?' I said. 'You keep changing your character like a damned witch.'

'Does your heart not inform you what you should believe about me?' she asked coyly.

'My heart informs me that I'm alive,' was my answer. 'If it stopped I should know I was dead.'

She laughed at that. 'Silly boy. I shall have to teach you the figures of Rhetoric, I see, as well as those of Euclid's system. And more of Anatomy than just the function of the heart.'

She had again insisted that we sit side by side on her sofa with the books between us, claiming that the relationship between tutoress (her preferred term) and pupil was an intimate one, requiring a matching intimacy of circumstance. Now she removed the books and writing materials to the floor and closed the gap with her body, so that our thighs were in contact with each other.

'Thigh,' said she with a wicked smile. She placed her hand on my knee and said, 'Knee. Anatomically, patella. And the thigh-bone is the femur. Now place your hand on my patella.'

Feeling foolish, I did so, but immediately removed it. She at once caught my wrist and replaced my hand on her knee. 'Shall we proceed further north, Heathcliff?' she said softly.

'Damn you,' I cried. 'You are either trying to make a fool of me or to seduce me. But don't pretend this is education.'

'It is exactly that,' she said. 'And a woman cannot be said to seduce a man. That would make her a "seductress," and as no such word exists, the concept cannot be said to exist. Ergo, I cannot be attempting seduction. I declare, you look very animated suddenly. It is warm in here. Would you like a window opened?'

'What is your plan, Mrs Durrant?' I demanded.

She repeated, 'Plan?'

'You seem determined to excite me,' I said. 'To tease me, to inflame me, and all while pretending that your intentions are a model of innocence. Am I supposed to be so stupid that I will not notice, and too unfeeling to care? It's a dangerous game. I'm made of flesh and blood too.'

'And more besides. See how you need lessons in Anatomy?' I gave her a very stern look and she said, 'Oh, Heathcliff, what dunces we both are at this. It seems I must be blunt to the point of indelicacy if I'm to let you know my feelings at all. Yet some things are not easy to say.' She hesitated, then said: 'You have just admitted I inflame you, and in a young man such susceptibilities are considered appropriate and not the least improper. Let a woman of any age display them, however, and she is in danger of being pronounced a hussy certainly, and far worse if the intention is to be truly hurtful. Yet my sex is not so much different from yours that separate standards of conduct should be applied to it in these matters. My body has its needs and its desires also. I cannot always be expected to be phlegmatic about them either, and at the risk of arousing your scorn I must say that the head does not rule the heart here. And I am being polite, despite what you may regard as my unladylike frankness, for the heart is not necessarily involved. I will not blame you if you walk out of the room this minute. But if you are prepared to listen I will say more.'

I gave a mumbled indication of my willingness to hear more.

'I realize,' she continued, 'that I have been unforgivably inept in my approach, Heathcliff. I have teased you cruelly, I know. That was to protect me from my own shame, my own embarrassment. For I am abashed even now, though you would never guess it to look at me. Heathcliff, I *do* want to educate you, sincerely, but I own I had another motive for these private sessions. Since you came into this house I have – may I go on?'

I had first to clear my throat before I could reply. Then I said, 'Yes,' rather hoarsely.

'I have yearned to have you as my paramour,' she said deliberately.

As if water had been thrown in my face, I drew back. 'Have you forgot who I am?' I fairly shouted at her. 'Are you insane enough to think I'll believe what you've just said?'

'It is the truth.'

'The devil it is!' I cried, getting to my feet. 'It would not surprise me if you had your husband stationed outside that door this very moment, waiting for some signal from you so that he could rush in and shoot me and go scot-free for it. I have no idea what you hope to gain by this lie, Mrs Durrant, but it is too much of a lie for me even to sham belief. And God knows, I'm credulous enough.'

She made no reply at first, but sat staring at the wall with moist eyes and a trembling lip. Then she said quietly: 'He is not beyond that door. He may be in hell, I don't care – I don't know or care where he is. I have ruined myself, Heathcliff. I want no sympathy and am not trying to earn any. I have stated a fact. My confession has ruined me. You may relate it in full to my husband when he returns. It no longer matters what you or he or anyone thinks of me. I have made myself worse than any of my husband's whores, and if I had the courage to take my life I'd do it joyfully. But I'm a coward. Get out, damn you. Don't stand there gloating. Get away. The sight of you reminds me of my shame and I can't bear it.'

I stood for a second or two, uncertain how to respond. Mrs Durrant did not, as I'd expected, fling herself down on the sofa and weep buckets of cold tears. She slowly leaned back and covered her face with her hands, and sobbed with what seemed great restraint. I had no doubt now that her tears were genuine, though I was still unsure whether she wept from shame, as she said, or for some devious purpose of her own. But I approached her and sat down beside her again, and felt her flinch.

'You must admit,' I said, 'you've given me cause to mistrust you.'

'Get away from me,' she hissed.

'I'll say nothing to your husband,' I promised.

'Say what you will. I don't care any longer.'

I said: 'I've been a monster too long, Mrs Durrant – Elizabeth. I've been too degraded, too often spurned and hated, to have any other expectations, except from one, and not even from her now.' I still had pity to spare for myself. It will no doubt delight you to know it.

'And I have lived too long in this house with a hateful, monstrous man to look elsewhere for those qualities,' said she. She removed her hands from her face and I saw that her eyes were wet and red. 'I do not pretend to love you, Heathcliff. But I do not hate you. And the kind of desire I feel has little to do with either.'

I nodded. Then I took hold of one of her hands, feeling the dampness of her tears on it, and clasped it in both of mine. I sensed that I was awkward and feared to squeeze the hand in case it hurt her.

'I'm not a gentle person, Elizabeth,' I told her. 'You will never teach me that. And I cannot love you either.'

'I don't require your love,' was her reply. 'But I fancy I can gentle you. In time.'

And she gave me a faint smile. So fragile was it that I did not contradict her.

15

By the end of the summer I could read tolerably well, and my curriculum was expanded. I made slower progress with my writing, however, and did not achieve until the spring of this year the proficiency of which you are now the sole judge.

Elizabeth praised me for an apt pupil, but insisted that the accomplishments of a gentleman – even a country gentleman – must include the cultured as well as the practical, and declared that to be passable in refined company I must evince an acquaintance with a range of subjects we hadn't yet touched upon. The notion of transforming me into a country squire seemed to excite her – her eyes became bright when she spoke of it – and when I saw her next (this was sometime in late August, I think) she had written a comprehensive plan for my education. I was to learn the rudiments of Geometry but much more of Arithmetic, something of both Geography and History, should touch upon Poetry and Rhetoric, master Grammar, Conversation and Manners. She would also teach me how to dress with taste and elegance but without affectation, how to dance and how to play at cards and dice.

A forbidding prospectus, was it not? Those would have been my sentiments had I not good reason to trust Elizabeth Durrant's abilities as a tutoress. She had a mind like a diamond, Cathy, hard enough to cut through any matter, yet always lucid, brilliant, many-faceted. Her intellect would have been remarkable in a man; in a woman it was wondrous. The tasks she set me were formidable, but her constant guidance and encouragement gave me the confidence to attempt them, and before long I was undeterred by any volume in her library. She had me read Lord Chesterfield's letters for their matter, Johnson's Ramblers and Addison's Spectators for their style, Pope and Swift for satire, Locke and Hume for their thought, Shakespeare for poetic excellence, Fielding and Richardson for diversion, and the classical authors in translation that I might allude to them in conversation and display my learning. You may guess how I struggled with the more long-winded of these fellows, with their elaborate figures and extravagant opinions and their frivolous flights of fancy; yet I stuck at them and was shown how to thresh them to get the grains from the husks, though more than once I felt the return of my old longing to consign all books to the horse-trough. Elizabeth also trained me to discuss my reading with her and give her my own opinions on all subjects, and in conversation to appear knowing even when I was ignorant – a sleight of mind is required for this which is a species of mental fencing, and no less dexterous an activity than the more lethal kind, though one that fewer gentlemen master, I was assured. The trick is to glean information from others without appearing to, and then to return it to them in the guise of an intelligently framed question, which in turn produces an informative answer, and so on.

Yet keen though I was to practise these skills, I had constantly to conceal all signs of my improvement from Mr Durrant and act the unschooled boor whenever I was in his company – which, thankfully, wasn't often. Ignorant of his role in my schooling, he absented himself often and for long periods that autumn, leaving me to be his wife's companion day and night. I continued to escort her to balls and supper parties until the end of the Season, when they became less frequent and poorer in attendance, and so less attractive to her. But not once did I lay eyes on Bassett, and not once did Elizabeth ask to be left alone with any gentleman, a request that our bargain entitled her to make. Yet she remained aloof from me when in company and obliged me to exercise a matching discretion, and neither danced nor supped with me or treated me otherwise in public than as her husband's servant. Only in the privacy of her apartments was our intimacy permitted to develop – but I will not torment you with an account of those sessions, Cathy, though you richly deserve one, and in the fullest detail. I know you too well to think you would read it in any case; just as I would tear to shreds any description by you of your intimacies with Edgar Linton.

Mondays were my sabbaths now. I took a rest from my books to drive the Round with Haskell and the bullies, and got to know it well, though every week saw the addition to it of more shops, inns and coffee-houses, and more shabby-genteel debtors. One Monday in particular I have good cause to remember.

It was quite early in November, a wet November after a wet October. Most of the streets were hub-deep in filthy black sludge quite unlike the mud that covers our northern roads after heavy rain; for this stinking ooze manages to creep over your boot-tops and gets stirred up by passing coaches so that the smell of it hangs over London like a gibbeted corpse. We had completed most of the Round in these conditions, having taken longer over it than usual, and found ourselves still in Cheapside by nightfall. From there we should have driven back to Westminster by way of Fleet Street, for the late increase of debtors made that our new route, many of them residing in that part of town. But instead Richards took us along Newgate Street and into Holbourn. When I asked Haskell where we were going he said it was a surprise, and I should get my answer soon enough and be delighted with it when I got it.

Before long I recognized the St Giles Watch House, where I'd first encountered the No Popery mob, and then, a little further on, we entered Broad St Giles's and halted by the Alms House. Rain was falling heavily – I could see it in the light of the coach lamps and heard it drumming on the roof.

'Richards'll take the coach back,' said Haskell. 'Where we're going we'd best be afoot.'

'I'll require to know more than that before I step out of here,' said I. I didn't trust Haskell and had no intention of letting myself be murdered in some wretched alley and left to rot in the mud.

'Stay if you've a mind to,' he replied, picking up a canvas bag that he'd had beside him. There was a clink from within it, as of two metal objects touching together. 'Tools,' he said with a grin. 'Will you come?'

'Aye,' I said, 'if you've a lantern.'

He answered that Twiss had one and cautioned me to ensure that my pistols were primed and kept dry. Reassured by this advice, I climbed down after him and found Twiss already waiting in the road with the lantern. In his other hand he carried his blunderbuss. He chuckled – it was a disagreeable sound, his chuckle – and bidding us mind the kennel, which was brimming, he raised the lantern aloft and crossed the street.

I let Haskell precede me and followed with my right hand never far from the butt of my pistol as they led me first into Dyot Street, then through several alleys where the muck came almost to my knees. Much of the time I could see neither Twiss nor Haskell, but followed the dim glow of the lantern, hurrying now and then when it got too far ahead of me. I had no desire to miss my way on such a night in such a place.

Of a sudden the light disappeared. I hesitated, fearing treachery, and half drew my pistols; but then, above the gurgling of the rain-water, I heard Haskell call: 'Heathcliff, here, in the doorway.'

They were both there, but Twiss had extinguished the lantern and was busy wiping the rain off his blunderbuss with a piece of rag. 'No sense in announcing ourselves,' he said obscurely. 'Better go up in the dark. But take care on the stairs; they're rotted through in places.'

'Why are we here?' I demanded. The only reply I got was a hissed 'Hold your damned tongue,' from Twiss, and a creaking from the first wooden step as he tried his weight on it.

It must have taken us all of five minutes to mount those infernal stairs. The unlighted ascent was made more perilous by the absence of a banister – I was obliged to hug the wall for support, fouling my clothes – and by the multitude of rats underfoot; I guessed that above half of the brutes were not indigenous to the building but had come in from the alley to escape drowning. I near broke my neck once by stepping on one, which squealed horribly and bit almost through my boot before it expired.

The final flight of stairs was so narrow that we had to go up sideways, but it brought us at last to the top of the house. Set into one of the crumbling walls was a door of sound timber, from behind which came voices – I heard a man's laugh, quickly followed by an oath from another.

'Two at least,' Twiss whispered. 'And they'll have that door bolted, sure. Have to ram it together.'

Since the landing was barely wide enough to accommodate the three of us, we had no space for a flying leap but crammed ourselves, with some difficulty, shoulder to shoulder, and, from a foot away, hurled ourselves bullishly at the door. It proved to be less stout than it had seemed, for our combined weight of about forty stone burst it open with such force that it was all but carried away. At least, its topmost hinge was wrenched

144

out, causing the door to heel, and we had almost to clamber over it to get inside.

We found ourselves in a gloomy, evil-smelling little room furnished only with a deal table, some simple chairs and a bed. An end of candle sputtered in a pool of tallow on the table, and by its meagre light two men were seated at cards.

One of them I knew instantly. And he recognized me, for his mouth dropped open and his eyes hardened, though he made no sound. So sudden and unexpected had been our entrance that neither of the card-players had summoned his wits sufficiently to get to his feet, and before they could think to do it Twiss had placed himself within a yard of the table and had his blunderbuss aimed midway between them. It pointed roughly at the candle; he had only to fire to take off both their heads.

'Move a hair,' Twiss told them, 'and I'll plaster that wall with your brains.'

My own contribution was a snarled: 'I'll be damned. Burns. Christmas has come early.'

Haskell laughed. He had crossed to the grate, where a sickly fire was going, and was kneeling by it. I watched him open his canvas bag and extract a flat length of iron such as smiths and wheelwrights use. This he thrust into the fire, stirring up the coals with it, then left it there to heat. 'Have some cheer for Christmas, shall we, lads?' was his comment. Next he pulled several lengths of thin rope from the bag, and, throwing some of these in my direction, he bid me tie Burns with them, and he would truss the other fellow. 'Leave his right arm free,' he added, 'and keep a watch on the door.'

To my disappointment, Burns gave me no trouble – I'd have relished subduing that one – and I soon had him neatly parcelled, and bound to his chair for good measure.

'Now get him as close as you can to that table,' Haskell instructed, 'and place the candle just out of his reach.'

Puzzled, I did his bidding, but not without complaint. 'I don't need him tied,' I said.

'I do,' Haskell answered. 'We're not here on your account. Now,' said he, addressing himself to Burns, who was sitting grim-faced in his chair, 'see if you can get the candle.' Burns looked as perplexed as I was by this, and said he'd be damned if he'd play children's games. I noticed also that Twiss had laid by his blunderbuss and had turned his back to the table – I presumed he was keeping watch on the door. 'It's little enough to ask,' said Haskell patiently. 'If you can reach the candle we'll let you go free.' Burns responded with a sniff, but stretched out his right arm with his fingers extended and strained to reach the candle. My estimate had been a good one, and he came very close to touching the thing. 'Shade further,' urged Haskell, whereupon Burns' face twisted with the additional effort, his fingernail just managing to scrape the tallow.

At that moment Twiss heaved himself on to the table. Before Burns could withdraw his arm Twiss had it firmly pinned under his broad buttocks. The hand writhed like a snake's head under a boot, then clenched into a fist, but the weight was immovable.

While Burns cursed and struggled, Haskell returned to the fire. He wrapped a piece of rag around the bar that was heating, withdrew it, then replaced it.

'You'll have spent what you took from Mr Sherall, I dare say,' he said, reaching once more into his bag. 'Drank it, did you?'

Burns managed a scornful laugh. 'Aye. It's in my guts if you want it.' To me he said: 'I knew I should have finished you when I had the chance.'

Haskell had drawn a wicked-looking hatchet out of the canvas bag. 'Mr Sherall can stand the loss,' he said, testing the edge with his thumb. 'Yours will be a loss you'll feel more.'

He came to the table with the hatchet and held it up for Burns to see. The fellow paled at the sight of the instrument and made a superhuman effort to free himself; Twiss had to hold fast to the table's edge to keep his seat.

'*Your* privilege, Mr Sherall says,' declared Haskell, offering me the damned weapon. 'Take your time over it. Two or three strokes will do as well as one. The lesson's in the doing.' And, placing the hatchet by Burns' wrist, so that the wretch could feel the steel against his skin, he pulled a kerchief from his pocket and tied it over the victim's mouth. 'I fancy he'll wail a bit while it's being done,' Haskell said, 'and we don't want to be interrupted.'

Burns' eyes were now busy in their sockets, rolling and fluttering in animal terror, as if attempting to escape from his head. I had little taste for the cold-blooded work required of me, however, and would have considered Burns' fear ample recompense had it not been for the others' expectations. Any hesitation of mine they would doubtless have construed as want of bottom, bottom being the main currency among bravoes. And I needed to retain their respect if I was to continue making the Round with them. Besides, thought I, Haskell would do the job if I refused, and why should it matter how I paid back Burns? He had shown himself to be a pitiful, cringing cur, and I swear I could smell his funk as I picked up the hatchet.

'As far above his wrist as you can manage,' Haskell directed, and Twiss obligingly shifted his bulk closer to Burns' shoulder. 'Mr Sherall's instructions were to shorten his reach appreciably.'

I did it, Cathy. Are you shocked by that? But at least I did it with merciful dispatch, which is more than Haskell would have done. Seizing the weapon, I brought it down

147

with all my force on the wretch's quivering forearm, some two or three inches above the wrist. The blade sliced easily through bone and gristle and buried itself fast in the planking, the severed hand flew off the table, and blood sprayed into my face.

Burns had time to give a single muffled shriek before he swooned – I've heard a fox shriek so with its leg broken by a trap – and the cloth over his mouth began to redden, which suggested that he'd bitten through his tongue. But that loss of blood was inconsiderable compared with the quantity that poured from his arm – you could tell his pulse by the rhythmic pumping of the stuff, and it was fast as a baby's. He wouldn't have lasted above two minutes if Haskell hadn't fetched the hot iron and applied it to the stump. I don't know where he learned the method, but I'll vouch for its effectiveness. The heat seared the cut artery closed with much smoking of flesh and sizzling of blood. It fairly turned to gravy as I watched, and the stench was indescribable.

'We should have made a good pair of surgeons, Heathcliff,' was Haskell's comment. 'We've contrived a damned neat amputation between us.' Then he loosed the hatchet, wiped it, returned it to the bag, and had Twiss recover the hand.

This grisly object we took downstairs with us, where Haskell nailed it to the outer door, using a nail and a hammer he'd brought with him for the purpose in the canvas bag.

16

I told you this incident took place early in November, but it must have been nearer the middle of the month; for it was not above four weeks later that Elizabeth suddenly declared herself to be suffering from melancholy and in need of a cure; and that I know was close to Christmas because Mr Durrant offered to take her to Bath if she would wait a week or two more for the holiday.

She refused to wait. She required a sea cure, she said, and had her heart set on Brighthelmstone; at which her husband snorted and averred she'd chosen that infernal place because she knew how much he detested it. But she had her way, and I was sent with her.

We travelled in the chaise, and since it was a fifty miles drive, were on the road all day, arriving at the Castle Inn by supper-time. Elizabeth's melancholy vanished long before we even sniffed the sea, the disorder being as fancied as the remedy, and she seemed uncommonly cheerful on the journey and sang to herself most of the way.

At the inn she ordered supper for two in her room, saying she expected her husband to join her shortly, and made separate arrangements for me. When I inquired, sarcastically, who was to be her husband, she replied with a sly smile: 'Not your employer, assuredly. Don't fret, Heathcliff, I'll give you some money and you may amuse yourself while we're here. Brighthelmstone abounds with young ladies on whom you can practise your new-learned manners. Like so many passive female Caesars, they are come to be seen and to be conquered.'

'And no doubt your male Caesar will be active here before long,' was my comment.

'Heathcliff!' she exclaimed with a laugh. 'Can it be that you are jealous?'

'You care nothing for your reputation, then?' I said.

'This would enhance it,' said she, 'and I'd have chosen a more fashionable place if I did not fear my husband. People of *ton* do not come to this smelly village, however, so I'm not known here. But why you should care is beyond me. You have said you do not love me.'

Since this was the truth, I could not answer her. But the sight of Colonel Bassett next morning, resplendent in his uniform and astride a handsome bay, fairly made my knuckles itch. His regiment was manoeuvring on the downs, it seemed, and the two of them planned to observe it fight a mock battle or some such thing. He'd provided her with a pure white mount, which she sat like a general, having more braid on her riding jacket than he wore on his own coat. The red cloth of their dress had me near to snorting and pawing at the mud of the yard like any bull.

'Ah,' said Bassett, noticing me for the first time, 'Snarler is with you still, I see. Will he jog after us?'

'You should not speak so to him,' said Elizabeth, shifting in her saddle. 'He has his dignity too, and things have changed. We owe our privacy to Heathcliff, if you must know it.'

'He looks less hang-dog, I'll allow,' commented Bassett. 'My apologies to you, Heathcliff.'

'Charles, I did not put on this riding habit merely to sit in an inn yard reviewing Heathcliff,' she said haughtily.

He soothed her with some compliment on her dress, but kept hold of both bridles to prevent her riding off without him. To me he said: 'I'm too well disposed towards you, Heathcliff, to wish to continue our quarrel. I dislike your kind heartily, but since you are obviously a man – though a poor one – I regret having called you a cur. Come, shall we have a truce?'

Cathy, he was insane enough to smile at me and expect me to forget his insults on the spot and be grateful for his paltry magnanimity. If he'd stepped down off the moon I could not have excused his behaviour.

'You may keep your truce for the devil,' I exclaimed. 'A moment since, I was a cur and now suddenly I'm an admirable fellow, am I? I can see why Mrs Durrant appreciates you. You're both of a kind.'

His face darkened, but before he could reply Elizabeth jerked her horse's bridle from his grip, turned the beast, and rode out of the yard at a canter. And fearing, possibly, to lose sight of her or distress her further if he delayed, Bassett denied himself the satisfaction of a retort but spurred the bay in pursuit.

I spent that entire day walking on the Sussex downs, and no landscape could have been more disagreeable to me. It exactly suits the southern character, being composed of soft, lush mounds with chalk the underlying rock. You feel you are treading on a marchpane cake, for those verdant hills are pretty and soft as a confection, and the temptation is to cut a slice with your fingernail. The weather, too, is appropriately clement. There was a squall or two in the afternoon and some hail showers – *we* should have considered it a passable day for April – but the talk at the inn later was of the storms, and of how severe the winter threatened to be.

Elizabeth proved herself to be a far sturdier specimen, however.

Bassett stayed in camp with his regiment that night, and she retired early, saying the ride had exhausted her. I made some unflattering remark about her want of a robust constitution, which she smiled at, and, advising me not to stay up late myself, she went to her bed. I continued drinking for an hour longer, then followed her advice.

It was as well that I did. My room was still in darkness when I awoke to find her standing over me, dressed for out-of-doors in a long hooded cloak.

'It wants an hour of dawn,' she said, in answer to my unspoken query. 'Now make haste and dress yourself. I've a mind to go sea bathing.'

'At this hour?' was my incredulous response. 'The guides will not be up yet.'

'Precisely my reason for wishing to go now,' said she. 'You shall be my guide. It will be delightfully private.'

'Aye, and deuced cold,' I warned, but I put on some warm clothes and we stole out and down to the sea like two ghosts.

A light frost lay over everything – even the foreshore was covered by it – and Elizabeth insisted that I carry her to the water's edge so that we'd leave only one set of footprints. I've said she had an impish turn of mind, like yours. Her notion was to confound any other early morning bathers who might be abroad, for she intended to leave one set of prints going into the sea and two coming out. 'And they'll think some man has made a tryst with a water nymph,' she said gleefully. But though some fishermen were about, they were offshore, and we saw nobody else all the time we were there.

'Now put me down,' she instructed when the waves reached my ankles. 'I shall require your services as a clothes-press.' Whereupon she commenced to undress herself. I'd expected her to be wearing a flannel bathing gown under her other clothes, but when her petticoat came off there was no garment beneath it, and she stood naked in six inches of water, shivering like a person in a fever.

'Elizabeth, you'll catch your death,' I chided, feeling more foolish than embarrassed. With her clothes bundled in my arms I felt like a footman about to serve dinner.

'No,' said she, her voice trembling. 'You have driven me to these extremes, Heathcliff, with your taunts, and you shall have me on your conscience.'

I laughed to see her so starved yet so proud. The memory of her appearance amuses me even now, and that is no mean achievement in my present circumstances.

I praised her courage and offered to take back my slighting remark about her constitution, but it would not do. She had formed the intention to bathe naked in the sea, and immerse herself she would. 'My only problem,' said she, 'is that it is like self-execution, and I cannot bring myself to do it. You must push me under. Imagine we are besieged by savages, and it is your last duty as my faithful retainer to spare me dishonour.' The idea seemed to excite her. She began to jump up and down, laughing as she splashed me. 'Oh, Heathcliff,' she wailed, 'all is lost. They have broken in the gates and swarm across the compound even now.' Here she pointed along the shore and seemed truly in a passion. 'Pray, strip yourself, dear Heathcliff, and perform your last service for your mistress.'

Her antics had me laughing like a fool. Without taking off as much as my hat, I quickly flung her clothes behind me to the shore – only one garment fell into the water – and plunged into the icy sea, pulling Elizabeth in after me.

She shrieked, drew several rapid breaths on rising to the surface, then went under once more. Each time she struggled free of the waves I allowed her a brief breathing space before ducking her again. She protested and laughed and fought me, her screams a child-like mixture of joy and terror. Until at last I was persuaded by the earnest tone of her shrieks to relent. She pounded me playfully with her little fists then, saying: 'Horrid Heathcliff. You've made me swallow some.'

'It's the recommended cure for melancholy,' I teased.

'Then I'd rather be melancholy,' she said, 'except that I am not. I'm wonderfully happy, and it is your doing, my dearest.'

'Dress yourself,' I told her. 'You'll be starved.'

Something in my tone must have been discordant, for she asked why I was not happy also. I said I was as happy as I could hope to be, and bid her hasten.

'That isn't enough,' said she, putting on the driest of her clothes and discarding the rest. 'You are still pining for that Cathy of yours, are you?' She gave a loud sniff as she applied herself to a stubborn button. 'You've said she no longer loves you. Young girls are capricious in that way, Heathcliff. I have been one myself and know their greatest delight is to torment men as wanton children torment cats. Cats have the good sense not to enjoy it, however.'

'Oh,' I said, 'you've outgrown that, have you? You no longer take pleasure in tormenting men. I wonder whether Colonel Bassett and your husband and myself, were we to confer on that subject, should entirely agree with you. If Bassett had not been in camp last night would he not be in my place now?'

'Certainly he would,' she replied without hesitation. 'But I should not have enjoyed the experience more in his company than I have in yours. Or less.'

'Then you are incapable of loving,' I flung at her. 'It is not possible to love two men equally.'

'Loving?' She left her buttoning to give me all her attention. 'Loving?' she repeated. 'If we have declared love for each other it must have been in our sleep, for I've no recollection of it.'

I muttered something about having to get out of my wet clothes and we returned to the inn without further conversation, under a dismal grey dawn sky.

There she became teasing again. She enticed me into

154

her chamber, saying she had a towel among her things; then insisted upon undressing me and wiping me dry, and had me perform the same service for her. After which, as I could scarcely go unclothed to my own room, she persuaded me to get into the bed with her, where we warmed each other until an hour past breakfast time.

We remained at Brighthelmstone all that day and the next. I was left to amuse myself as I could while Elizabeth gadded about the county with Bassett, going on horseback to Lewes, and to Arundel in the chaise – they hired a coachman, to my chagrin, without consulting me; I'd have relished refusing to drive them myself. And in the evenings they danced and played at cards, the innkeeper having got up these entertainments for his genteel guests.

Elizabeth took care to keep me apart from Bassett, liking us both too well, as she put it, to see us brawl ignominiously in the mire like chairmen. 'Besides,' she added, 'he has fought with labourers many times aɪd invariably wins such silly contests, having been instructed in boxing by Johnson himself – who *is* Johnson?'*

'I shouldn't care if he were the devil,' I sneered. 'And I'll risk a thrashing if he'll meet me.' I had confused my pronouns, but got no correction.

'Don't commit the error of doubting his courage, Heathcliff,' she advised me. 'It is simply that he feels the world is already too dull a place, without our having to repeat experiences in it. He likens you to the savage Indian who believes he might acquire his enemy's qualities by defeating him in combat, and wonders if you have Indian blood or are an anthropophagus, who would not scruple to eat a man's flesh to achieve the same end.'

*Probably Tom Johnson, Champion of England from 1787 to 1791.
– W.L.

'Does he say so?' I answered angrily. 'Well, you may inform him that I covet no single quality of his, least of all his insufferable arrogance.'

'Oh, I've told him that,' she said gaily. 'And he has promised to devise a quite different test of your character for some future occasion. I cannot wait to know what it is, can you?'

I was all for seeking Bassett out at once, to fight him in any fashion he cared to choose, with any weapon from mace to cannon; but Elizabeth restrained me, saying it was not such a duel he had in mind, and that in any case he would require time to make preparations. 'Now,' she said, 'forget this nonsense and come down to the dance. There are some pretty girls at it and this will be your last opportunity to have fun before we return.'

Her notion of 'fun' so horrified me that I shut myself up in my room for the rest of the evening and would not have quitted it had all the fiends of hell come bursting through my window.

Next day it rained, and I had a miserable journey back to town.

Christmas was celebrated about a week later. Though it is a lively enough affair in London, townsfolk have not our way of doing things, and I found myself missing the cheer of the Heights, and Nelly's cakes and mulled ale, and even Joseph's unseasonable gloom.

Nay, my cruel darling, they were not all I missed. I could not wrench my thoughts away from you, though I tried hard to divert them. What I remembered in particular was that Christmas when you returned from your stay at the Grange and I got a thrashing from Hindley for anointing your fine new friend with hot sauce. I was confined to my room, and you were still mine then, enough to abandon Linton to his howling and climb in through the skylight to keep me company.

Do you recall what we talked about, Cathy? We discussed Christmas and said what a mockery we thought it. We blasphemed and defied God to bring down the house on our heads for our blasphemy, and when He showed no willingness to oblige us we called on the devil, then declared *him* a scoundrel for not making an appearance either. You said Old Nick was giving a Christmas party in hell to celebrate his success at hoodwinking the world, and that was why he couldn't answer our summons; and I said God must be Guest of Honour at it, and that explained *His* absence. But it raised our spirits, and the memory of it did as much for me this past Christmas.

The New Year brought colder weather – a few snow flurries and freezing mud in the streets – and the usual increase in the Bills of Mortality. I had begun to read newspapers, having nothing to do in the long evenings but read. I read until my eyes burned. London was become an abomination to me. I yearned for fields, for the feel of earth between my fingers and under my feet, hated the brick and stone surrounding me with a passion I would not have thought it possible for inanimate things to inspire. And it seemed my body was weakening with every day of idleness, my constitution getting softer, until I sweated in my dreams with the fear of waking to find myself transformed into a Linton. Does that make you smile?

Weeks passed unmarked by an event of consequence, yet I felt – God, it was the strangest feeling – I felt at the same time content and ill-at-ease. I seemed to be waiting for something – how can I express it? – for some event, some change, though I had no idea what to expect. Nelly would have called it a premonition; I've heard her use the word to describe dreams that foretold events, saying the dreamer was given a key that would fit but one lock, and that one exactly; that he had a duty to go seeking the lock, though he might never find it. Well, what I've found does not correspond to my presentiment. Tell it to Nelly, ask her what it means.

But I must continue my narrative while I have time. I'm weary. I sleep badly and write away my nights by the light of a single candle. Its flame makes frenzied patterns of my words, dizzies me. I see faces in it, but only yours is clear. There is not much more to come.

Mr Durrant was seldom out of the house last winter, so I had few opportunities to be with Elizabeth and got my lessons irregularly. And since the same circumstances governed our more intimate meetings, we soon hit upon the plan of combining both, in order to make the most of each other's company. Consequently, whenever her husband's absences afforded us a few hours of freedom, Elizabeth would inform the servants that she felt tired or unwell and would retire to her bedroom, leaving instructions that she was not to be disturbed on any account. After a safe interval I would join her. She had a magnificent bed with carved mahogany posts and a domed silk tester, and I learned much in it: English and Latin grammar, and some fine phrases in the French tongue as well.

One afternoon towards the end of February we were lying together so, covered loosely by the counterpane – the fire had been going all day and the room was nicely warmed – and having abandoned Livy, were reading a Gothic romance Elizabeth had got from the circulating library. It was an idiotic story with an Isabella for its heroine, so you may guess how little I like it; but Elizabeth was delighted by the thing and insisted that I read some of it to her, saying my voice was exactly suited to the matter. One infernal phrase she had me repeat a dozen times, a description of an ideal hero with large black eyes and manly locks like jet – I believe it went so.

'Dear Heathcliff, it is yourself!' she cried gleefully. 'Mr Walpole* must have seen a vision of you when he wrote those words. Are you not proud to be his heroic archetype?'

I laughed at her foolishness and said I felt myself closer to Manfred – he was a different character in the story.

'But he is a villain and a tyrant!' she exclaimed, horrified by the suggestion. 'He reminds me of Alex. I detest Manfred.'

'Then you should detest me,' I answered, 'for I like him best and would do precisely as he does were I in his role.'

'How dreadful you must think yourself. Are you saying that you care nothing for the feelings of others and would kill and torture indiscriminately to get your way?'

'I would do as much,' I said, 'if I had his power and exemption from the law, and considered the measures justified by the ends.'

'That is extraordinary, Heathcliff,' she said, exhibiting signs of vexation. 'I have heard Alex express the same proposition in almost identical words. Come, say you are teasing me.'

'I assure you I'm in earnest,' I returned. 'And what is more, you know it. I believe it is no accident, either, that you see a resemblance between my character and his – bad natures fascinate you.'

Her reply would have interested me. Unfortunately she had no time to make it, for at that moment the door was flung violently open and her husband stormed into the room.

---

*The Gothic romance is Horace Walpole's *The Castle of Otranto*.
– W.L.

159

17

At first it appeared that his extreme agitation had struck him dumb. He stood and stared at us as if confronted by some unspeakable horror from Walpole's story. Then he said, in a barely controlled voice: 'Oh, you have been an artful bitch, Elizabeth. I'll give you credit for that.'

She retained her composure wonderfully, replying: 'You must have had a dull afternoon with your little girls, Alex, to have returned so early.' She had the effrontery to yawn before adding: 'My own being equally dull, I thought to have Heathcliff entertain me. And there is not a warmer spot in the house. Why don't you join us? You look ridiculous standing there.'

'Take care,' said her husband, 'not to provoke me too far. I am in a murderous frame of mind, I warn you, and could dispose of two as easily as one.' He now turned his attention to me, his face distorted with hate as he said: 'You chose to ignore my earlier advice, Earnshaw. You must expect to pay a heavy price for showing such miserable judgement. I believe I could justify shooting you where you lie.'

'I believe you could,' I replied, wondering how much he'd overheard of my conversation with Elizabeth. 'And if I were you I'd attempt it. But if you quit this room to fetch a weapon, do not expect to find me lying here with my chest bared for your bullet when you return. I am not so honourable, being merely a low ruffian you've taken from the street.'

'Bravo, Heathcliff!' interposed his wife. 'Alex, in no sense is Heathcliff prepared to remain where you decide to leave him. He has not been idle these last months, and I have helped him put himself beyond your influence. I'm too proud of my handiwork, however, to allow you to destroy it unopposed. So if you kill Heathcliff you must kill me also – I shall insist upon it. Otherwise my testimony will send you to the gallows.'

Durrant seemed to give this careful consideration, placing his finger to his lip. Then, nodding slowly, he said: 'Yes, it would be unlawful; and that would not do. Very well, Earnshaw, kindly remove yourself to other lodgings within the hour. My reason may not rule my passions much longer.'

'Wait, Heathcliff!' cried his wife as I made to throw off the counterpane. 'You will require certain assurances from my husband before you depart. Will he not, Alex?'

The other said: 'I have already promised I will not shoot him if he quits my house at once.'

'You know that is not sufficient,' said she. 'I refer to an assurance that you will not send Haskell after him to murder him. Heathcliff may be naïve enough to trust you, but I am not; and he is certain to know more about your activities than is good for him. I insist that he have some surety – if it be only your promise to let him alone, given in exchange for his that he will keep your secrets.'

Durrant gave her an astonished look. 'He has neither the means nor the motive to hurt me,' was his reply. 'And let me remind you that you are hardly in a position to *insist* upon anything. I dare say the fellow will be thankful to get away from this house with a whole skin.'

'Take care, Heathcliff,' she warned. 'Don't be deceived by his soft, complaisant manner. I'd rather he stormed and threatened the punishments of hell – his softness is quicksand.'

'And yours, madam,' he breathed, 'is the whisper of the succubus. Begone, Earnshaw, before she persuades me to prevent you.'

I said coolly: 'Mr Durrant, cuckolds enjoy certain

privileges, including temporary licence to insult and threaten the adulterous pair – but beware of exceeding your permitted limits, for I've no surer way of obviating my murder than to send my potential assassin to hell in advance of me.'

This speech of mine could not have got a more mixed reception. Elizabeth applauded it, but her husband was thrown into an access of fury, and, clenching his fists, took two or three steps towards the bed. White-faced and trembling, he thundered: 'You damned insolent beggar! You might as well place a pistol to your own head as speak so to *me*! By God, you'll suffer now!'

I had leapt out of bed to confront him, but as I was wearing nothing but my shirt, he had the advantage of dignity, and mine was not much improved by a sudden outburst of shrill laughter from Elizabeth.

'Whisht!' I said. 'Will you anger both of us?'

'You may be sure that is her intention,' said Durrant, apparently the calmer for having his rage diverted.

Elizabeth made an effort to control her laughter – it was chiefly hysterical, I suspect – and managed to say: 'It was the sight of you, the two of you so,' before she fell once more into incoherent mirth.

'Look at her,' said Durrant contemptuously, indicating the frivolous woman writhing on the bed. 'Was she worth it, Earnshaw? Was she worth what she'll cost you?'

I gave no answer but collected my breeches and made a hasty exit.

My wages during the past months, together with my share of the takings from the Round, amounted to a considerable sum. I had accumulated above two hundred pounds, having spent very little while at Hill Street, and in consequence it did not take me long to find lodgings to my mind – a suite of apartments in a house in Great Marlborough Street, fitting my new station as a landless gentleman in want of suitable employment.

I had lately purchased a good suit of clothes, and so looked the part; and the jingle of my gold made up any deficiency in my appearance, character, or history that may have impressed itself on my landlord. I paid him £25, an advance of six months, and a further £10 for my dinners during the same period.

Thus fixed, I went from the house early on the morrow to seek employment, found none, and after repeating the process every day for a fortnight with no success, abandoned the attempt. Thereafter I ventured abroad only in pursuit of pleasure, which I found in abundance, being plentifully supplied with the means to purchase it. You have reason to appreciate, Cathy, that a taste for comfortable living is as soon acquired and as hard to be rid of as any disease, and the only physic for it is more of that which produced the first symptoms. So by April I began to worry, having reduced my stock of medicine to such a level that at my current rate of spending I calculated it would be entirely exhausted before the summer. I set to considering how I might replenish it – I'd tried gaming but had proved unlucky at it – and after rejecting several other possibilities, resolved to go upon the high-toby, this time for profit rather than pleasure.

I have often wondered, these past weeks, whether Destiny is a grave justice like the Fielding who has lately died, or a comic one, like his brother; and whether the highway life, if I'd adopted it, would have made me rich and returned me eventually to you, or would have brought me at last to this same infernal place. I cannot shake the feeling that all my life I have been led here, even while supposing myself strong-willed, as a fierce bull may be led by the nose to slaughter and never know it.

One mild April morning I stepped out into Great Marlborough Street to begin my new life with the purchase of a suitable horse. I looked, as was my custom, to right and left in case Haskell should be lying in wait for me, and saw instead of Haskell half a dozen thief-takers and another fellow who pointed at me, and cried out that I was the one, and urged the constables to seize me directly. He was an old man, dressed in the livery of a footman, and at first I didn't know him. But he knew me. He'd recognized me a day or two since in Oxford Street, and having followed me to discover where I lodged, had laid an information against me. Now the officers were come with a warrant to search my apartments, and this fellow seemed in a transport of joy to be with them.

'You've changed your looks, I'll allow,' said he as the search was made, 'but I'd know you in a camp of gipsies on a moonless night. You destroyed an Hepplewhite table, and you're going to hang for that.'

Only then did I remember him, and if two of the officers had not held my arms I'd have twisted his head off his scraggy neck. Minutes later they found the volume of Blackstone annotated in Lord Mansfield's own hand – the footman identified it almost with reverence; and this, with his other evidence, was enough to convict me for my part in the riots of June, 1780.

Summer has come again, the anniversary of my departure from Wuthering Heights has come and gone. They have put me in a fire-blackened cell in a part of Newgate Gaol that escaped destruction. I am chained like a beast, Cathy. I rot away here.

Tuesday morning, a little after sunrise – I can tell by the shadow of the grille upon the wall how high the sun is.

I'm to be hanged on Friday.

So my history is at an end – unsatisfying, is it not? Yet I regret nothing of what I have done, only my failure to achieve my purpose. It is wasteful to have struggled with such determination towards death, when a minimum of effort would have got me there as surely. I am not afraid of it – it's a trivial annoyance – but I wonder about it.

Yesterday I sent the Ordinary packing. He came prating to me about my soul and bidding me to devote my remaining hours to its salvation. He had the air of a debt-collector, Cathy, who has been put off for years and now knows he must be paid at last. He was gloating. I told him I'd supported the devil's party all my life and had no cause to change my allegiance now, at which he raged and commenced to bluster – I'll swear he thought himself in the satanic presence even at that moment. 'By noon on Friday,' said he, 'you'll have discovered who is master of the universe, and my only wish is that I might witness the effects of that revelation upon your black soul.'

'Step where I can get at you,' was my cry as I rattled my fetters, 'and I'll arrange for you to have a commanding view.'

That was sufficient for him. He'll not venture here again.

However, his mouthings set me to thinking about survival; for I'm convinced the soul does survive the body's death, particularly if it be a strong-willed soul, as mine will be. If only I could be sure distance would not thwart it, I'd promise to give you no peace, Catherine Earnshaw. You'd have me with you day and night. It would be an exquisite, lovely haunting, though you deserve a horrendous one. Still, if two hundred miles can be managed by a spirit, you'll see me yet.

Wednesday in the forenoon. I'd resolved to write no more to you, having convinced myself in the comfortless hours of the night that you care nothing for me. I despair when I think so, and then hell does not wait for Friday but begins and ends with an image of you reading this letter. Edgar Linton stands behind you and reads over your shoulder, laughing as he points out an infelicity here, a mis-spelling there. And you laugh with him. You deride my hopes, my pretensions, my pride; scorn my love; ridicule my anguish. Oh, darkness is unrelenting, Cathy. It affords no distractions, numbs the reason and enlivens the imagination, goading it to produce the cruellest phantasies. I hoard my candles like a miser to stave off that tormenting darkness with its flaysome images. How strange it is that I, who fear nothing on earth or beyond it, cringe like a milk-blooded coward at the very thought of your contempt. I couldn't stand it. I'm promised a quick end if I elect to die game; yet I'd willingly be tortured out of existence, then drawn and quartered, if I could be certain of your grief. Shakespeare has it wrong: it is not conscience that makes cowards of us, but the prospect of losing what we most cherish. For others that is life; for me it is your esteem.

Then day comes, and I receive my meagre allowance of sunlight and hear the criers abroad in Newgate Street and Old Bailey, and my terrors seem foolish to me. I cannot believe you have changed so much. Again I take up my pen, to set down more of my thoughts. I shall no doubt continue to write as long as I'm able.

The Keeper visited me not an hour ago. He's a cheerful fellow, full of good advice about diet and how to hang heavy on the gibbet – it shortens the agony, he informs me, to relax all the muscles at the moment of turning-off, though few manage it. 'You'll tend to strain and be tense,' he warned me, 'but it does only harm. Hang heavy.' I was fortunate, he said, having the weight to do it; there was a child due to be turned off with me, a boy of twelve, who weighed less than eight stone and would be made up with lead. 'Help him if you can,' I was urged. 'You appear to have spirit enough for two. In return I'll give you this advice: make a game showing

166

and the mob will let your friends have you instead of the surgeons – that's no way for any man to end his days.'

I thanked him and gave him a further £10 garnish. The rest of my money I have no use for. If Bragg leaves me any I'll enclose it with the letter.

I neglected to tell you who Bragg is. He is my neighbour, a sharping cove who can split a card with his fingernail and rub the spots off dice, seemingly. He has robbed me of thirty or forty pounds these past weeks with his doctors and his high and low fulhams,* but it has made the time pass and I've learned why I cut no great figure in the gaming hells – the sharpers know one another there, and work in concert to gull the inexperienced.

Why do I tell you this? Because I cannot bear to lay down my pen and want more interesting matter to occupy it; because writing is become an obsession with me; because I feel myself uncannily close to you when I have my pen in my hand, and so damnably alone at all other times. A gaoler sits with me day and night – that is the rule for condemned prisoners – but he is scarcely better company than the vermin I'm plagued with here, and I have to remind myself to regard him in the light of a human being. There you have my condition in epitome; life will be no loss to me, Cathy.

Wednesday in the afternoon. Elizabeth Durrant has been to see me – an unexpected visitor, to be sure, but a welcome one. My gaoler consented, for a consideration, to find other business, and we were able to talk freely.

As soon as Elizabeth had satisfied herself that we were not overheard, she began to speak in rapid, urgent

* This sentence contains some 'sharping' terms – i.e., those employed by fraudulent gamesters. The references are to adulterated dice. – W.L.

whispers, bidding me listen without interruption and without any show of anger; for she suspected the gaoler was just beyond the door and did not wish me to alarm him by bellowing.

'Now I'll tell you why you're here,' she said then. 'It is not as you imagine, Heathcliff. First, know that you owe your predicament to my husband – there, I wanted to say that before anything else, so that if we are disturbed you will at least know your killer. Since that day he discovered us together he has been seeking a way to pay you back with the law's assistance, and now – no, just listen – now I will tell you how he contrived your execution. It's a fiendish intrigue, Heathcliff, but if you gnash your teeth so you will not hear it.'

I could scarcely restrain myself and clutched in impotent fury at my top-hairs while she continued: 'You once told him, I understand, that a man called Burns had been with you during the rioting – ah, you remember the name. Well, it seems that Burns is no friend of yours, for when he was asked where you had busied yourselves last June he fairly tripped over his tongue to incriminate you. That is how my husband learned you had taken part in the destruction of Lord Mansfield's house in Bloomsbury Square.'

'I should have cut out his tongue too, it appears,' I muttered.

'Hush,' said she. 'Let me finish. How my husband contrived all this without involving himself I cannot tell you, but I know that one of His Lordship's footmen had reason to remember you, and was as eager as Burns to bring you to justice, so eager that he perjured himself. He did not recognize you by chance in Oxford Street, Heathcliff. He waited outside your lodgings in Great Marlborough Street until you went abroad, then followed you, and testified at your trial that his sighting of you was fortuitous. That's all of it. Two of your enemies, guided by the evil genius of a third, have brought you almost to the gallows, without once arousing your suspicions.' Here she reached out and took both my hands in her own. 'I'd have come to you sooner, but he has watched me as closely as your guard yonder watches you. Today I got my first opportunity to give him the slip, and somehow I must manage it again tomorrow.'

'I do not understand,' I said, 'how the footman knew where I had my lodgings.'

'Did I not tell you?' said she. 'Haskell followed you across half London that day you went from Hill Street. My husband has known where to find you ever since.'

'I'd go to hell with joy,' I breathed, 'if I could take the damned villain with me. Can you get him to come here, Elizabeth, so that I can strangle him with these chains?'

'Hell will wait for you both,' was her sharp retort. 'I'd thought to find you more sanguine about Friday. Do not forget you have a vixen for an ally as well as a fox for an enemy, and I want him repaid as much as you do. Now, raise your head – I wish to inspect something.'

Puzzled, I did her bidding and let her scrutinize my lower jaw and neck and touch my beard with her slender fingers. This completed, she got up from her chair and announced that she must go. 'I've much still to arrange,' she said. 'But I'll be back tomorrow and will inform you then of the plan. Do not shave off your lovely beard meanwhile, Heathcliff. I like it, and it will help to keep you alive on Friday.'

I pressed her, but she refused to say more, except that all would be well if I continued to trust her.

And though I trust her intentions, I cannot trust her judgement. Escape is impossible from this place. It is a fortress. The doors are double-locked and constantly guarded, and no purse is long enough to buy these gaolers

169

– they derive too much income from garnish to risk their position here.

If Elizabeth comes again tomorrow I will entrust this letter to her.

Thursday. Elizabeth is not yet come, though yesterday she was here by this hour – I judge it to be after two o'clock. In all probability her prison has proved itself as strong as mine. So I'll give this to the Keeper, who seems an honest fellow.

I spoke to the boy for almost an hour this morning. He shook uncontrollably all the time I was with him, though whether from fear or gaol fever I cannot say. He has confounded his mind with contradictory expectations, being convinced on the one hand that God will not permit him to die before he has lived – he is not quite twelve years old – and fearful, on the other, of riding alone in the cart to Tyburn. He regards me as an older brother and urged me to sit beside him on the morrow, which I've agreed to do. He is afraid the crowd will jeer at him and make him blubber, and by promising to drub him all the way to the gibbet if he shows milky blood I've managed to comfort him. Odd, is it not? I've substituted my fist for the rope in his terrified imaginings.

Well, my darling, I am done. God has no reason to spare me, and I've little faith in Elizabeth Durrant as my saviour. But she has tried, and if I've not made you too jealous, you may wish to write and tell her I bear her no ill will.

Inform Nelly and Joseph of my end; it may afford that pious pair some satisfaction. And tell Hindley Earnshaw and Edgar Linton that I intend to depart this life with the bitterest imprecations I can summon on my lips; for I'm told a hanged man's curse has wondrous potency, and I covet their lovely company in the dark regions.

As for you, Cathy – my heartless, cruel, adored darling – I can find nothing to say to you that does not burn me worse than the rope. Death will be a balm to me after this agony of a labour. My blessing and my curse I mix for you, for you must know that you have been the source of all my joy and all my suffering in this existence, and that I am, in death as in life,

Yours, Heathcliff
June, 1781

18

1803. – How remarkable are the vicissitudes of fortune! And how infinite her capacity for surprise! Not a month ago I pronounced my poor heart quite dead, Cupid's arrows having so lacerated it that I truly believed it proof against further injury; yet it seems I am still capable of being provoked to amorous affection, and this latest shaft may prove the deadliest of all and make of me a Saint Sebastian, martyred for love.

But I run on too fast and risk confounding my reader when it should be my purpose to enlighten him.

I wrote in February of the circumstances in which Mr Heathcliff's letter came into my hands. What I omitted to mention was that my eagerness to discover how he had extricated himself from his predicament was then eclipsed by a far more urgent need to resolve a situation of my own. I had recently fallen victim to the charms of a delightful young creature, the only daughter of a Buckinghamshire gentleman, and having reason to believe that she was not entirely cool towards me, felt encouraged to pursue her into the country. There the progress of my amour detained me until the end of Spring, when, alas, displaying that inconstancy for which her sex is justly notorious, the lady suddenly reclaimed her affections and bestowed them on the second son of a local baronet. My disgust was such that I immediately entertained the notion of retiring once more from the world, and only the memory of my last wretched experiment with solitude brought me to my senses. Experience is the greatest teacher.

Upon my return to London it occurred to me that the most salutary occupation for a mind in turmoil must be a disinterested one, and that such a mind, engaged by another man's misfortunes, could not fail to find temporary relief from its own problems. Accordingly, I resolved to distract myself from fleshly pursuits at the commencement of the Season by devoting my energies entirely to ghosts; namely, to discovering, if I was able, what course events had taken in the life of Mr Heathcliff twenty-two years ago.

I was not hopeful of learning much. Twenty-two years are quite a spell – two-thirds of my life hitherto – and the rolling ocean of life leaves nothing undisturbed or unchanged; and memories grow blurred. Yet I had as my point of departure Mr Durrant's house in Hill Street, and there I decided to begin my inquiries one morning last month.

My task soon proved even more difficult than I had anticipated. I was all day knocking at doors before I hit upon the right house; and then I received the disappointing news, from a servant of the present household, that though the Durrants had resided there once, nobody of that name had lived in Hill Street these twenty years. I supposed I must consider myself fortunate to have learned this much, thanked the fellow, and had gone a few steps when he called me back. A moment's reflection had served to remind him that his master had subsequently corresponded with the previous owner about some outstanding domestic matter, the letters having been delivered by a footman who was still in service with the household. This ancient was at present about his master's business in the City, but if I would return on the morrow his memory might be profitably searched for an address.

Return I did. The footman was produced, assisted in his recollections with a quantity of silver, and the result, after ten minutes' grinding of the mental mills, was Grosvenor Square. Thither he had taken letters in 1783 – he was certain of the year, he said, because it had been the hottest summer in his life-time, and the subject of those happy epistles had been water supplies or something related but less delicate, it seemed.

Grosvenor Square being no great distance away, I repaired to it directly and presented myself at the likeliest mansion fitting the description I'd been given: an imposing dwelling in the Adam style, with vaulted window recesses at ground level and a Grecian upper façade of columns supporting an ornate pediment. The door was opened by a young servant who, in answer to my inquiry, declared in brusque tones which no novice could have distinguished from downright rudeness that he knew nothing of Durrants, and that in his opinion I had been misdirected. I reserve a tone of my own exclusively for domestics of his humour, and made use of it to thank him for his opinions. And had not my wasted labours put me out of temper I should have been satisfied with this; but, as my dear mother was fond of saying, I have a stubborn disposition, which is never more evident than when my designs are frustrated by the ignorance or indifference of underlings, and though weariness should enervate us, its effect upon me is often the paradoxical one experienced by gamesters who have suffered heavy losses: it strengthens my resolve to hazard all on a final and decisive throw of the dice. I therefore gave this disobliging lackey no opportunity to exercise his tongue further, but demanded to speak with his master or his mistress if either should be home. My manner was peremptory enough to send him scuttling within.

He returned presently and, bidding me enter (most civilly), conducted me into a large, tastefully furnished apartment, where it seemed I must await his mistress.

Some minutes went by, which I occupied with perusing a copy of *The Times* I chanced to find on a low table, before the door was opened to admit – if the Sistine Chapel may be said to have a painting ceiling this apparition may be called a woman.

Would that my poor pen could do her justice. I believe she defies description, being not only the handsomest creature it has ever been my pleasure to behold, but peerless in any gallery of portraits – and portraiture flatters as the critical eye does not. Yet in her both art and nature work in harmony, the dark curls and ringlets of her hair forming a frame for the immaculate beauty of her countenance, the black velvet gown in which she was clad an elegant case for her shapely form; and to these the grace of her carriage added its own master-stroke, so that the whole was a flawless composition of female pulchritude, a veritable Platonic Ideal of Womanhood.

It would not do to estimate her age, save to say that she was of mature years, but I doubt there is a woman in England twenty years her junior who would not unhesitatingly exchange that unlived portion of her life for such an exquisite appearance. It was all I could do to answer without stammering like a tongue-tied schoolboy when she said, in a voice of unimaginable sweetness:

'You have some business with me?'

'I venture to hope, madam,' I replied, 'that my business, trifling though it is, may not be too quickly concluded.' She did not acknowledge the compliment, but looked inquiring, whereupon I continued: 'My name is Lockwood. I regret this unforgivable imposition, but the quest I am engaged on has brought me to your house, and it is my earnest hope that I may learn from you where I must go next.'

'Quest?' she inquired, with a hint of a smile. Oh, that hint!

'Forgive me, madam, for not being direct,' was my next remark, uttered with little sincerity – had I not feared to try her patience I should have taken a sweet hour or two to come to the point. However, I said: 'My quest is for Mrs Alexander Durrant. Your servant informs me that the lady does not reside here, though I believe that has not always been so. May I take the liberty of asking you whether you know Mrs Durrant's present whereabouts?'

She did not reply immediately, but touching her finger to her chin and inclining her lovely head some degrees from the vertical, gave the appearance of cogitation. Even these artless gestures delighted me so extravagantly that I own I was in some despair of concealing my regard for her. Yet her answer, when she gave it, sobered me considerably. 'That lady no longer exists,' said she.

I confess I had not considered this possibility, assuming that the vigorous, robust young woman Mr Heathcliff had known twenty years ago would now be settled into a dignified but still active matronship. 'I am heartily sorry to hear it,' was my response.

'Are you?' I got back from the lady. 'Why? The loss is not a personal one, is it?'

'Indeed not,' I returned, 'but the demise of a beautiful woman is always a loss to the world of men.'

She laughed outright at this, somewhat to my surprise. I'd thought it a gallant sentiment deserving of less equivocal appreciation. 'How preposterous you are, Mr Lockwood, to lament the loss of a person about whom you can know nothing.'

Her speech made me defensive. 'That is not entirely true,' I replied, 'and were she not in her grave – '

'Oh, you've put her underground, have you?'

'Forgive me, madam,' was my perplexed reply, 'but it was you who told me of her death.'

'I said she no longer exists. Three-quarters of the living world could be said to share her situation, Mr Lockwood, though it's a philosophical point I'll not pursue at present. She has a successor, however, and if you will explain your errand plainly I may arrange an introduction for you.'

She now had me wondering if I was the object of some outrageous private jest, for her manner was unquestionably playful. I smiled as I answered: 'Nothing but idle curiosity brings me, I fear. My intention is merely to ask her for the sequel to a tale of which I have the largest part already.'

Her face seemed to undergo a subtle transformation; an alertness entered her beautiful dark eyes, signifying perhaps that what had gone before was harmless play, and that here at last was matter serious enough to justify her full attention.

'Pray continue,' was her only comment.

'There is little I can say,' I protested. 'Mr Heathcliff's letter does not – '

'Heathcliff?' She showed signs of extreme animation. 'You have a letter for me from Heathcliff?'

'Not for you, madam,' I said. 'It was addressed – '

'You must be very dull, Mr Lockwood,' she interrupted, 'not to have guessed that *I* am – *was* – Mrs Durrant. Be good enough to give me my letter.'

I hemmed, totally at a loss. She seemed so excited by the prospect of a letter from Mr Heathcliff that I hadn't the heart to disappoint her with the truth. 'It is not recent,' I began, then faltered. 'Perhaps I should explain some things to you.'

She was shaking her head impatiently. 'Confound you!' she said. 'I have waited twenty years to hear from him, and I will not be delayed another minute. My letter.'

She held out her hand, and I had no choice but to put the letter into it. Immediately she turned her back on me and began fumbling at the pages, unfolding them in such haste that I fancied I heard one tear. I had not been invited to seat myself and so stood looking out of the window while Mrs Durrant began to read the letter. She was not seated either, and I dare say we would both have remained on our feet until dinner-time if her reading had not been curtailed.

After only a few moments, however, she said: 'What cruel joke is this, Mr Lockwood? Do you mean to insult me?'

'Nothing is further from my thoughts,' I answered. 'You'll allow that I tried to warn you the letter was an old one and addressed to another.'

'I did not think you could be referring to *that* letter,' she said. 'I wonder he has kept it all these years. Is her companionship not enough for him?'

The acrimony of her tone made me uncomfortable. 'Perhaps you would like me to go,' I ventured.

'Oh, do not be so ready to take offence,' she said. 'It ill becomes a man. Besides, your curiosity is not yet satisfied, and nor is my own. Tell me, how is the wretch?'

I hesitated, but then, determined not to repeat my mistake, said distinctly: 'Mr Heathcliff is dead, madam. He has been dead two years.'

I expected the news to produce shock or agitation, but she accepted it quite calmly, and only nodded. 'Did he die violently?' she inquired.

'Peacefully,' I said, 'though in a rather odd manner.'

'Pray don't tell me, Mr Lockwood. I prefer to be alone now. But I should be pleased to have you dine with me tomorrow, and then we may talk all evening.'

'Your servant, madam,' I said, bowing.

'And I will keep this letter, if I may. I knew he'd written it, but I have never read it.' Her request embarrassed me, and I must have shown my reluctance to comply with it, for she added: 'You need not fear for my feelings, sir. I know what to expect from Heathcliff,

178

and we rarely get the chance to see ourselves through another's eyes. I dine at six.'

I returned the next day, having occupied myself with thoughts of her throughout the intervening time. I was now as eager to learn more of my hostess as I was to know the rest of Heathcliff's history. Was she a widow? Had she subsequently married Colonel Bassett? Had she driven Heathcliff away and come to regret it?

We dined *à deux*, and conversed on neutral topics during the repast. I found her very amiable and well-informed, and, if it is possible, even more delightful to look upon than she had been the day before. Once I allowed my eyes to stray while in the act of pouring wine, and spilled some on the cloth. She laughed, being too used to such accidents not to know what caused them.

'I was inexcusably rude to you yesterday, Mr Lockwood,' she said as the meal was ending. 'I trust you will forgive me.'

'I am prepared to forgive you anything, madam,' I replied, 'if you will relieve me of the intolerable burden of having to address you so impersonally.'

'I wondered how long that would take you,' said she. 'You may call me Elizabeth – none of its diminutives, mind, for I detest all of them – and I shall call you Lockwood. There, I've shocked you.'

She had, I own it. I have a propensity to be shocked by forwardness of any kind. It is the consequence of a very formal upbringing.

'I care little for the proprieties,' she added. 'I am a free woman, Lockwood, and have been one since my husband was dispatched to the infernal regions. But you'll become accustomed to me. Well, have I any more of your unvoiced questions to answer?'

I protested, rather feebly, that no such questions had been in my mind.

'Fie,' she laughed. 'Poor liars should make it their particular virtue ever to tell the truth, however disturbing it may be. Come, shall we make ourselves comfortable?'

Her conduct was so unpredictable that I hardly knew what to expect, but to my unspeakable relief she did no more than conduct me to the drawing-room, where, both of us being settled comfortably, she said: 'Now, Heathcliff is dead, you tell me. So I suppose I can wait an hour or two to discover how he ended his days. First I will satisfy your curiosity to know how he avoided ending them prematurely. He never spoke of it, did he?'

'He was always most secretive about that period in his life,' I confirmed.

'How like him.' She made a slight movement with her head – I suppose it signified fond regret. 'I have read over his letter,' she continued. 'His eye was jaundiced, of course, but so is everybody's; otherwise his account of events accords well with my own recollections. So I shall go from the Wednesday. And since I'm as forthright as Heathcliff you must promise not to be bashful. Oh, I'll edit my narrative to make it fit for an entertainment – that is what you require, is it not? But I refuse to be a censor for you. I fear Heathcliff's avenging spirit too much to turn his story into a romance suited for young ladies in a seminary.'

I was not flattered by this remark, but as I had no wish to offend her by saying so, I agreed to her terms and then reclined in happy expectation of the dénouement to this obscure episode in Mr Heathcliff's life.

19

Do not wonder why I resolved to have Heathcliff, or you will drive yourself mad. I have my own reasons for doing anything, and they are often perverse – I like to be perverse. And besides, you know enough to guess at my motives. All I need tell you is how the thing was managed.

I don't know for certain how strong the old gaol was – it has since been rebuilt, of course – but I believe it was still very strong even after the mob had finished with it. At any rate, I began with the assumption that an escape from Newgate could not be planned in a single day, and was left with the choice of rescuing Heathcliff either while he was en route to Tyburn or from the scaffold itself. Further reflection soon convinced me to reject the first of these alternatives as impracticable – you'll appreciate that if you have ever seen the procession of condemned criminals pass through Holbourn: the tumbril is surrounded by dozens of armed officers, mounted and on foot, and is so carefully guarded that nothing short of an army could effect a rescue. So it had to be the gallows, and cunning rather than force the means.

All this may sound uncommonly cold-blooded to you – or so your face tells me – but do not confound a cool head with an unfeeling heart; had the vapours been called for, I should have contrived an excellent womanly fit of them. As it was, I had formed a plan that required certain arrangements to be made with particular care and in extravagant haste. It is why I stayed less than half an hour with Heathcliff that Wednesday afternoon: I had three other calls to make.

My first was to a coppersmith not far from Newgate, a very skilled fellow who had once made me a handsome burnished grate with pierced fender, and for whom no work in the metal was too difficult. I explained what I wanted: a shaped piece of copper, flexible enough to be moulded but too strong to buckle, of just such a width and thickness, and with a flange of an inch along its upper edge and slots cut in certain places near the bottom. I said it was to be used in the repair of a marble statue that had got damaged, but he looked unconvinced. I soon distracted him, however, by demanding that he have the thing ready for the morrow. That was impossible, he said, even if he worked the night through. 'Dispatch is my chief requirement,' said I, and claimed I was come to him because none of the other smiths I'd approached had been able to promise the work so quickly, one or two having intimated that it could not be done in a night by Vulcan himself. This challenge and a double fee had him persuaded. I helped him choose a suitable sheet of copper, then left him to cut it to the required shape and dimensions.

Next I called at the house of a surgeon in Fleet Street, where I was until four o'clock arranging matters for Friday. I had a particularly gruesome request to make of him, and he regarded me with horror when I made it and refused at first to comply; but I prevailed upon him by means of another heavy fee to supply what I wanted, after which I insisted that he describe certain of its properties and instruct me in its preparation. I have made you curious, I observe. Well, Brewster – that's the surgeon – was curious too, though he should have divined what I was about, knowing what was required of him on Friday.

Finally, I hired a cart and a driver for Friday. I engaged the carter on purpose to wait just beyond the Tyburn enclosure at eleven o'clock on the day, thence to carry a hanged man to Fleet Street for resurrection by a surgeon. It was a familiar commission to him, and he was satisfied with half the agreed sum in advance, the remainder to be paid on prompt delivery of his load.

This done, I returned to Hill Street, stopping on the way at a saddler's, where I purchased two stout girths with brass buckles.

I told my husband I had spent the afternoon at a friend's house, and even gave him the name of the lady. I'd been an hour with her before going to Newgate, and had persuaded her to be what lawyers call my *alibi*. But the device, having worked once, could not be employed again on the morrow.

Consequently, I slipped out of the house in the early hours of Thursday morning, before even the servants were stirring, and was knocking at the smith's door by nine o'clock. All was not well with him, however. The copper he'd been using had proved to be of too fine a gauge, and though he had followed my design exactly, the contrivance, when completed, had wanted the necessary rigidity and must be re-made. If poor Heathcliff had seen me then he would have had good cause to doubt me, for I was thrown into distraction by the news, having only twenty-four hours in which to save him and no other plan. But luckily the smith took pride in his craft, and promised to have the work finished for two o'clock if I would return then. As I made to go, he said: 'I think I've guessed what you'll be using this for.'

'Have you?' I responded calmly.

'If it's intended for a certain boy not far from here,' said he, 'you've ordered it too unwieldy for the lad to manage.'

I said: 'It is not for that boy, but for his neighbour.'

'Oh,' he said, 'I'd hoped you were saving the lad. Still, it won't work for a man either.'

When he had told me his grounds for thinking so, I said: 'I've an answer to that, and since you've guessed my purpose you can spare me a deal of trouble by completing what you've begun.' And I gave him, in its wrapping of oiled paper, the stuff I had got from the surgeon. He sniffed distastefully at it, but said it would do nicely, and even made some suggestions for improving my design; which I was pleased to accept.

I passed the next few hours at a friend's house in the Strand, then called at the New Exchange, where I bought a light shawl suitable for wearing on chill summer evenings. This I put around my shoulders before returning to the smith, who, when he beheld it, nodded approvingly and showed me a small private room behind his forge that I might use.

Less than an hour later I entered Newgate Prison. I was muffled in the shawl and dabbed frequently at my nose with a handkerchief. Heathcliff's gaoler admitted me with expressions of sympathy, but all he received from me in return was a harangue. I declared that I'd been in perfect health the previous day and owed my cold entirely to the horrid damp atmosphere of the gaol. I said it was a wonder to me how any condemned man lived long enough even to feel the hemp about his throat, and generally went at the poor fellow like a fishwife; until in the end he fairly fled from the cell, clutching his bribe. I dare say he would have gone as readily without it, so keen was he to be out of my society.

As soon as I heard the bolt slammed to, I pulled Heathcliff – poor Heathcliff had no idea what I was about – I drew him into the far corner of the cell and bid him observe.

Then I unwound the shawl.

'What the devil's wrong with your neck?' said he.

'Nothing,' was my reply. I believe I gave a nervous laugh as I said it. 'It is not *my* neck, it's yours. And I wish you joy of the uncomfortable thing. Here, help me off with it – quickly. If your shadow out there chances to peep through the grille we'll need two of these devices.'

Now I'll tell you what the contrivance was. I suppose it most closely resembled a Greek hoplite's corselet, being a single sheet of copper moulded to the neck and shoulders, but not extending as far as the chest. It fastened under the arms by means of two straps, and completely enclosed the neck once the wearer had pinched the edges of the collar together. That flange I referred to ran along the line of the jaw, where it would be concealed by beard, and Heathcliff's long hair would perform the same duty at the sides and back. Its purpose was to support the halter, though most of the weight would fall on the body straps – the new scaffold breaks the neck of its victims, but twenty years ago the wretches were left to dangle and kick until the breath was squeezed out of them. My copper neck sheath was designed to protect Heathcliff from that fate, since it would both shield his windpipe and distribute evenly what must otherwise have been an intolerable strain on his jaw parts. A happy addition had been made by the smith, who remembered what I had forgotten – namely that a man's throat is not smooth, but like a range of hills with its veins and pipes and cartilage; so for greater strength, which was consistent with verisimilitude, he had hammered the collar piece into lifelike ridges and lumps. It was, indeed, a work of considerable art.

But the final touch, the *sine qua non* of Heathcliff's neck armour, was its covering. A man's neck, however swarthy he be, does not resemble worked copper; and conscious of this, I had got from Brewster the grisly contribution I mentioned to you. It was a portion of human skin, taken from the neck and shoulders of an anatomized corpse, complete with hairs and stretched across the whole surface of the copper. How it was secured I don't know, but it had given me quite a shock when I saw what the smith had made of it – I had not imagined it would look so convincing. There were even creases in it, which would disappear when the neck was tensed and reappear when it was relaxed.

Heathcliff had been giving me what he called his 'gaumless' look, and had so far made no move to take off his shirt.

'This is madness,' said he. 'Am I expected to die in this thing? Elizabeth, it will suffocate me quicker than the rope, and with less dignity.'

'Then consider it a mercy,' I said snappishly. 'And if you don't make haste and get into it you will lose whatever chance of survival it offers you.'

Reluctantly he began to remove his shirt, and then, while I transferred the armour from my shoulders to his, fumbling with the fastenings in my urgency, fearful of being caught in the incriminating act at any moment, I explained the theory of the device to him.

'Wear it continuously,' I told Heathcliff, attempting vainly to pinch the neck band closed. 'You'll have to do this. My hands aren't strong enough. Make it as tight as you can bear; and try not to hold yourself so stiffly. I know it's difficult – I've been wearing the wretched thing for an hour – but it may help if you remember that your existence depends upon this deception.'

'And do you remember,' he complained, 'that I must dangle for half an hour with all London looking on.'

'Oh,' I answered airily, 'you'll probably lose consciousness after ten minutes. Besides the hangman will cover your face with a cloth. Accept it. And ask him not to pull on your legs.'

He had the collar fixed now, and smoothed his hair and beard down over its edges. The result was amazing.

186

With his shirt on once more he looked like any thick-necked ruffian, and would not have warranted a second glance; though it remained to be seen whether he would deceive the hangman. Confidence made me flippant, and I said: 'It is like the false rumps ladies sometimes wear, Heathcliff. You may start a new fashion in false necks for male malefactors.'

But this put him out of temper, so that I was obliged to soothe him with little kisses and promises.

'This time tomorrow,' I whispered in his ear, 'you will have revived. You'll be drinking brandy in a surgeon's house in Fleet Street, and after we'll set about paying back your betrayer.' Nothing could cheer Heathcliff like a promise of revenge, and I soon had his black eyes lustrous with the contemplation of it.

'I'll think of that while I'm swinging,' he said. 'Thank you for reminding me why I cannot quit this life yet.' He gave me an odd smile then. 'I was about to ask you to take a letter I have written, but I'll not do that now. If your device should fail tomorrow, however, I charge you to recover the letter from my body and see that it is delivered. Will you?'

I promised that I would, though if you must know the truth I had no intention of honouring my promise. That little bitch in Yorkshire would get no satisfaction through my agency. I would gladly have let her suffer the torments of doubt and self-reproach all her days.

There was little more we could say to each other, so with a final word of advice – I urged him to take up the rope's slack before the cart was drawn away, or the sudden pressure would buckle the collar and tear its covering – I wound the shawl about my neck again and called for the gaoler to let me out. He scrutinized me as I passed him, no doubt to ascertain that I was not Heathcliff in disguise, and I saw him peer into the cell too. I smiled to hear Heathcliff say: 'Aye, I'm still here. Did you think I'd got out under her skirts?'

I did not have to sneak out of the house next morning. My husband was only too anxious to have me witness Heathcliff's execution and insisted upon taking me with him to Tyburn. Despite the weather – it was a showery day – a large crowd had gathered, many being there to comfort the boy; and since of the three who were to die he would undoubtedly attract the most attention, his presence afforded Heathcliff an advantage, though I was sad to own it.

They arrived five minutes before eleven o'clock, in a single cart, accompanied by the Newgate Ordinary and preceded by the City Marshal with his mace. Heathcliff had his arm around the boy, a doll-like figure dressed all in black, and seemed to be encouraging him, for the child managed a brave smile and nodded at something his companion was saying. That selfless act of Heathcliff's earned him vociferous approbation from the watching mob, ever ready to find a new hero, and a grudging acknowledgement from Mr Durrant. But I knew it for hypocrisy and could not forbear to sneer a little at such philadelphian gestures by the elect towards the damned.

'Pity,' said my husband when the halters had been thrown over the cross-bars. 'He'll die the gamest of the three, and without a whimper. I'd lay good money on it. Hold your eyes there, Elizabeth. I insist that you witness the result of your work.'

'I thought it was yours, Alex,' I answered, but my words were lost in the cheering – Heathcliff had waved his fist in the Ordinary's face, and the mob was showing its appreciation. He seemed preternaturally calm, almost happy, and I was anxious lest he should forget my instructions and allow the device to be detected. It was unobservable from my station, some two hundred feet from the gibbet, but the hangman was not a yard away from him, having stepped close to adjust his knot. I

188

believe I did not take a breath for half a minute, waiting for him to be alarmed by that unnaturally hard neck, and thanked God for what happened next, for it proved a perfect distraction.

The boy had been placed on Heathcliff's right, the halter around his white neck, the cloth over his face; and while the executioner busied himself with the others, he was left to wait and pray. The waiting must have been too much for him, however, poor child, for he suddenly commenced to scream and struggle violently, making such pitiful sounds and movements that the mob was roused to fury. I heard cries of: 'Turn the lad off!' and 'End that boy's misery, damn your eyes!' They were not to be denied.

Abandoning Heathcliff and his third charge, the hangman hurried back along his platform to attend to the little one. At first he appeared to try expostulating with him, but when his words had no effect, the mob's vociferations having meanwhile mounted to a crescendo, he clearly had no other course than to turn off all three simultaneously. And this he did by signalling for the cart to be drawn away.

A moment later all three bodies were hanging and the crowd was silent.

The small figure twitched only once, then was still. The last of the trinity jerked vigorously for above a minute before settling into the quiescence of death. Heathcliff, in the middle, hung motionless from the start. So still was he that I could not tell whether he was dead or merely insensible, or feigning insensibility.

'Hm,' remarked Mr Durrant. 'I'd have said he would last longer. His weight must have assisted him to a quick end.'

I was about to reply when, to my unspeakable horror, I saw that the hangman was pulling on the boy's legs. And I watched in mute disbelief as he stepped across to the next

189

body, which was Heathcliff's, and briefly added his own weight to the load on that rope. Heathcliff showed no sign of life. I was forced to conclude that my contrivance had been ineffective and all my efforts vain.

My husband had taken my arm to lead me back to our carriage, and for a moment I was too shocked to resist him. But then I recovered myself and shook him off, crying: 'I will not let him be anatomized, Alex. We both owe him a decent burial, and I have arranged that he shall have one.'

'My dear Elizabeth,' the fiend replied, 'you may have the privilege of burying every one of your paramours after I have finished with them.' With that he climbed into his chaise and was driven off through the crowd.

For half an hour Heathcliff was left to dangle at the rope's end. When he was eventually cut down the mob enclosed his body to protect it from the surgeons, and four fellows carried it to the cart I had hired.

Then I climbed in with the body, which was as lifeless as a stone, and the driver sped us towards Fleet Street.

20

Brewster had everything ready for the resuscitation – I believe he had attempted such a procedure once before – and commenced by laying Heathcliff on a couch and removing the neck armour. He struggled with it for some minutes before he got it off, the metal having become distorted just below the jaw-bone, and marvelled at its ingenuity; though he feared it may have facilitated rather than prevented death. Heathcliff's throat bore the imprint of the copper flange and was lacerated in one or two places. His face was a very dark red and set in a frown, so that I could not help thinking how fitting it was that he should have died in a fury, and wondered if his last thoughts had been of me, his unwitting murderess. It chilled me to contemplate those last moments of his.

But though no pulse had been detected, no evidence of life, Brewster did not abandon hope. It was possible, said he, for breathing to be imperceptible, and he had known men presumed dead to revive hours after burial. He got an assistant to let Heathcliff a quantity of blood, while he himself placed a bellows to the purple lips, a cloth soaked in spirits being applied to the other end of this instrument so that volatile air should enter the lungs. Then Heathcliff's windpipe was pressed and rubbed, and when this had no effect he was turned over and pounded at the base of his spine. Afterwards the surgeons held a blanket over the body and circulated fragrant steam under that canopy. They rubbed him with turpentine and peppermint water and various other substances – but to no avail. And at about one o'clock Brewster pronounced Heathcliff dead.

I was left alone with him then, and sat staring at his dark, permanently scowling countenance. A bottle of brandy being at hand – that had been tried too – I poured myself a measure and sipped at it while keeping my vigil. After an hour, however, observing not the least indication of vitality and being too weary to stay longer, I made arrangements with Brewster for the funeral – Heathcliff was not to be buried until Monday, in case he should revive – paid him a sum of money for it and returned home.

The rest of that day and all the next I was in a state of constant uneasiness, despairing and hopeful by turns. At any moment I expected to receive news that Heathcliff had miraculously revived, yet at the same time I entertained the conviction that it was impossible. My husband was uncommonly cheerful about the house, and knowing that his joy and my misery had a single cause, I longed to push him down the stairs so that I might celebrate *his* broken neck; and would have done it had he allowed me the chance. But he had ever been too cautious in his comings and goings to put himself in the way of such an obliging accident.

He spent Saturday evening drinking and playing at cards with some of his friends. I retired earlier than was my custom, but did not sleep, being as much disturbed by my thoughts as by the revellers downstairs. I read a little of my bedside book, a romance by Miss Reeve in the Gothic vein, then snuffed out my candle and lay in the darkness. Still I did not sleep, for my waking phantasies were so fearful that I dared not risk my dreams. I could imagine nothing but horrendous walking corpses bent on vengeance and terrible bloody happenings in mediaeval castles – that surprises you, I see. You think me too rational a person to confound reality with the absurdities of romance. Well, that is generally true. Remember, though, that I blamed myself for Heathcliff's death and that in the night we are all children. The most ungodly villains fall on their knees and pray at the approach of death, and cry out for their mothers. And darkness is a reminder of death, Lockwood. I have always been mortally afraid of both.

I must have dozed. I began to dream. In my dream there were sounds at the window of my chamber – first a knocking, then a scraping, and finally the strident squeaking of summer-dry wood in its frame as the window was raised. I knew instinctively what caused the sounds. My slumbering mind provided me with an awful picture of the cause: a ghastly cadaverous face framed in the grey rectangle of the embrasure, its eyes alight with an unearthly light, malevolent points of fire afloat like candle flames in pools of yellow-green putrescent tallow. I tried to cry out but my throat was choked by a bloody hempen rope, and in my terror I reached out and groped sightlessly for my tinder-box, reasoning as if with full waking mentality that only light would dispel the illusion. You cannot imagine my horror to realize that I *was* awake, in the brief second before my groping hand was arrested by the grip of another, colder hand, and Heathcliff's face appeared inches from my own.

Had he not stifled my scream with his free hand, I should have alarmed the whole of Mayfair. Then his lips parted and he gave a soft laugh, and said:

'Whisht! I'm no spectre, Elizabeth. Though it pleases me to see I can be taken for one. Now, can you be trusted not to cry out or light your candle or do any other thing to alert the household if I release you?'

I nodded. I still did not believe he was real. Yet his grip had been substantial enough, for when he relaxed it I had little feeling in my wrist or lips – the pressure of his strong fingers having numbed them. Now he seated himself on the bed and took my hand in a much gentler hold.

'You were not entirely wrong,' he said then. 'I have been dead – for a spell.' He laughed again as my eyes widened. 'No, Elizabeth, *you've* nothing to fear from me, chuck. I'm as corporeal as you are. But I have visited the undiscovered country of which Hamlet speaks, and I have returned. Do you believe me? I cannot prove it, alas, nor have I any desire to. It is enough that *I* know it exists. You have no idea how sustaining such knowledge can be. I have never felt more alive, Elizabeth. Ah, if it were possible to describe it . . .'

'Try,' I said. My childish terror had passed. Suddenly I wanted nothing more in the world than to share Heathcliff's vision of the life to come, though had I known how the experience was to transform him I should have been less eager. But of that you will hear more presently. 'Tell me,' I urged him. 'Tell me everything you can recall.'

'Oh, it is not like a dream,' he answered. 'I can recall it totally. To describe it is the hard part. It is like attempting to dress a child in man's clothing – nothing fits. Language is inadequate, irrelevant. It's a wordless world. Nor can I tell you what I saw, since there is nothing to see. It has no pictures, no sounds, no sensations. The senses do not function after death; yet the myth persists that pain is possible in hell, and in heaven joy. Well, in the most peculiar fashion that is so, but not in a way priests would recognize. God does not sit there on His awful throne, nor His horned and scaly counterpart.' Here he ran his fingers through his long hair and half closed his eyes. It was a gesture I had seen him employ when a difficult point of grammar continued to elude him in our lessons. 'What troubles me,' he continued, 'is that I did not have time to learn if the dead can return. *I* did. My body was not lifeless, so I was able to inhabit it once more. But I have a longing to know how the incorporeal manage their peregrinations, for I'm convinced they do, somehow. There, I've told you nothing, though I've made you damnably curious, have I not?'

'When did you revive?' was my mundane question.

'Last night,' he replied. 'I know not when exactly, except that it was quite dark and still in the room. I was lying on satin – and at first I thought I must be here, in my bed along the hall. But then I became aware that my couch had high sides, which I could reach out and touch with ease. There is such a bed at the house where I lived in Yorkshire, and I supposed I must have got there, somehow. Until further exploration revealed that it was a coffin, not a bed. I was out of it damned quick then, I can tell you. Shall I tell you what I did after that?'

I could only nod. I was trembling too much to speak.

'I waited till it was light,' he went on, 'and let myself out of the house – I assume it was the surgeon's house, in Fleet Street. From there I walked to Golden Square and harnessed a team to the coach your husband keeps in a yard nearby. Then I made the Round, two days early.' He smiled at the memory. 'I hadn't the benefit of Haskell's company, or that of the other bravoes your husband employs, but it seemed I didn't need them. I frightened a good many of his customers with my very presence – they believed a dead man in a ghostly coach was come to collect his dues, and they were right, Elizabeth. I have robbed that villain whose name you bear of near a thousand pounds – I doubled all charges today. If I let him live he may reduce them again next week, or not, as he pleases.'

I found I had to moisten my lips with my tongue before I could say: 'You plan to kill him?'

'I've a mind to,' he said, 'unless you can dissuade me. I know he's below. I saw him through the window before I climbed up here. And since I'm already dead I cannot be suspected of the crime. I plan to murder him, as

195

he murdered me, then sentence myself to transportation afterwards – America appeals to me. It's a rough continent where a rough gentleman, such as myself, may make his way. Do you object, Elizabeth? You'll be left free and wealthy by my action.'

At a loss how to respond, I said: 'I won't deny that you owe him a death. And I've no objection, save this: you say his "customers" saw you abroad today. Does that not mean Haskell could persuade them to give testimony? He would have reason to.'

'I hadn't thought of that,' said Heathcliff, stroking his neck – it must have been very tender still. 'No matter. When he comes to bed I'll confront him, and he shall determine his own future by his conduct.'

We spoke no further but waited in the darkness for what must have been almost half an hour. I heard the hall clock strike two, then the quarter, and a few minutes later the guests began to take their noisy leave. Roisterous good nights were called, doors slammed, and carriages could be heard in the street. A short while after, we caught the sound of my husband's tread on the stairs, then along the hall, its irregular rhythm suggesting a quite advanced state of inebriation. Heathcliff put his finger to his lips until the foot-fall had died away and Mr Durrant's door had closed behind him. When all was quiet again, he said: 'I want him in bed and dreaming, as you were. I plan to terrify the blackguard to death if I can, and leave no mark on him.'

I own that prospect delighted me so, I could hardly contain my impatience, and as soon as Heathcliff declared it safe to go I was at the door. We carried a lighted candle with us, which illuminated Heathcliff's face grotesquely and projected a ghastly shadow of him upon the wall. I had to stifle a chuckle at the sight of it.

My husband's snoring became audible the moment we opened the door of his chamber. We need not have concerned ourselves with stealth – he was sprawled, fully clothed, on his bed, stinking of brandy. His candle lay on the floor, no doubt having extinguished itself by its fall, and it occurred to me that a less fortunate man would have set the bed on fire and saved us a deal of trouble.

Heathcliff signed to me that I should conceal myself behind the clothes-press, and setting his candle on the floor, where it cast an eerie glow over the lower part of the room, stretched himself across the bed and carefully placed both his hands around my husband's throat. I watched, filled with a strange excitement, as Mr Durrant commenced to moan and thrash about in his stupor, doubtless absorbing the disagreeable sensation into his nightmare. Gradually the pressure was increased. His movements began to grow more frenzied, until at last his eyes opened and he became aware that the relentless grip on his throat was not imagined.

Had he been faint-hearted he would have expired on the spot. Had there been a shred of conscience in him, the horror of discovering his nemesis suddenly upon him in the night must have been unendurable. Yet there was nothing of horror in Mr Durrant's countenance, only a momentary widening of his eyes in disbelief, which was immediately replaced by a look of recognition and intense hatred. It was a disappointment to me, I own, that the shock had not turned him into a gibbering baby at the least, but Heathcliff was evidently satisfied with the effect he'd produced, for he suddenly relaxed his hold and, straightening himself, gave a derisive laugh.

'You may as well show yourself,' he said. 'This husband of yours is less easily deceived than you were, Elizabeth. He merely thinks I have a charmed life.'

'You are there too, are you?' said Mr Durrant as I came out from behind the clothes-press. 'That explains everything. And now I suppose you intend to watch him torture me to death and gloat over my last agonies.'

'I would gladly pay for the privilege,' was all I said.

My husband made to shift his position, but before he could move far Heathcliff's weight was on him once more. 'If you attempt to move or to cry out I will certainly finish you,' said he. 'You've more courage than I gave you credit for, Mr Durrant, which disposes me to mete out a different punishment entirely. Had you demonstrated fear a moment ago I believe I should have killed you.'

'Unless you do, Heathcliff,' I urged, 'you'll never have peace from him. He'll devote the rest of his life to seeking you out. I know him. He does not let go once he's tasted blood, and he has tasted yours.'

'If he leaves me breathing,' said the disadvantaged villain on the bed, 'I'll make you sorry you said that.'

'Do you hear him, Heathcliff? He threatens me. If you care for me at all, you've no choice but to finish him now. Don't forget how he betrayed you.'

'I don't deny it,' said my husband calmly. 'It was politic. Heathcliff would have done the same had our positions been reversed, and knows it. He doesn't want my life, do you, Heathcliff? He wants my success. He wishes to *be* me. Is that not true?'

'Be silent, damn you!' said Heathcliff. 'I am considering what to do with you. Have you any money in the house?'

'Oh, yes,' answered the other, 'a considerable amount. But it's cleverly hidden, and you may torture me all you like without learning its whereabouts from my lips. And she doesn't know where it is. So what is your next question?'

'My God, you're a cool devil,' said Heathcliff admiringly. 'I wish it had been possible for me to like you.'

'So do I,' he got back. 'But *she* has made that impossible. Now, either kill me or begone. I have drunk too much and require sleep – temporary or permanent.'

Heathcliff's indecision had angered me. I regarded them both with loathing, seeing two small boys daring each other to a contest and and becoming firm friends in the process. I believe at that precise moment I'd have settled to see either of them spill the other's blood. But what happened next took me quite by surprise.

Heathcliff suddenly began to laugh. 'I have it,' he declared, collapsing anew into merriment. 'God, it's perfect. So neat, Durrant. I shall relieve you of your burden. I'll take her away with me.'

We both stared uncomprehendingly at him. 'Do you not see the beauty of the concept, Elizabeth?' said Heathcliff. 'That simple action will accomplish everything. You will attain your liberty; he will be robbed of his most precious possession; and I shall have a mistress and a hostage in one person. He says I wish to *be* him, and by heaven I will – in all that matters. Well, what are you waiting for? Go and pack some things.'

I made no move. I was too stunned to move. Of all possibilities, this was the last that would have occurred to me.

'He'd find us,' I said in desperation. 'He would relish the hunt and can afford it. Your little bit of money would not support us for long.'

Heathcliff's face hardened. 'Are you refusing to go with me?' he said in a dangerous voice.

'It is not that, Heathcliff,' said I, cautiously.

'Then what is it?' he snapped.

Before I could frame an answer my husband interpolated: 'Let me tell you what it is. She has enjoyed playing the coquette with you, Heathcliff, but now that you have broken the rules of her game she is angry with you. It seems you have spoiled her pleasure by showing your ignorance of those rules. Shall I explain the rest, my dear, or will you? No, you would only lie, and your lies are so pretty he might believe them. I will tell you, Heathcliff. Let her deny it if she wishes!'

'Hush!' said the other. '*She* shall explain.'

'He is attempting to set us against each other, Heathcliff,' I said. 'It is just that I require time to prepare.'

'She will not go with you, Heathcliff. Nor should you expect her to if you care for her. It would be like transplanting a hothouse flower to the polar regions. She'd shrivel in a day. Why not be grateful for what she has already given you – a little education, in and out of bed, and your life? And don't make the mistake of imagining that I want her for myself. She would dearly love to see me dead, for then she would be free to marry again, with my money as her dowry. Oh, yes, I'll leave her that when I go. I love her too much to see her left penniless. The experience would destroy her soul, and though I am prepared to keep her captive while she stays with me, I would not destroy her soul. That is love indeed, is it not?'

'Do not listen to him, Heathcliff,' I said, angry tears burning my eyes. 'He is insane with jealousy and will say anything to divide us. You've said yourself how false his love is. He wants to keep me here so that he can torture me at will.'

'Then come with me,' urged Heathcliff. He sounded perplexed now. 'That will settle all arguments. Why do you resist? I'm no longer a boor, am I? I will not disgrace you in company. And I have some of his money, which will suffice until I can get more. Why? *Why* won't you come?'

'You've learned nothing, have you?' persisted the other. 'If she abandons me she loses everything in life that she values – rank, dignity, fortune, esteem – all of it. And in return, what would you provide? You're an outcast, a convicted felon, a nameless, landless gipsy. An alliance with you would put her in limbo.'

'Is he right, Elizabeth?' demanded Heathcliff. 'Is that what you think?'

'Oh, you believe him, do you?' I said, feigning indignation on purpose to change the issue and gain time in which to think. Heathcliff's proposal had caught me unawares, and I needed desperately to recover my composure.

But I was given no time.

'I demand to know now if you will go with me or remain with him,' said Heathcliff. 'If I'm to be rejected again, I insist upon hearing it direct. You must spit in my face and say it, Elizabeth. Do you understand? Come over to the bed here and choose between us.' When I hesitated he raised his voice. 'Come here, I say!'

Slowly I crossed the room and stood by the bed. The candle had burned low, and by its pale light I could see both their faces – Heathcliff's white and pained; my husband's cruelly triumphant against his pillow. That damned face. How I detested that wicked face of his. Had it shown a different expression – one of love, perhaps, or one of despair – I might have behaved differently. But no prospect of penury or disgrace could count for much beside that of living any longer with such an odious man. I would rather have endured any man's hatred than another day of his suffocating love. I took Heathcliff's hand and gave it a squeeze of assent.

My husband's response was a disdainful sniff. 'Tell her to pack her gyves,' he said to Heathcliff. 'You'll need them if you intend to keep what you've won.'

21

Within an hour, while it was still dark, we were on the road to Dover; and in the afternoon we sailed on the packet to France.

At first, I own it, I entertained the gravest doubts about travelling abroad with Heathcliff. I could think of no way to explain him. As you know, the French do not value our English manners, and Heathcliff's manners, barely passable here, would be considered intolerably uncouth in Europe. I dreaded that he would make us both a laughing-stock.

But during the passage I happened to overhear two French dandies speaking of a third gentleman, who was standing at the rails letting the spray break over him. The sea was not calm, though it was quite a fair day, and he had managed to get his cravat somewhat damp in the process, an act verging on lunacy in the eyes of the two fops observing him, for I heard one say: '*Qui est ce fou là?*' and his fellow reply: '*Quelque Milord anglais, sans doute. Plus grand le seigneur, plus outrée sa folie.*'

'Heathcliff,' I said with a gleeful laugh, turning to my companion, 'you are hereby elevated to the peerage. You shall be an English – nay, a Scotch – milord as long as we are in Europe.' He gave me a mistrustful look. 'Do not look at me so,' I said. 'It's a perfect plan for introducing you into the genteelest coteries. You may use as much northern dialect as you wish and speak a little execrable French and be as rude as you please in company. Nobody will think ill of you, for I'm sure that is how barbarous Scots lairds are expected to behave. *Quelle tromperie!*' I clapped my hands with excitement as a new thought suggested itself to me. 'And, Heathcliff,' I cried, 'you must be impossibly rich. There is no better way to justify what must be our frugal mode of living than to attribute it to the niggardliness of a northern Croesus.'

To my surprise, he seemed pleased with my scheme, and helped me choose a name for him. We settled finally for Lord MacHeath, after the highwayman in *The Beggar's Opera*. It sounded Scotch, and we thought it an excellent jest.

Thus His Lordship and I posted across France, Switzerland and Italy in the finest chaise that could be got at Calais (it was important that we should not stint ourselves in the matter of our conveyance or of our dress), making, in effect, a Grand Tour of the best and most interesting places in Europe. From Calais we went by way of Amiens first to Paris, then to Versailles, but I did not risk a presentation to Their Majesties. Paris, however, detained us above a month. You must know it is the liveliest town in the world, and I did nothing but dance and dine out and go to plays and the opera and gorge my eyes on the modes in the Rue St Honoré. Heathcliff, delighting in his role as the thrifty Scot, teased me cruelly, refusing to buy me any but the meanest gowns, but I got revenge by limiting his play at cards, for which he seemed to have a decided penchant. Play in Paris is very deep – the betting is in hundreds of louis – yet I convinced my Lord MacHeath that his wagers must be more modest to demonstrate parsimony; though his habitual success at the tables gave me cause to regret my cleverness.

Heathcliff did not like Paris, despite the opportunities it afforded him for gaming. He complained that he could not distinguish the men from the women, since both sexes spoke in the same affected manner and tittered behind their fans and had mincing gaits. He could mimic the Parisian fop most effectively. In truth, I shared his view of the gentlemen, though not of Paris. Apart from its elegance and modishness, it has one outstanding virtue: women do not age there. *Jeunes filles* and *grandes dames* alike are judged not by any chronological measure but by their conduct and appearance, so that a gay and sprightly grandmother may out-Pompadour her more sober juniors at an assembly. Paris gave me back my girlhood. I flirted deliciously with several well-made young men during our stay, though I was serious with none of them and made no clandestine rendezvous. One bold monsieur brought me a basket of roses, however, and was thrown down the stairs of the hotel by Heathcliff for his pains.

'If you are to be so jealous of every poor man who looks at me,' I teased, 'I will make myself ugly on purpose to spare them your brutal discouragement.'

But I had misjudged his mood, seemingly. He shook his fist in my face and snarled: 'Take care I don't do that for you. You'd smile a lot less prettily without teeth, madam.'

'La,' I said, throwing my arms about his neck. 'If you make my mouth all bloody you will find it disagreeable to kiss.'

He was never proof against my kisses. Whenever we quarrelled he would retreat within his walls and hurl threats at me from the battlements; whereupon I would lay sweet siege to him until he capitulated. Hellenic guile always overcame Trojan fortitude, and always will – it is in the nature of things.

Everywhere we went in France we were received with the utmost kindness and courtesy. In those days I had many friends among the Haute Noblesse (they have been decimated since), and we stayed at various châteaux en route to Italy, sometimes for several weeks together. My own connexions and Heathcliff's spurious nobility secured us all the comforts and attentions we could have wished for, and we very nearly stewed to the bone in the luxury of it, my *petit avare* and I. He played his part admirably.

One evening I remember particularly. We were staying at a château on the Rhone. It was towards the end of that summer and, as is the custom there, our hosts held a *fête champêtre* in the grounds. They illuminated the lawns with torches and coloured lanterns, and engaged dancers and musicians to perform for us while the servants brought out a sumptuous supper – only the French know how to do that properly. My mood was very frivolous. All the guests save Heathcliff were wearing bucolic costume, he being considered delightfully eccentric for declining to make a pastoral figure. We had been riding in the afternoon and had passed through one of the count's villages (that was our host): an indescribably filthy place crowded with the most dreadful hovels and filled with half-naked children. One pretty, fair-haired creature, scarcely modest in the flimsiest of cotton rags, and dusky as a little sweep, had caught both Heathcliff's eye and the count's. Monsieur le Comte had beckoned to the child, and when she had come shyly up to him and made her curtsy, he had sat contemplating her for a few moments before dismissing her with a wave and a muttered '*Trop sale.*' Then, with exaggerated politeness, he'd offered her to Heathcliff. I saw a look of undisguised malevolence and disgust cross Heathcliff's face, but he said nothing; merely produced a gold louis from his pocket and handed it to the child, which earned him a deal of applause and not a little teasing. But in a strange way it had enhanced his reputation, and he was thought very clever for it.

I tell you all this to explain why Heathcliff was behaving so oddly, though I do not think it explains it at all. Heathcliff believed it did, however, for he mumbled something about rustics being plentiful enough in the villages without their having to be aped within the grounds. And as I told you, our hosts excused him. Well, the night being warm, we reclined on the grass after supper, listening to the music and watching the dancers.

Monsieur le Comte had hired a party of gipsies to play their music in the rose garden and to tell the guests' fortunes. I wanted to have mine told, but Heathcliff would not be persuaded to go with me. He seemed uncharacteristically pensive – he was often sullen, as you must know, unless he changed greatly in later years – far too pensive to my mind, and I was attempting to tease him out of his study by pulling his long hair and pretending to fret.

'We must learn our future, Heathcliff,' I said, tugging at his arm. 'I want to know how soon my husband will die, and I'm afraid to go alone where there are gipsies.'

He half turned to see me better. 'So you would have a gipsy accompany you, is that it?' was his response.

'You are different,' I said lightly. 'They are sinister.'

He gave a dismal laugh and, furrowing his brow, said: 'And you consider me innocuous, do you?' Then, 'Don't look so terrified, Elizabeth. I intend *you* no harm.'

'Will you come, then?' I urged, not caring for the turn this conversation was taking.

'In a minute,' was his reply. 'First answer a question of mine. It has been troubling me since we came here.' With a sweeping gesture he indicated the house and grounds, magnificent in the light of the lanterns. 'How do they become so rich?' he said.

It was my turn to laugh now. 'Heathcliff, you are astoundingly naïve at times,' I told him. 'They tax their peasants.'

'Is that the whole answer?'

'It is the whole answer here and elsewhere,' said I. 'The richest lords in England have estates and tenants too. There is a finite quantity of wealth in the world, and the rich have become so by appropriating the largest share of it. It follows mathematically that what remains must be the smaller portion, and that is what the poor have.'

He gave me a bitter look. 'So damned simple, is it?'

'All great truths are simple,' I replied. 'And this is too splendid an evening to be spoiled by philosophy. Even the French are being frivolous tonight.' I pulled at his arm once more, but still he resisted.

'What a perverse law of nature it is,' he murmured, 'that the weak should always support the strong.'

'They are numerous enough,' I said impatiently. 'Don't you wish to know if you will ever be rich?'

'Oh, I will be,' said Heathcliff, prodding his chest with his thumb. 'This gipsy tells me that. But I'm not certain it is enough. Once I believed it would be. Now I am doubtful.'

'Well, it is enough for me,' I declared. 'And I am going with or without you to find out how long I must wait.'

With that I stood up and began walking towards the rose garden. Heathcliff caught me up before I'd gone very far, however, saying he'd decided to see for himself if gipsies were as loathsome as people said they were.

A small group of swarthy figures in colourful costumes had clustered about the path, and a crone with a bristly chin was seated at a little table in their midst. I did not much like the look of her, but when I hesitated Heathcliff nudged me forward. The hag signed to me that I should seat myself opposite her, which I did reluctantly; whereupon she seized my left hand and commenced to examine it.

'You wish to hear only the good things,' she said in surprisingly good French. 'You are afraid of the rest.'

'I declare that is true of everybody,' was my comment.

She shook her head and pointed a bony finger at Heathcliff, who was standing a little way off. 'Not of him,' she said. 'He knows his fortune and does not like what he knows. But he is not afraid.'

'You are supposed to be telling me mine,' I reminded her rather sharply. 'Can you divine whether I am a married person?'

She grinned, nodding towards Heathcliff. 'You are, but not to him. To a gentleman you have no love for.'

I could not help laughing at her cleverness. I said: 'That is hardly an instance of second sight. If I am in another man's company, then it follows that I cannot love my husband greatly.'

'That man yonder does not love you,' she said maliciously.

'He is brooding about something,' I snapped. 'He loves nobody when he broods, not even himself. And you will not be paid if you continue to talk nonsense. Now, tell me if I'm to be very rich and how long I must wait.'

'You will be,' came the reply, 'and before very long. But it will not please you.'

'Indeed it will,' I laughed. 'And you'll allow I'm the best judge of that. Heathcliff, ask her if you will be rich too.'

I said this last in English, but my tone must have conveyed its import to the wily crone, because she said in French: 'He will. He will have everything he strives to get, except what he desires most. And the same is true of you.'

'And of the whole world,' I scoffed. 'It seems one has only to know a little of human nature to tell fortunes – and to make them by the same means, I shouldn't wonder. Well, here is a prediction you cannot make by guess-work. I wish to know if I will die young.'

The old woman shook her head slowly. 'You know that already,' she answered, 'since your youth has gone and you are still alive to regret it.'

That was more than I could tolerate. Standing up, I flung some coins at her, damned her impertinence and stormed away. Heathcliff did not follow immediately but stayed to talk to the wretch, though what they said to each other or how he made himself understood I have no idea. Perhaps they talked gipsy gibberish together. At any rate, when I asked him about it afterwards he changed the subject, and it was never raised again.

A few days later we set out for Switzerland, a salubrious but dreadfully dull country which I would have gone through at the gallop had not Heathcliff insisted upon our spending a few days there. He took great delight in its mountains and made daily excursions from our hotel at Geneva to climb them, like some blessed pilgrim. I would not go with him. I consider mountains as much a blemish upon a landscape as pustules are on a human face, and wish some method might be found to disguise both effectively. We quarrelled a few times on that subject. I accused him of being a rude mystic, and he made some unflattering countercharges. The truth of it is that I had begun to find his society irksome. I was having to drag him to parties under protest, and he rarely laughed or made witty conversation. His only interests seemed to be cards and mountains. Once I made the mistake of saying that I preferred my husband's company, since he, at least, was no miser, and loved nothing and nobody better than me. We were in the post-chaise when I made that unfortunate remark, and Heathcliff responded by bringing us to a halt and thrusting me into the road with a 'Go to him, then. You may walk all the way, and see if he welcomes you at the end of it.' And I was left to walk above a mile back to Geneva in the twilight, an experience I would not repeat for a kingdom.

Italy was better. For me it was. Heathcliff seemed rather to thrive on cold weather, being a wintry person, but I kept him occupied in Rome and Florence and Venice with antiquities and works of art, so that he quite soon knew as much about them as I did. He also acquired a little of the Italian tongue, which, with his few French sentences, was as much education as he got abroad. He was very comical to hear in any language but his own, and sometimes sounded like Mrs Malaprop even in English, for he was ambitious enough to attempt a word before he had mastered it.

But I perceive that all this interests you very little, Lockwood. You are impatient to learn how we fared on our return to England, and I will satisfy your curiosity as soon as we have had some coffee.

22

We were away a twelvemonth in all, and the last few weeks were among the most miserable of my life. Our stock of money had diminished alarmingly, which, together with the excessive heat and dust that plague all tourists in southern Europe during the summer, made us as snappish and ill-natured as wild beasts. It got so that Heathcliff would no longer permit me the little comforts that render travel bearable, obliging me to sleep in filthy beds at the meanest hotels and eat unpalatable food. And for want of additions to my wardrobe I must wear the same dusty clothes for days together, until I had the aspect of a miller.

In short, MacHeath had swallowed and digested Heathcliff, and was become a disagreeable, tedious character. There was a physical transformation too. He had matured during our year abroad, his youthful form and callow manner giving way to manliness, so that his appearance and bearing, at least, were much improved. And this metamorphosis was to serve him well in England.

We arrived in London early in July of the year 1782, and even my extreme fatigue could not detract from the joy of that homecoming. Everywhere there was vivacity and splendour, elegance and animation. The streets were filled with carriages and chairs – the Season was at its climax – the shops overflowed with the latest fashions and the very atmosphere seemed vibrant to me. I experienced a most poignant longing to dive headlong into that stream of life, there to refresh myself and cleanse my memory of recent privations. But if I had any notion of resuming my old life, Heathcliff soon disabused me of it.

For several days I had been giving consideration to my future, and had decided that my best course must be to return to my husband. A few tears of wifely contrition would suffice to solicit his forgiveness, and a year of solitude having no doubt convinced him of my value, he could not fail to permit me my autonomy in exchange for my promise to live under his roof. I thought it a very neat plan; and, convinced that my travelling companion had grown as weary of me as I had of him, I confided it to Heathcliff.

'You have got your revenge,' I reasoned, 'and I have tasted liberty. Now it will be to our mutual advantage if we separate, Heathcliff. You still have your fortune to make, and I hunger for the main dish.'

'You believe he would take you back?' said he, grinning.

'Depend upon it,' was my answer.

'And I am to agree, meekly, to this one-sided arrangement?'

Not caring for his tone, I said: 'Heathcliff, I believe you are barking in the manger. You no longer have any use for me, but you would keep me in order to deprive my husband of my society. That is exceedingly churlish of you.'

He responded with a sneer. 'Oh, but I do have a use for you. I have given you a year of my time, provided you with that taste you mentioned. And now you owe me a year in return. A year's labour, Elizabeth, as in Biblical times.'

'I am not an apprentice lad,' I snapped, 'to be indentured. You forget yourself.'

'Nay,' answered the tyrant, 'it is you who forget me. If you abandon me before I release you, you'll be found on a dung-hill.'

'You are quite mad,' I said, not a little disturbed by his strange manner. 'Have you forgotten who saved your miserable life a year since? And do you suppose your absurd threats will reduce me to a shivering, complaisant heap of flesh?'

'I should think very little of you if they did,' he replied. 'There are certain aspects of your character that I still admire, and one is your good sense. Now, hear me out. I fancy you will not object too strongly when you learn what I have in mind.'

He explained his plan to me then. He said he had saved sufficient money to take a house in London for a spell, and to keep us both in modest comfort until he could get more. This he proposed to do with my assistance before the end of the Season, by winning large sums at cards from the wealthiest people in town. That was his precious scheme.

'It's quite ridiculous,' I objected. 'How do you expect to accomplish this gaming miracle? Will you threaten to leave the *beau monde* on dung-hills unless you are permitted to win at Faro?'

'I shall take care of that part of it,' was his reply. 'All I require from you is an introduction to your quality friends, the ones with loaded pockets.'

'Oh, certainly,' I sneered. ' "Lord M., this is Heathcliff Earnshaw, a gipsy my husband once employed to cut throats. I taught him to calculate myself, so you may be confident that he will not cheat you. He merely wishes to win himself a fortune so that he can afterwards spit in your face." La-la. Heathcliff, I suspect the French climate or the water has addled your brains.'

'We deceived Europe,' he said with animation. 'Why shouldn't we deceive London?'

'Oh, God! He's wandering. London crawls with Scots. MacHeath would not survive an hour.'

'No, confound you, I have another character for London,' he cried impatiently, but I was too helpless with laughter to heed him. I should have known better than to ridicule him. Before I could avoid it his blow caught me on the cheek. Luckily he'd struck me open-handed or I might have been badly injured. But it was enough to bring tears to my eyes and I tasted blood in my mouth. 'Now,' said the villain, 'will you listen? I am not the fool you think me. I have it worked out. Few of the quality folk know me, and you'll allow my appearance has altered considerably this last twelvemonth. I could be a country squire down from the north for the Season – I have just the fellow picked out. Could I not pass for a country gentleman?'

I nodded to humour him, being too busy dabbing at my mouth with a handkerchief to speak.

'You should not have angered me to that degree,' he said. It was the nearest he could approach to an apology, though it expressed no moral sentiment. 'In future you'll know not to do it.'

'You forget another thing,' I flung at him. 'My husband will not tolerate the humiliation of your presence in London. As soon as he has learned your whereabouts, he will not be idle. And this time don't expect me to save you.'

'Nay,' he replied with a short laugh. 'He has tried killing me once. He won't attempt it a second time. But I intend that he shall know where to find me.' This puzzling statement was all I could get from him on the subject.

He took a house soon after, in a middling part of town near Covent Garden; and there we established our *ménage scandaleux*.

It proved less difficult than I had anticipated to introduce Heathcliff to the *ton*, and vastly amusing. Fashionable London had heard, though not from his own lips, that I had abandoned Mr Durrant; and one or two of the keener ones had sniffed out intelligence of a Scotch nobleman. Now, it seemed, I was cohabiting with this handsome Yorkshire squire – you may imagine the effect upon their moral sensibilities, those that had any. But I own I quite enjoyed my new notoriety, and you may be sure I did not disappoint my slanderers. When truth (or what passed for it) threatened to make dull gossip, I would invent amorous adventures for myself as a glutton invents feasts or a soldier brags of battles he has never fought. I had been shut away too long not to make capital out of my liberty, and determined that if Heathcliff could have a new character at all, I should not wear my old one into holes.

Thus we found ourselves invited into every salon of consequence in London, where Heathcliff was introduced as Mr Edgar Linton of Yorkshire, my paramour of the moment. He delighted in the name – it held associations for him which I could only guess at then – and had a complete character for Linton. At first I was afraid that he might betray himself, but he soon convinced me otherwise; his conversation was exactly that of a landed northern gentleman and magistrate, being of tenants and rents and the untrustworthiness of servants.

He was exceedingly proud of his magistracy and talked of it often. 'Mr Linton is from one of the best and oldest families in the north,' I would say, presenting him. 'They have been magistrates since that office was created.'

'How interesting,' was one lady's response. 'But are you a lawyer, Mr Linton?'

'Indeed not, madam,' said Heathcliff, with a clever little look of disdain. 'My family considers the profession next to shopkeeping. I have some acquaintance with the law, however, or the rogues with whom I have to deal would soon confound me.'

'Do you have to do with many scoundrels?' was the next question. 'I should not have thought them in abundance outside the larger towns.'

215

'Upon my soul, madam,' replied Heathcliff, 'there are bandits in my native hills beside whom your London felons would seem mere innocent babes. I could tell you tales of villainy that would make you swoon.'

And being pressed, he gave several horrifying accounts of dark and bloody deeds that had the entire company wide-eyed in fascination. I now know the source of one of his stories, that of a certain rogue whose hand was severed in vengeance. But I was quicker to recognize another, a cool-as-you-please recital of the circumstances of his own hanging and rescue. Of course, he omitted to identify himself with the tale's protagonist, and its artful 'mort' he called Moll Scutworth. He told it so like a ballad that I could not keep my face straight and made some excuse to quit the room for fear of betraying us by my giggles. Thereafter, whenever he was in a wicked mood, he would torment me by relating that tale to a company.

Most of all, he liked to talk about legal matters of a different kind. He had supplied himself with a small library of legal tomes, including all of Blackstone, and would study them by the hour, as the pious do their Bibles, getting whole passages by heart. Inheritance was his favourite subject. There was nothing he did not know about it. He became as hobby-horsical about estates in possession and expectancy as ever Toby Shandy was with his sieges – though he was less genial in his exposition. His advice was often sought too – he was considered very learned – and I think he must eventually have become tiresome if the gaming that is the curse (and blessing) of such assemblies had not always diverted him.

His games were Quinze and Faro, and Hazard when it was played. He would sit all night at cards or dice, his purse at one elbow, a bottle of brandy at the other; and as the latter emptied the former would invariably fill. Play was never very deep – no doubt Fox gave away more in vails at Brooks's than Heathcliff ever won at private tables – but it was not unusual for him to bring home two hundred pounds after a lengthy sitting, which is no mean sum. We did not want for the necessaries of life, at any rate, even if we were not lavishly supplied with its luxuries.

Publicly, that was our mode of living in the weeks following our return – parties almost every day, sometimes a rout or a picnic, and always cards. But though Heathcliff could be amiable, often wonderfully entertaining in company, in private he was a vastly different man. Moroseness being his natural state, he reverted to it whenever he was relieved of the necessity to impress his benefactors – for so he regarded my wealthy friends. Then he would shut himself away like some Eastern mystic and meditate for hours in a darkened room, never moving or calling for anything; though I would hear him sigh at intervals, and he'd start like a wild beast if I interrupted him.

Yet even when he did not seclude himself I had the strangest sensation that he was absent in spirit. He could sit a whole day in a room with me and never utter a word or give me a single glance. His confounded law books interested him more than I did, seemingly, but I could have stood that. His meditations too, vexing though they were, I regarded as an understandable preoccupation. But what truly disconcerted me was his indifference to me at other times. It is difficult to express this as delicately as you would wish me to, so I rely upon your curiosity to overwhelm your modesty when I tell you that Heathcliff remained distracted even at the most intimate moments of our life together. You must know that at such times a woman requires more than the mere physical presence of a man; yet that was all I got from Heathcliff, and neither tenderness – of which he was incapable – nor the pretence that he loved me. The rest of his life might be

217

a prolonged deception, but in that he was scrupulously honest. I received the impression from his manner that I did not signify, that another would have suited him just as well. He showed no awareness of *me*, Lockwood, and it was unbearably mortifying.

Once I asked him, at a particularly poignant moment, where his thoughts were.

'Transported with the rest of me,' he answered, smiling.

'You may think that a clever answer, Heathcliff,' I returned, 'but it does not satisfy me. It is impossible to deceive a woman in these matters, and since I know that you have been mentally truant I demand to be told who my rival is.'

'It grieves you that you have one, does it? Perhaps I was anticipating supper.'

I struck him playfully on the chest. 'Heathcliff,' I chided, 'it is not genteel to let a veal pie take precedence of a lady. And I'm too well acquainted with your appetite to suppose you would. No, if I have a rival, it is that Cathy person you dote on.' There was no response from him, so I climbed upon his chest and, grasping one of his fingers with both my hands, commenced to bend it against the joint. 'It shall be wrung from you under torture,' I announced, 'as befits an Inquisition.' His lip curled slightly, though whether with pain or amusement I couldn't tell. But he said nothing, nor made any move to dislodge me. 'Now,' I resumed, 'we shall begin with your true name, sir. It is not Edgar Linton, is it?'

'Assuredly it is not,' said he with a sneer.

'Then what is it?'

'Heathcliff,' was his reply.

'Good. And the rest of it?'

'Just that. There is no more.' He spoke so quietly that I was obliged to lean forward to hear him. His countenance was devoid of expression.

'Is it not Heathcliff Earnshaw?' I prompted.

'Nay,' was all he said.

'Then it must be Heathcliff Heathcliff.' I laughed. 'A decidedly odd name to be entered in the Book of Heretics, but 'twill do. Now, Heathcliff Heathcliff, I have some very grave questions to put to you. Failure to answer truthfully will necessitate a turn of the screw, so take care. You are accused of this heresy: that while you are at your devotions to me your soul flies to another. Is that true or false?'

'I have never denied it,' he answered.

I twisted his finger nevertheless, then said: 'Her name?'

'Catherine Earnshaw,' he replied hoarsely. 'Her name is Catherine Earnshaw.'

'Ah!' I exclaimed. 'That name is explained at last. Do you love this person?'

His response was an indistinct whisper. He seemed to be looking through me. I gave his finger another nasty wrench, but he might have been carved out of wood for all it hurt him. 'Do you wish you were with her now?' I asked, and saw him incline his head almost imperceptibly. 'Why?' I demanded.

'Because she is my life,' was the unwelcome reply. And to my embarrassment I observed that his eyes had grown moist. 'She is my life,' he repeated.

'Weeping will not avail you here,' I said sternly. 'Only a recantation will do that.' His finger had turned white. I pushed it further back. 'Recant,' I demanded. 'Damn you.' Strong as his finger was, I believe I had it strained to breaking point; yet still he gave no sign of pain, and I was obliged to relax it or hear the bone crack. 'Heathcliff,' I said, 'dear Heathcliff, why are you so cruel to me? Is she prettier than I am?'

'Nay,' he said, 'not half so pretty.'

'Is she wittier, then? Is she more amusing?'

Nay again.

'Then *why* do you prefer her?' I cried with genuine vexation. 'Why do you love her better than you love me?'

He hesitated so long that I thought he would deny me a reason, and took hold of his poor finger again in order to make him answer. But before I could twist it he said: 'They cannot comprehend it. She, herself, does not. The word is at fault, that promiscuous word they apply to beasts and women and God – Love. She loves Linton as you would love a lap-dog, but I love her as we are supposed to love God. There, I can put it no better.' He gave an odd smile, then said: 'But I've the law on my side. I have a lien on her soul, and if she refuses to pay her debt to me in life I'll take possession after.'

It was the speech of a madman, and it roused me to fury. 'If you expect to make me jealous,' I scoffed, 'you must do better than that. I've no intention of entrusting you with my soul, Heathcliff. You'd only stake it on a throw at Hazard.'

'Make you jealous?' He seemed puzzled. 'Why should I wish to make *you* jealous?'

'Because we are alike,' I told him, worrying his finger again. 'We are both selfish, hard, immoral intriguers; and we belong together. Yet seemingly we must hurt each other. In your place I should use jealousy as my chief weapon, since it's easily the cruellest.'

'Let go,' he said, suddenly aware of my grip on his finger.

'No. I want to hurt you as you've hurt me.'

'Let go unless you wish me to strike you,' he growled, showing his fangs. 'Or is that what you're hoping for?'

I own it was. He was never more complaisant than when he had hurt me, and I had come to rely on the device of goading him to violence; though lately I was having to suffer more to win less. The game was hardly worth the candle.

'God, you're a cunning minx,' he said. 'You're to be pitied, Elizabeth, if you can find a fool to waste his pity on you.' And to demonstrate his contempt he swept me aside with his arm, so vigorously that I fell to the floor.

I was wary of him after that and for the next few days avoided him entirely. You will think this an uncommonly obscure remark, Lockwood, but I could not decide whether I loved him or hated him – love and hate are neighbours; one opens and the other closes the circle of our passions. And though he was without doubt the most brutal, ungenerous and selfish man I had ever known, he made all the others seem insipid by comparison. Several times during those weeks when I lived with him at Covent Garden I had it in mind to desert him – and there was opportunity enough – but each time the thought of his desolation prevented me. I could not bear to think of him friendless. I believe I was so foolish as to regard him in the light of an unlovely brute that, being spurned by the world, could no longer distinguish friend from foe and for self-preservation snapped at all who approached him. How wrong I was, you will learn in a moment.

23

By the end of the summer we had still received no indication that my husband knew we were in London. Our hosts, anxious to spare me embarrassment, avoided inviting Mr Durrant to their assemblies, and he was never once spoken of. Yet Heathcliff, at least, had made no secret of our residence at Covent Garden, and I was convinced that my husband had kept himself informed of every detail of our movements, preferring to hatch his revenge rather than act precipitately.

I was not greatly surprised, therefore, when a footman I had known at Hill Street called late one afternoon with a message for Heathcliff. I had been in my dressing room, and by the time I descended the servant was gone. But an excited gleam in Heathcliff's eyes informed me that something of moment had occurred.

'I saw him from the window,' I said. 'What did he want?'

'What I have wanted,' was the reply. 'A cordial invitation from one gentleman to another. Your husband has asked me to dine with him this evening.'

'Where?' was all I said.

Heathcliff grinned. 'At White's. And that is more than I'd hoped for.'

I stared at him incredulously. 'You're not mad enough to go? He's plotting something. I've been expecting it.'

'Do you think I have not?' said he. 'Don't waste your anxiety on me, Elizabeth. There are others who will need it more, I can promise you.'

I pressed him for an explanation of that remark, but he would not give one; though he assured me I should be given a full account of his evening when he returned. And having dressed himself with particular care, he quitted the house an hour later.

I waited for him until past two o'clock, then went to my bed in a state of great distraction. I don't know how long it was before I fell asleep.

The morning was well advanced when I awoke, and the absurd notion entered my head that I would never see Heathcliff again – as if by sleeping late I had permitted some calamity to overtake him, which by wakefulness I might have prevented. I hastened downstairs, very agitated, only to find Heathcliff sitting cheerfully at breakfast, some papers spread before him on the table. To my confusion he gave me an unusually hearty greeting and bid me take coffee with him. I had never seen him so animated and in such obvious good health. His eyes, though reddened with fatigue, seemed unnaturally lustrous; and his hand, I observed, was a good deal steadier than my own as he poured the beverage.

'I thought you were – ' I began, then stopped myself.

He shifted one of the pieces of paper as I seated myself, apparently fearful that I would spill coffee on it. 'That I was dead,' he supplied.

'I was about to say that I thought you were Fanny,' I said, reaching for a slice of toast. (Fanny was our maid-servant.) 'As for your being dead, Heathcliff, I gave you up at two o'clock and slept remarkably well afterwards. You advised me not to waste my anxiety on you, so I did not.'

'Bravo!' said he. 'If I believed you, I would congratulate you on having improved your weak character. Unfortunately, I suspect you were solicitous enough to sit half the night imagining any number of romantic deaths for me and fretting tearfully about each one. Notwithstanding your hard exterior, Elizabeth, you are pulp at the core, like all your kind. It will be interesting,' he continued, before I had time to bridle up at the insult, 'to see what your husband's heart is made of, when I reach it. I made a preliminary cut last night, I think, and met no obstruction. But I've some layers to go through yet.'

'Am I supposed to understand your metaphor?' I said, biting into my toast.

'You will when I explain it. And if you undertake not to interrupt I'll share my triumph with you now. But no protestations, if you please. No cries of "Outrage!" or "Unfair!" I want none of your hypocrisy.'

I shook my head, affecting nonchalance. In truth I was too intrigued by his exordium to wish to delay him.

'Very well,' he resumed. 'As you know, I dined with him last evening. At White's. What a shameless place that is, Elizabeth. It is your world in miniature, perfectly painted and without a sign of the inferior – any intrusion from my world would be a blemish. Indeed, had I not been your husband's guest, they would not have allowed me past the door; I'd have been considered too profane to enter that temple – for so it is, a temple dedicated to Fortune, and Mr Durrant must be one of its priests. They burn bank-notes for incense and their orisons are the odds at Hazard.' Here he laughed and shook his head. 'Well, at any rate, they know how to feed their members; which they must do, because once play has commenced none will quit the tables, and then sandwiches must suffice.

'After we had eaten an excellent meal, your husband came at last to the business. Perhaps the wine had put him in a mellow, reflective mood – he didn't bluster, but spoke very softly to me. To hear him, you'd have thought us old friends whom a respite from our affairs had brought together for the first time in a twelve-month. He told me how he'd extended his interests – it seems he owns half London now – and asked about my own fortunes. "It is plain that you've prospered," said he.

' "Then why inquire?" was my reply. "You are as well informed about me as I am myself. You must know I've been in Europe and that here in London I'm admitted to the best coteries, and that I win at cards. What more is there?"

' "How is Elizabeth?" He asked it almost with diffidence.

'I lied on purpose to vex him. I told him you were the most fascinating woman in creation, vivacious and charming as ever, and happy to be my mistress. I said all Europe had envied me and that you loved me more dearly than life. Ah, the expression on his face, Elizabeth. Pure greed, it was. I've seen men look so at a pile of gold on the baize. He fairly slavered as he pictured you, and there was bile in his mouth – I saw him swallow it with difficulty. God knows what he can see in you.

' "I appear to have misjudged you both," he said sadly. "I thought she would return to me after a week – not for my own sake, but because she would find life with you unendurable. But I forgot that you possessed the one commodity I could not buy her – youth. And you've shared it with her, seemingly. She must prize it even more highly than I imagined."

' "Come, Durrant," I interpolated. "You must own that I have made her love me."

' "Yes," he said, giving me a curious look, "that was my second error. I did not believe you cared to love or be loved, Heathcliff – or must I call you Linton?"

' "Heathcliff will do when we are alone."

' "No, let it be Linton. You've earned that privilege. Well, Mr Linton, you have proved yourself worthy of my respect. I thought you desired only wealth, but I begin to suspect there are no bounds to your ambition. You have become a gentleman and possess the most fitting adornment to a gentleman's life, Elizabeth Durrant. I made myself absurd, a figure of ridicule, to get and keep her. I laboured like Hercules to achieve my present position, whereas you – you won as much with minimal effort in half the time. I salute you."

' "Is that why you invited me here, Durrant?" I said then. "To salute me? Or will you seek to persuade me, by threats or entreaties, to return Elizabeth to you? If that be your plan, I advise you to abandon it. You are powerless to rob me of her. All London knows I'm living with your wife" – he winced at this – "and the very cause of your humiliation ensures my safety from your assassins. Besides, Elizabeth would resent you if you murdered me, and you'd lose the little affection she has retained for you."

'So eagerly did he swallow the hook, he nearly choked. A quantity of wine trickled from the corner of his mouth, and he leaned forward to hear more of that little affection. "She cares for me, then?" he breathed.

'I said: "She cares more for me, I assure you."

'He reflected a moment or two, then said: "What will you take to relinquish her and return to the north? You once told me you desired to be the first gentleman in Yorkshire. Well, I cannot make you that, but I can help you approach it. Two thousand pounds, sir. I'll give you two thousand – let it be guineas – if you'll go tomorrow. What do you say?"

'I laughed scornfully. "You put a low price on love, Mr Durrant," said I. "Nay, I have all I desire already, and you've just told me how valuable she is as an adornment. She is not for sale, sir."

' "Five thousand," said he between clenched teeth. "Damn you, you'll get no more out of me."

' "Cast your infernal gold into a warming-pan," was my answer, "and take it to bed with you." Are you not proud of me, Elizabeth? Did you think I loved you more than five thousand guineas? Well, your husband was as surprised as you are. His tongue froze in consequence, so that when I got to my feet he was obliged to grip my arm to prevent me from departing. "What?" I said. "Another offer?"

' "You like to gamble, do you not?" said he. "Gaming is not unknown here, Mr Linton, so it occurs to me that a little play might be a good way for us to forget our differences. Or settle them."

' "With all my heart," I replied. "I should enjoy nothing better than to relieve you of some cash, since you're so anxious to give it away."

'We repaired to the gaming room, a splendid saloon furnished only with chairs and baize-covered tables, but sumptuous in its decoration and blazing with hundreds of little tapers in crystal chandeliers. The room was less crowded then I'd expected – it was still early – there being a dozen fellows at cards and half that number dicing at a table marked for the purpose. All wore the vestments appropriate to their devotions – wide-brimmed hats adorned with flowers, and leather cuffs; some had their coats reversed and others had put on surtouts of coarse cloth, which must have stifled them. It's a strange ritual, is it not? But they serve a whimsical mistress in Fortune.

'Your husband suggesting Hazard, I agreed readily and was introduced to the dicing company. I forget their names, but one was heir to an earldom and two others were Honourables. Illustrious company, at any rate. I gave them the briefest of bows and scant attention. At one time I should have thought myself in heaven to have the chance of doing battle with gentlemen of the first rank; but last night I was loaded for fox, not grouse.

' "We are agreed upon a main of seven," announced one lisping macaroni, who was caster. "Is that acceptable to you, sirs?"

'We said it was, and play commenced. The fellow casting had abominable luck and a culpable ignorance of the odds that was matched only by the length of his purse. I bet consistently against him, winning a moderate amount, and your husband did likewise.

'Before long, however, the dice passed to another, who had better luck. He threw a nick too often for my liking, and I lost on his casting as much as I'd won on his predecessor's. So I was even. We were waging fifty pounds at a throw in table betting, the cup being still cold; I've heard of bets at White's made in tens of thousands in the hottest play, and of entire fortunes passing across the tables in a night. But I was prudent at first and hedged my bets, taking sixty pounds to thirty with your husband against my own table wager of fifty on the main; so that when the caster threw his chance, I won my sixty for the loss of but fifty.

'Mr Durrant paid me, saying: "The game is called Hazard, Mr Linton. It does not seem to me that you are prepared to hazard much."

' "You'll find I'm bolder on my own casting," was my reply. I had good reason to say it, too.

'Eventually the dice came to me. I threw six for my chance, which gave the company odds of six to five against me. Bets were laid accordingly – fifty here, an hundred from the lordling, nothing from your husband.

' "No wager from you, Mr Durrant?" I said. "The game is called Hazard."

' "So it is," says he, reaching into his pocket. He pulled out a paper and very slowly placed it within the circle. "That," he said, "is a note in the sum of two thousand pounds, Mr Linton. Will you agree to answer it?"

'I'd expected no less of him, Elizabeth. In his place I would have done the same. But you will appreciate my difficulty here. If I accepted his bet – and I could hardly do otherwise – I must lay down every penny I had in the world to answer the sum. So I hesitated.

' "I will withdraw the bet if you wish it," was your husband's comment, at which one of the fops playing with us murmured that he should. His meaning was plain. He thought the play was become too deep for me. Well, it suited me that they should all think so, and I did my best to make my hand quiver as I picked up the dice box and knocked it upon the table at your husband's note.

'At once Mr Durrant called for me to cover with a stake of my own, which drew an "Upon my soul, I thought you two was friends" from the macaroni. My response, however, was a nod. And taking up my purse, I flung it into the circle with your husband's note.

'But this did not satisfy him. "I doubt you have five hundred there, sir," said he. "I'd prefer a note of hand."

' "You've my word," I answered, enjoying myself hugely. "If the word of a gentleman is not sufficient for you, pray say so plainly."

'I watched him writhe, Elizabeth. He exercised masterly self-control, I'll allow, and every muscle in his face had work to do. But in the end he managed to subdue himself, and muttered some indistinct formula of appeasement.

'I picked up the dice and replaced them in the box. Then I shook the thing for fully half a minute before I cast.

'If I had not understood it hitherto, I discovered at that moment why gaming fascinates us so. There is an instant, as the dice roll, when your entire being seems concentrated into the compass of those two chance-tossed bones; you cease to be human and time cannot touch you; and what has always been of greatest importance in your life suddenly becomes irrelevant. Your very existence no longer matters, so intense is the experience. It is a little moment of death, Elizabeth, and nothing in life can exhilarate us like those little moments of death.

'Six was my chance. Six I got – two treys. I was not surprised, and I did not exult, but simply reached out to recover my winnings, which included a quantity of the others' gold as well as your husband's note. Mr Durrant's voice checked me, however.

' "Let it stand, Mr Linton," said he. "I doubt that you can repeat your chance on the next throw, and I'm willing to increase my stake on it if you'll agree."

'My response was unhesitating. "Do you have a sum in mind?" I inquired.

' "Five thousand."

' "Damme, I'll match that," cried another. "This is what I call play, sirs."

'I did not even glance at him. He did not exist for me. None of them existed save your precious husband. I swear I could smell his blood, Elizabeth. "I think not, Mr Durrant," I said deliberately.

'He showed some surprise, then quietly asked why I'd declined his bet.

' "Because the stake is insufficient," I answered. "I've a mind to be a landlord and would prefer that you wager certain of your properties instead of cash."

' "Ah," said he, "of course. And which of my houses do you covet, Mr Linton?" When I told him which ones I wanted he smiled broadly. "Those are my highest rents, sir. They are worth five thousand *per annum* to me. Do you expect me to risk them on a single throw of the dice?"

' "I do," I replied coolly. "I'll cover the bet with a property of my own. I've no need to name it. It is one you know well."

'I saw by his eyes that I had him. It's unmistakable, that gleam of cupidity. I fancy he could imagine you naked on the baize, Elizabeth – no, hold your tongue until I've finished; then you may say what you like. I assure you your husband saw nothing improper in my wager. His sole concern was to decide if he could trust me. "Is it that mare we discussed at dinner?" he inquired.

' "The same," I said. We'd impressed the company, it seemed. I heard one of the idiots say he'd like to see

230

the mare worth five thousand *per annum*, and another answer that he'd sell his entire stable for less. But they had the good sense to talk among themselves and did not intervene.

' "Agreed," said my adversary at last. "You've six to make. Pray cast the dice."

'It wanted a few minutes of nine o'clock, I think. What were you doing then, when your fate was being determined at a table in a gaming club? I spared you a thought, you may believe, as I shook the dice box. And how I shook it! The rest of them heard the rattle of bones, but I heard sweeter music. I'd tell you what I heard if I thought you'd comprehend it. No matter. I'll just say I cast the dice, knowing how they would fall even before they touched the table. One showed a four, the other a deuce.

'Your husband looked as if I'd shot him. His face was pained and grey, and it was all he could do to support himself in the chair. I needn't tell you why. The loss of a few houses meant nothing to him. But what he'd failed to win! Ah, I knew what he was suffering; I knew it intimately. And it made me glad to see *him* suffer so. I'd have sacrificed all I have in the world for the privilege. I made a wish then, Elizabeth. I wished I might have the pleasure one day of seeing that same look of anguish on two other faces – no, not pleasure, rapture. That I might know the bliss of causing it and be assured that they were aware I'd caused it. I'd expire fulfilled with such an assurance.

'But your husband is no believer in luck, it seems. Having taken a minute to recover his composure, he sprang to his feet and cried: "You've cheated me, damn you! You palmed the dice."

' "I think you are too fond of that mare, Mr Durrant," I said in a steady voice. "It has made you rash." I showed him my hands, then shook each of my sleeves to demonstrate that I had no concealed dice about me.

' "In your pocket, then," he groaned, near to weeping with frustration and rage.

' "I'll turn them out to humour you," said I calmly, "though I'd be justified in responding less charitably. No, better yet. The dice I threw are still upon the table. Cast them yourself, any number of times. If they're false you'll get six each time."

'This was acceptable to him. And after he'd thrown them four or five times, getting treys and fours and sixes, and once ames-ace, he mumbled a curse and, promising to send the deeds of my properties with a servant, quitted the room.

'I stayed through the night and squeezed the rest of them dry. Then I returned home, having had the most successful night of my life. Mr Durrant's man called an hour ago with these deeds. I shall be wealthy now, Elizabeth; as rich as I have always dreamed of being, and I did it in a single night. Do you think you can guess how it was managed?'

I could not say a word, Lockwood. I had listened to his madness without protest, but now that I had a chance to express my horror I found it impossible to speak.

'Then I'll answer for you,' said Heathcliff, grinning. 'You think I substituted a pair of fulhams, do you not? Well, I have them, that's true. I had them at White's, in my waistcoat-pocket. Two low men, contrived to fall a trey at every roll. I got them from a fellow in Newgate, and I've used them to advantage several times – they served me particularly well in Paris. But not yesternight. Nay, I had no need of them yesternight. I *knew* I could do no wrong at that table. It is uncanny, and I can't explain it. But I *knew*, as surely as if I'd been playing with the doctored pair. Here. Here they are in my pocket still.' He produced the things, though God knows what he thought to prove by it, and rolled them on the table. 'See – a pair of treys. Yet I swear I did not use them.'

I found my voice then, and very icy it was. 'Why bother to convince me of your probity?' I said. 'You are undoubtedly the most evil creature I have ever encountered, Heathcliff, and there can be no villainy you are incapable of. Indeed, I should have been better pleased to hear that the dice were not square; then you might have argued that I was never at risk. As it is, you've used me worse than a whore, and I'll never forgive you for it.'

To my amazement, he seemed puzzled by my outburst. 'Used you?' he repeated. 'How have I used you?'

'If wagering a person on a throw of the dice does not warrant the term,' I said angrily, 'I should like to know what does.'

He laughed, Lockwood. The fiend laughed. 'Oh, so that has offended you, has it? I forgot you've a woman's sensibilities, Elizabeth. Well, you were in no danger of being lost, I assure you. And if I'd thrown seven instead if six, why, I'd have paid your fool of a husband with my mare and let him bring suit to get his redress. Shall we have the coffee heated?'

'I see you now for what you are,' I said bitterly. 'God knows, it has taken me long enough. You, too, regard me as a property; only you have no love for your property and would willingly exchange it for a house, or a horse, or whatever your devilish ambition required. Beware, Heathcliff. This property has a will of its own and the power of movement. Do not be surprised if it chooses its next owner for itself.'

As soon as I'd said it, I wished I had not. I did not owe him the courtesy of a warning, and I could tell by his expression that I'd been unwise to give him one.

'I've not finished with you yet,' was his chilling reply, 'either of you. And until I have, I'll let you do nothing that might interfere with my plans.' A moment later he brightened. 'I have it,' he said. 'I'll celebrate my good fortune by taking you to buy a new gown.'

24

I had my new gown, but owed it not to any nascent spirit of kindness or generosity in Heathcliff; contrariwise, the prospect of wealth, and later its pursuit, made him more niggardly than ever. He would walk to inspect his new properties rather than hire a chair, stinted the housekeeper and checked her accounts like a common book-keeper, haggled with our servants over wages and with shopkeepers over prices, and generally earned himself a reputation for parsimony. When he spent freely it was to flaunt, which, paradoxically, he was fond of doing; formerly he had been content to establish the Linton character by insinuation; now he must flesh it, seemingly. But though he was unable to perceive it, the jest had become stale.

Once he evinced a signal prodigality. Two or three weeks after the incident I just described to you he decided that we must give a supper party of our own at Covent Garden – I had taught him that reciprocation is the essence of hospitality – and with characteristic single-mindedness he devoted himself to preparing for it. He had it in mind, I suspect, to be the talk of the Season. Every one of our hosts of the past months was to be invited, and no expense spared to provide them with an ambrosial repast. He supervised everything himself, calling on me whenever he doubted a particular – for all must be proper and according to the best custom. Thus we had six kinds of wine because I said one was not sufficient; and food for fifty, though only thirty were asked, because I remarked that a poor table was not genteel. I also expressed the hope that he would not bore the company in his usual manner with legal dissertations, but would rehearse himself in some lighter, more agreeable topics; and had the satisfaction later of seeing him pore over every newspaper and magazine he could find in search of titbits of gossip with which to spice his conversation.

I own it was with spiteful pleasure that I watched him receive our guests and commence to bludgeon each of them with his carefully prepared conversation, like a footpad waylaying travellers. How they writhed under his verbal assault, and how well-informed and interesting he considered himself. But it was a two-edged blade I'd forged, for the company's mortification soon became my own; while Heathcliff, aware only of his own brilliance, was too thick-skinned to notice what effect his soliloquy was having. Or, if he noticed, did not care. I had never known him so loquacious or so possessive, Lockwood. Everything was *his*, and had to be acknowledged as such. It was *my* food, and *my* wine and *my* house, and *my* good lady – as if he must establish his proprietorship of the very words in his mouth before he'd consent to release them.

It was all I could do to keep from falling to my knees in thanksgiving when the meal ended and the ladies withdrew. But a more subtle ordeal awaited me in the drawing-room.

'Mr Linton is an exceedingly well-informed gentleman,' remarked one lady, with a sigh of pity for her captive knight in the neighbouring room. 'A man with his fondness for conversation must find provincial living very dull.'

'Indeed,' ventured another, 'I have found it most restful to be relieved of the necessity to give my opinions; that can be quite irksome at assemblies. Talk gets terribly in the way of a good evening.'

This for an hour, and I dare say it would have been two but for the interruption. I heard the sound of raised voices, and that of the supper-room door being flung open. Glad of the excuse to quit the room, I hurried to investigate, and found Heathcliff in the hall, dragging one of our guests towards the street door. He'd made a wonderful choice, having no lesser person than a baronet by the scruff. Both were flushed with excessive drinking and exertion, though Heathcliff's must have been the stronger head, for he staggered less and spoke without slurring his words.

'This is *my* house,' he was saying (though he did not own a brick of it), 'and if you insult me in it you must expect to be thrown out.'

'Get your damned hands off me,' protested his victim. 'You'd need twice your strength to keep me *in* your infernal house.'

I opened my mouth to intervene, but Heathcliff gave me such a vicious look that I held my peace. 'There's a lesson in manners being given here,' was his boorish explanation. 'Why, he scratches like a lass. Did you see that, Elizabeth? My lady here has claws.' With that he applied his boot to the other's breeches and sent him out of the door.

It seemed I was to be spared no humiliation that night. Our guests had by now assembled in the hallway and were clearly preparing to depart, the incident having provided a welcome pretext. Heathcliff began to urge them back inside, saying there was no necessity for them to disturb themselves. He had redressed an insult and that was an end to the business.

It was an end to more than that, as he was to discover. Even while he was speaking, coats were sent for, excuses half-heartedly made; and I heard a few polite valedictory murmurings in my ear. The atmosphere reeked of commiseration.

Heathcliff began to comprehend what he had done. To my horror, he actually attempted to hold back the departing guests physically, by interposing himself with drunken gracelessness between them and the door; entreating them to stay for a hand or two at cards. 'You needn't fear my luck tonight,' he was saying. 'I'm well-bred enough to lose in my own house.'

The only reply he got was a request to stand aside, and the gentleman who uttered it came perilously close to having his ears boxed – Heathcliff raised his fist, but thankfully a moment's reflection convinced him of his error and he stood grudgingly aside.

A few minutes later he kicked the door shut behind the last of our visitors and turned his glare upon me. He was fetching his breath in gasps, like a man who has run a race. I knew the sign well. It signified a degree of violent passion that rendered him unfit for human society. Nothing would do while his mood lasted. He'd foam to hear reason and think conciliation a species of affront.

'I suppose you enjoyed that little farce, did you not, bitch?' was his challenge to me.

Accustomed to such refined language from him, I returned calmly: 'So I'm to pay, am I? Well, have no fear, Heathcliff. You've managed it beautifully. As long as I am associated with you, I shall share your disgrace and the ostracism that will inevitably accompany it.'

'What damned disgrace?' he mocked. 'I see no disgrace. Do you take me for some flutter-fingered molly to be devastated by a show of bad manners? They need your lessons more than I do. Nay, I'm just wondering what possessed me to endure them under my roof as long as I did. They're carrion. What passes for animation in them is nothing more than the twitching of dead muscles. They've poisoned my air.'

And pushing roughly past me, he staggered into the supper room, where I heard him throwing open the windows and crying 'Noxious!' like a madman. Truly I thought him insane, and wondered whether I should have to fetch help to get him to Bedlam before the night's end. His ravings were interrupted now and then by the discords of breaking china and glass – I assumed he was flinging the supper dishes against the walls. 'They're expensive to replace,' I called mockingly.

'My brass, i'n't it?' came the response, and emboldened by that much sanity, I ventured within.

He was in the act of battering a decanter of wine against the table, having cleared a space to serve him for an anvil by sacrificing half the supper things. The walls and carpet were hideously stained with wine and gravy; these dark splashes so strongly resembled blood that I had the impression of confronting an executioner in a slaughter-house, and gave a little shudder.

'You would do better to finish that work in the morning,' I suggested. 'You'll be fresher for it then.'

My sarcasm did not have the anticipated effect. Heathcliff put down the decanter and turned to look at me, but with a softer expression than I deserved at that moment. Perhaps the violence had soothed him as a child is often soothed by his tantrums. At any rate, he spoke almost gently.

'I'm fit to be humoured, am I?' he said with a little laugh. 'Aye, that's fair. But say no more to me tonight, lass. Your soft voice reminds me of *theirs*, and I can't guarantee your safety if I hear it again before the morrow.'

I had no intention of saying more to him, then or at any time. Nodding my assent, I led him quietly to bed.

Early next morning, while the villain still snored, I packed my few things and quitted his infernal house.

As you will appreciate, it was not an easy matter for me to decide where I should go. I considered Hill Street a poor refuge – it was the first place Heathcliff would hit upon his search for me (I never doubted that he'd pursue) – and I wasn't anxious to exchange one oppressive *régime*

239

for another. Nor could I venture very far, having little money, and he was acquainted with my London friends.

But it is not my nature to despair, and after meditating a while upon the problem I remembered that Charles Bassett's residence was unknown to Heathcliff. Accordingly, I made my way to his house in Hanover Square, only to learn there that Charles was gone to Heshton Manor in Buckinghamshire, for the coursing. That was Sir Thomas Wales's seat. I knew Sir Thomas slightly, and though in other circumstances I would not have been so forward as to present myself uninvited, I felt that my situation was sufficiently extreme to warrant the intrusion. I therefore took the next stagecoach into Buckinghamshire and arrived at Heshton late the same afternoon.

I have never received a warmer welcome in my life. So overcome was I with relief and joy to be among kind, sympathetic friends, that I wept in earnest. Being much comforted by the company – the house was full of cheerful guests – and restored by an excellent dinner, I then related my misfortunes to Charles, who promised that I should never again be troubled by Heathcliff or my husband if he could prevent it. And Sir Thomas assured me that I might stay as long as I pleased.

Thus began a blissful week of country diversions. Though autumn was well advanced, the days were still mild and we went coursing and purlieu hunting, our evenings being given over to dancing and the more refined pleasures. Once some villagers entertained us with a play, though that was somewhat spoiled for me by the resemblance one of the fellows bore to Heathcliff. I could not banish him from my thoughts, Lockwood, try as I might. His image obsessed me. In the woods I saw him behind every tree, every bush: a sudden rustle of leaves, a twig crackling – that, to my frenzied imagination, was Heathcliff lurking in the undergrowth.

In the house, particularly at night, I saw his face pressed against windows and heard him skulking about outside. I sensed his damnable presence everywhere. Charles made light of my fears, but I could not easily accept his assurances, knowing Heathcliff as I did. Obstacles that would deter ordinary men he would consider laughable, and I'd no more rely on his forbearance out of decency than I would expect a ravenous wolf to feed decorously at table.

One evening, as I was dancing a gavotte, I happened to glance towards the window and received the shock of seeing him peering in. His eyes glittered like a snake's in the reflected light, and I fancied I could make out his fangs, sharp and white against the glass. I gave such a startled shriek that the musicians ceased playing immediately; but when I was asked what had alarmed me I felt too foolish to name the intruder and merely said I'd seen a face at the window. A few of the men dashed outside at once, but though they searched the grounds for half an hour and even set the dogs loose, nothing was found. We'd had no rain for a day or two, or I'm certain they would have discovered footprints below the window.

The following day Charles took me riding. After a chilly night a mist had set in, which, there being no wind to disperse it, persisted throughout the forenoon. I should tell you that Heshton lies in a pretty village in the Chiltern Hills, bounded on either side by wooden slopes to which the mists often cling. In order to escape the disagreeably damp atmosphere of the park, therefore, we resolved to climb to higher ground, though this meant taking a rather treacherous path through the woods. I did not like it much. It was fetlock-deep in leaf-mould and very slippery in places. Yet I'd have been content had not the woods been so hushed and eerie. The mist had deadened all sounds, so that even our horses' snorting seemed subdued and their hooves muffled, like those of smugglers' beasts.

As there was not quite space enough for me to ride abreast of Charles in comfort, I kept behind him, and found myself unaccountably apprehensive in this station. Several times I turned in my saddle to look back, but each time I saw nothing, only the denser mist below.

The air was clear at the top. We rested our mounts after the long climb, then had a gallop at leisure for perhaps an hour, which warmed our animals nicely but left me anticipating a hot drink and the manor's cheerful fires.

'Is it possible to descend by a different way?' I inquired as Charles directed his horse towards that hateful path once more. His reply was a chuckle, and a promise that I should find it more agreeable going down, since a steep descent would get me sooner to a fireside. And it was steep, alarmingly so. Twice my pony stumbled and came close to unseating me before we had covered a quarter of the distance to the park. But at least the mist was tenuous now, though that was poor consolation, for it allowed me to imagine how far I would have to fall should I be thrown.

Suddenly Charles reined in his horse. Thinking he feared to get too far ahead of me, and desirous to evince some spirit, I brought my pony alongside of him. It was then that I saw what had arrested him.

Some yards below us a horseman had stationed himself athwart the path, on purpose to block it. He was barely distinguishable in the hazy atmosphere and looked, at that distance, an unearthly figure. The sight of him was enough to freeze the blood; but he did not freeze mine. I knew him. I knew him without having to see his face; and my certainty that it was Heathcliff, openly confronting us at last, relieved me of all terror. That must sound very strange, yet it is the truth. I'd feared him as a spectre, Lockwood, in the night: the idea of him, not his mortal flesh and bones.

'Are we to be robbed, do you think?' muttered my companion.

'*You* are,' said I. 'And it is *me* he intends to steal, Charles. That man is Heathcliff.'

Charles responded with an oath and urged his mount recklessly down the declivity. I followed at a more cautious pace.

Heathcliff it proved to be below. He sat motionless while we approached, and I observed as I came nearer that he carried a brace of pistols in holsters at his saddle, after the fashion of highwaymen. How cowardly I thought him to come armed when he must have guessed that my protector would be weaponless. The same notion had apparently occurred to Charles, for his first words to Heathcliff were: 'Do you intend to take Mrs Durrant from me by force?'

'I'll take her any way I must,' snarled Heathcliff. 'I've no honour, Bassett. Attempt to prevent me and I'll shoot you.'

'Then you're a contemptible coward as well as a scoundrel,' cried Charles. 'Mrs Durrant has informed me of your aspirations to gentility. Do you think you can be a gentleman without honour? Even that cut-throat husband of hers isn't totally regardless of it – forgive me, Elizabeth.'

'She owes me a debt,' said the other. 'I never fail to collect my debts.'

'I owe him nothing,' I interposed. 'Ride him down, Charles.'

Poor Charles seemed puzzled. 'Whatever the sum is,' he assured me, 'we'll settle it and be rid of him.'

This drew a laugh from Heathcliff. 'That is hardly possible,' was his comment, 'since the debt is herself.

Now, will you dismount, Elizabeth? I've no desire to be accused of horse-stealing.'

Instead of complying, I said to Charles: 'Are you just going to sit and do nothing? Ride him down as you would a common highwayman. He's no better than one.'

Charles appeared to consider this for a moment. Then he said: 'No, I'll not ride him down. But if he has bottom for it I'll gladly ride down against him.' He indicated the slope below us as he spoke. I saw Heathcliff's brow corrugate with suspicion, and he glanced down to measure the steepness. 'Well,' Charles taunted, 'is it too dangerous a course for you?'

Heathcliff grunted. 'So this is your notion of sport, is it?' he said. 'Why should I not simply take what I want?' Yet even as he said it he was turning his horse to face downhill.

'If I win,' said his adversary, 'will you agree never again to force your presence on Mrs Durrant?'

'Charles, that is absurd,' I said.

'Whisht! I'll give him my word. My word as an aspirant to gentility.'

'Charles, he's mocking you,' I cried. 'He'll try to kill you. You don't know him as I do.'

Heathcliff grinned. 'And you shall start us, Elizabeth. You'll enjoy that, won't you?'

I protested. I said it was madness, and refused to be a party to murder or self-murder. But I confess I felt a strange excitement at the prospect of such a contest.

'We need not race,' said Heathcliff slyly, 'if you'll undertake to return with me to London.'

'I'd sooner gallop to hell myself,' was my reply. And having delivered it, I raised my whip and, crying, 'Off!' brought it down viciously upon the flank of Heathcliff's beast.

My intention had been to startle the creature, so that it would throw its rider; but I had not taken into account the excellence of Heathcliff's horsemanship, and though the animal reared and looked in danger of falling, he managed to keep his seat. My action had given Charles the advantage, however, and he had disappeared into the mist with a start of several lengths by the time Heathcliff was able to follow. I heard the latter cursing his mount and hurling even more scurrilous imprecations back at me for spoiling his chance.

'He's your superior in everything, Mr Linton,' I yelled, then, laughing to myself, commenced my own descent. I went as quickly as I dared and halted often in order to listen. Though they were out of sight I could judge their progress by the sounds they made in their headlong career towards the park below: branches snapping and the muffled percussion of hooves; and once a shout – whether of dismay or triumph I couldn't tell; nor from which throat it issued. But it was followed not long after by an indescribable rending noise, and close on that a dreadful clamour compounded of human and animal cries of distress.

I do not exactly remember – or I would describe them – my feelings as I approached the scene of the disaster. I suppose I hoped to find Heathcliff its victim, but not dead or dying: a happier consequence would have been a sprained ankle or the like – as much, at any rate, as would teach him a little humility and send him home lamed from his pursuit. I believe I did not permit myself to contemplate the other possibility.

The calamity had occurred near the foot of the hill, where the path was narrowest and overgrown by brambles. I saw a fearful sight. To the left of the path, by a beech tree, one of the horses lay on its side, kicking feebly. Both the poor creature's forelegs appeared broken and its flank was horribly gashed. I recognized it at once as Charles's horse and surmised that the animal had collided with the tree, there being smears of blood on the trunk too. But at first, seeing no sign of its rider, I hoped he had been thrown to safety, and that I would find him dazed but unhurt behind a bush. I had no sooner framed this thought than I heard a groan from the far side of the beech, and, dismounting, hurried to investigate it.

I found them both there. Heathcliff, pistol in hand, was bending over Charles, who lay on his back among the leaves. A glance was sufficient to inform me that, far from having escaped harm, he was severely injured. His face was scratched raw by brambles and his left cheek, doubtless torn away by its contact with the rough bark of the tree, hung down to his jaw. But he had suffered an even more hideous wound. Through a rent in his breeches, two or three inches above the left knee, protruded a jagged end of bone. Fortunately, it seemed not to have pierced the femoral artery, though he'd lost a quantity of blood and might yet die of the injury if we did not soon get him to a surgeon.

I entreated Heathcliff to fetch his horse – it had wandered off – so that we might help Charles on to it and take him back to the house.

'We'll say he was thrown,' I promised. 'Your part in this need not be mentioned.'

'He's a fool,' said Heathcliff. 'I'd overtaken him and he chose this place to try to pass me. You think I forced him from the path, do you? Well, ask your honourable friend – he'll tell you the truth.'

'I don't care to apportion blame just now,' I snapped. 'Charles will die unless we help him to a surgeon immediately. His leg will mortify.'

'He's asked me to be his surgeon,' said Heathcliff, flourishing the pistol. 'If we move him we'll kill him in any case, and I intend to do as much for his horse.'

I saw Charles nod weakly. He was in too much pain to speak. 'You suggested it to him, I'll be bound,' said I sharply. 'Well, you may shoot the animal, Heathcliff, but you'll have to be content with that. Men are not brutes.'

'You needn't fear,' said Heathcliff. 'I'll not risk the gallows for him. But it's a distinction you must teach me someday, that between brutes and men. I've never had it clear in my mind.'

With that he stepped around the tree and fired a ball into the horse's brain.

25

Leaving my pony to find its own way home, we rode to the next town on Heathcliff's horse. There he hired a chaise to return us to London and sent back a surgeon to attend Charles. Poor Charles. Months later I learned what had become of him. The surgeon, fearing to wait, amputated his leg in the woods and afterwards conveyed him to Heshton, where, as soon as he was recovered, Charles took his own life. I wish I could be sure his death has been added to Heathcliff's black account – I, at least, held him responsible for it – but I happen to believe the wicked make their own rewards in life and laugh at eternity. Besides, Heathcliff must thrive in hell. Adversity always suited him. He seemed to draw his strength from it, as weeds are often nourished by rank soil which poisons worthier growths.

He certainly thrived in London that winter, though London had set its face against him. He had made himself an outcast by his churlish conduct – we might both have been lepers for all the company we got – but I alone suffered. He no longer cared what the world thought of him, and my mockery no longer touched him. I wept, I entreated, I reasoned, I threatened. He was stone. Once, when I asked him why, since he obviously did not value my society, he persisted in keeping me in his house, he said: 'I'm not sure of it myself. But I must have you here. It will not be for long.' I believe he regarded me as his talisman.

As first he would quit the house only for short periods, locking the doors and windows to incarcerate me. But soon, requiring to absent himself for longer spells, he

248

found another means to ensure that I did not wander. One afternoon he returned from one of his expeditions in an uncommonly bright mood. I was upstairs, but I could hear him laughing below and talking to another person. After a while he came to the foot of the stairs and called: 'Elizabeth, we have a visitor. There is a gentleman here who has expressed a desire to meet you. So take care to make yourself presentable before you come down.' You must appreciate, when I tell you this, that for weeks I had set eyes on no other human being – Heathcliff scarcely deserved the title. I could not believe my good fortune, therefore, and having devoted half an hour to my toilet – it would have been longer, but I was impatient – I descended, as elegant as I could make myself and with the highest expectations.

I have never been the victim of a viler trick. Heathcliff was nearly sick with laughter when I entered the room and at last beheld his 'gentleman', for I almost swooned at the sight of him. He was real, Lockwood, but you may have an idea of him if I say that my waking mind could not have imagined a more monstrous creature; only nightmare could have improved upon him. He stood at least six feet high, yet appeared squat, so gross were his proportions. And his face – that was as grotesque as any mask, being hideously scarred and set in such a grin that I wished never to see its frowning counterpart. His skull, hairless and mis-shapen as it was, might have been formed from a ball of wax left too long before the fire.

'This is Mr Twiss,' said Heathcliff, enjoying himself hugely. 'Lately in your husband's service, now in mine. Have you no greeting for him, Elizabeth? No matter. You'll have time enough to become acquainted with Twiss – he's an excellent fellow. He is to be your – what was that phrase? – your constant companion. Do you like her, Twiss?'

'She's a 'andsome woman,' was the reply. 'They said she was.'

'She has more talents than are evident in her face, Twiss. If you'll let her, she may amuse herself by exercising them upon you. Do you know how to read?'

The monster growled some incomprehensible reply. Heathcliff construed it as a negative, for he said: 'Splendid. Perhaps she'll teach you – after she's first made you suffer the torments of a goaded beast. Then it will be Latin and dancing lessons. And when she tires of you, she'll abandon you like an out-of-fashion bonnet. I wish you joy of her.'

Such was my introduction to Twiss. Thereafter, I saw more of him than I did of Heathcliff, who was rarely in the house, day or night. I neither knew nor desired to know where he went, but I doubted that it was honest work he did. The signs were familiar. He would talk to Twiss in whispers about his 'rents' and his 'customers', and count coin into the night, and lock away his papers in an iron strong-box, and keep loaded pistols by his bed. Sometimes he would be gone from the house three or four days together, and would return looking as if he'd not slept an hour in all that time. Yet he never yielded to exhaustion; fanaticism drove him too hard. When he did sleep it was restlessly. I stood at the door of his chamber one night and heard him mumbling in his sleep. Most of what he said was incoherent, but among the gibberish I distinguished the words: 'Not yet. Not enough yet.' It disquieted me. The unremitting force of his will always disquieted me.

Strangely, though I loathed him deeply, I never feared Twiss. Yet he was a savage man with a quicksilver temper; beside him Heathcliff could seem quite gracious and amiable. Soon after he came into the house I tried his mettle and was amused to discover that in taciturnity and gaucherie he surpassed even his master. I invited the brute to take tea with me one afternoon and tried to engage him in conversation, but without evoking any response save the noise of a pig at the trough. Eventually, tiring of the sport, I abandoned caution and said: 'Twiss, do you still owe any loyalty to my husband?'

'Said you'd try that,' was the clipped response.

'Who said I would try what?' I demanded, vexed by his disregard of pronouns.

He gave me a sour look. 'Don't waste your time. Sherall's done up, or soon will be.'

'I suppose Heathcliff pays you more,' I said.

'That's the one,' was his obscure reply. He wrenched his features into a smile. 'Aye, that one's a rum cove and knows a good man.'

Evidently this signified more than I supposed, for I got no further with my catechism. Whether gratitude, admiration or venality was the cause, his loyalty to his new master proved unquestionable, and I soon abandoned my attempts to subvert him.

I will not trouble you with an account of the wretched months that followed, except to say that after the servants deserted us I languished in that house with just its two brutish inhabitants for company and occupied myself with schemes of escape and revenge. None of them availed me. I was never allowed out of doors. By day Twiss kept watch over me and at night the doors and windows were locked, the keys being hung on a chain about his neck.

Then, one day at the beginning of summer, my ordeal came suddenly to an end. Heathcliff had been gaming all night in one of the hells, as was his custom – no decent house or club would admit him – and at about ten o'clock he returned, drunker than I had ever seen him, and with an odd expression on his face. I could not tell what it signified, but it was neither of his habitual moods – gloom or exultation – and I determined to keep out of his way. Drink usually had little effect on him, but when it did it invariably worsened a bad nature, so that at such times I would consider myself fortunate to avoid his blows, if not his insults. On this occasion, however, he surprised me by soliciting my company. He had something to tell me, he said; and dismissing Twiss, invited me to breakfast with him.

You will understand why I was wary, Lockwood. I had no idea what to expect and sat in silence waiting for him to speak. But he did not speak. I poured coffee for us and sipped at mine; his remained untouched. He just sat gazing at the table, as if this was some form of torture he had recently devised and wished to test on us both. When I inadvertently dropped my spoon into my cup he gave no sign of having heard the sound.

Finally, unable to stay quiet longer, I said: 'Heathcliff, if you have something to tell me, pray say it. God knows, you've never been garrulous, but you are excelling yourself this morning.'

He started out of his reverie, 'Oh, I forgot about you,' he said. 'You may go now. That is all I wish to say to you.'

His capricious humour made me peevish. I said: 'You did not seek my company simply to inform me that you've no desire for it. Unless the brandy has quite destroyed your wits. I've suffered more – '

'No, you fool,' he interrupted. 'I mean that you may get yourself out of my house. Go wherever you please, but do it quickly, before I decide to keep you for sport.'

Discretion urged me to go at once, without another word; curiosity and mistrust counselled otherwise.

'What are you plotting now, Heathcliff?' I demanded. 'I won't be tricked.'

His reply was almost gentle. 'I've ceased plotting, chuck,' he said. 'I no longer have anything to strive for. You're safe from me now, and you may inform your husband that I want nothing more from him.'

'You've succeeded in ruining him, then?'

He smiled. 'Alas, no. Though I came close. I have reasons of my own for desisting.' After a pause he added: 'Finish your breakfast first. You needn't fear that I'll change my mind.'

My manner belied my feelings as I chewed toast and drank off the last of my coffee. I was slow and leisurely in my movements, manifesting none of the agitation I felt, for I would not give him the satisfaction of seeing me scuttle away like a hare loosed from the jaws of a greyhound. He seemed unaware of me, however, and relapsed into his own meditations.

Just as I was about to push my chair back from the table he said: 'It is odd how a chance encounter can transform one's life.' I had the impression that he was talking to himself, that my presence in the room was irrelevant to him. But I stayed to listen. 'I met a fellow not two hours since,' he continued in the same distracted tone, 'who imparted a simple piece of gossip to me. To any other living person it would have been no more than that. Yet to me it was annihilation. It has rendered my life, my hopes, my plans – everything – quite meaningless. Do you not find that interesting, Elizabeth? You've cause to know how strong my will has always been. Well, it has evaporated. If you should choose to stab me to the heart with that knife, I doubt that I'd prevent you.'

He was pitiful. But I did not pity him. Instead, I was tempted to accept his challenge, and might have buried the knife in him had I not feared retribution from the law. Besides, I prefer more subtle means of laceration. I said: 'I find it interesting, Heathcliff, though impossible to believe. Have you discovered, at last, that human wishes are vain? I could have told you that. Any child knows it.'

'Nay,' he answered, 'this was merely a miscalculation. But it has cost me my existence. The irony of it is that had I not chosen to use the detestable name of Linton I'd be ignorant still.' He struck his head with his fist, exclaiming: 'The fool mistook me for him! He actually congratulated me on my marriage to Cathy!'

'Ah,' was all I said. He did not hear it.

'I had him almost throttled before they dragged me off. He'd read of it somewhere – in one of the Yorkshire journals, I imagine – and supposed – '

He broke off, suddenly aware that he had revealed too much.

I was smiling now, a smile of scorn and triumph mixed, such as only a woman's lips can form. Our nature arms us with it against men, as she provides the tigress with claws, and I see by your expression that you know it, Lockwood. 'Heathcliff,' I said, 'your simple item of gossip has delighted me beyond measure. To see you annihilated recompenses me for the misery you've caused me, and I thank you with all my heart for communicating your distress.'

'Do you think I care if you taunt me?' was his reply. 'It's your privilege. Exercise it all you will, but do so from a safe distance.'

'How fickle you are,' I laughed. 'You said I might stab you to the heart with impunity; and since *she* – Mrs Linton we must call her now – since she is at your heart, you can hardly blame me if I impale her too.'

'Take care,' said the stricken tyrant, controlling himself with difficulty. 'I told you I've no reason to continue living. I'd not scruple to make you her proxy and exact my due with less compunction for it. So go while you're still able.'

'I think it very mean of you,' I retorted, 'to deny me my little moment of pleasure. But I'll go, and gladly. First you'll hear this, Heathcliff. It's no gibe, but the truth.

'For three years you've struggled to make yourself a fit partner for your precious Cathy, and we both know how you have achieved your ends. Now you make the remarkable discovery that you've been sacrificing to a stone goddess, and you blame her, as if the fault were hers and not your own. She never did love you, Heathcliff. Yes, clench those fists of yours – I'll say this if you kill me for it. What has she ever done for you? *I* have saved your wretched life; *I* have given you an education; everything you have you owe to *me*. You should go on your knees to me, entreat me to forgive you; and I wish you would, so that I might respond by laughing in your face.'

A dangerous look had entered his eye, and, perceiving it, I retreated towards the door. 'Yet you say your existence is ended,' I continued. 'I own that surprises me. I would have prognosticated a different course for you. Knowing you as I do, I'd expect you to return tomorrow and play the ogre to Linton's knight, carrying the fair Cathy off to your lair – why, you could build a folly for the purpose, in the gothic manner – and incarcerate her there while you plotted her husband's ruin. I'm sure that would revivify you. And if you thought she'd tolerate you for a minute, I'm certain you'd do it.'

He advanced menacingly, but I already had the door open. 'You may keep my paltry wardrobe for Mrs Linton's use,' I flung at him as I prepared to make a hasty departure. 'My husband will supply me with a new one.'

I ran from the house as if a legion of devils were at my heels, for I considered my flight an escape from hell, and though my lungs were soon gorged with the unbearably sweet upper air, I neither stopped nor looked back.

26

It was two years since I had last seen my husband, and the alteration I found in him shocked me. Not only had he lost a deal of weight, but he seemed to have aged alarmingly. He appeared shrunken and abject, no longer filling his clothes, so that I received the impression of a frail old servant wearing the cast-offs of his sturdier master. In short, he had the look of a tired, defeated wretch.

You must not think me without pity when I tell you that I stiffened in his embrace and despised his welcoming tears. I felt compassion for him. But I found his ardour repugnant because those clinging arms were weak; they sought more comfort than they afforded; they did not satisfy my need, which was to be loved with a man's whole strength and to answer with all of mine. I have often wondered since what I wondered then – whether such a love is possible, untainted by idolatry or the jealousy of ownership. Mr Durrant never showed himself capable of it, and Heathcliff, it seemed, must be either master or slave in his loving; and he was the same in all his passions, the intermediate state being unendurable to him.

When he had done with fawning upon me, my husband fell to questioning me. His questions were puzzling, and he trembled as he asked them. Had Heathcliff treated me ill? Was I ever permitted out of doors? How had I contrived my escape?

I answered that I had not escaped but had been released, then asked Mr Durrant how he knew I'd been Heathcliff's prisoner and not a willing guest in his house.

'So the fiend didn't tell you,' was the reply. 'Then why do you imagine I never fetched you back? Why do you suppose I did not pull down his house brick by brick?'

'I supposed you thought I wished to be there,' I said truthfully.

'At first I did,' he owned. 'You went willingly, and I heard you were happy enough in Europe with him. Not a year ago I saw him at White's, and he informed me then that you were contentedly installed as the proud mistress of his house, that you loved him more than life and me considerably less. But to learn that you esteemed me at all gave me hope. I entreated the blackguard to return you to me, but he laughed at that; so I attempted to bribe him, thinking he loved gold more than he loved you and would gladly make such a bargain.'

'How much was your offer?' I asked.

'I forget the sum,' he said. 'At any rate, he refused it. Though I didn't know it then, he wanted every penny I possess, and had a scheme to get it.'

'Why didn't you offer him every penny, Alex?' I said teasingly. 'Am I not worth so much to you?'

'I know you too well,' said he. 'Had I impoverished myself in order to prise loose that damned leech, I hardly think you would have come back to me, Elizabeth. Besides, he would not be bribed. The largest part of his payment was not to be money at all, but my humiliation, my suffering. That same night he won some properties from me at Hazard – legitimate ones. And do you know what his stake was? You were his stake, my dear. Would you have loved him still if you'd known that?' When I made no reply he took a deep breath, then continued: 'I thought that was an end to his demands. I thought I should hear no more of him. Oh, I considered sending Haskell after him, but I still hoped you would return to me of your own accord and feared to destroy that hope by killing the villain. He'd said you loved him. So I held off. Did you, Elizabeth? Did you love him?'

'You seem to know that I was his prisoner, Alex,' I said. 'That should answer your question.'

'You were not his prisoner then,' said he. 'Or, if you were, I didn't know it. I decided to wait. I have ever won with patience what others have lost by precipitation. But again I made the error of underestimating that cunning devil. He should have been a general. We'd still have America. His first stratagem was to turn Twiss against me – you're acquainted with Twiss, I'll be bound. He managed that piece of work magnificently, Elizabeth, as I afterwards learned from the fellows he'd paid. They were a couple of St Giles ruffians he'd engaged to waylay Twiss, as if to assassinate him; which they must do crying "This is from Sherall!" – Heathcliff being close by to intervene and rout them. "He cannot afford to pay you, Twiss," says he afterwards, "and since he can no more afford to leave you at liberty to peach on him, this is how your employer has you dismissed." Twiss, having the wits of a stunned bull, not only believed his saviour but thereafter became his devoted slave – you'll have seen that for yourself, I don't doubt. Now do you begin to comprehend Heathcliff's intrigue?'

'It sounds worthy of you, dear Alex,' was my comment.

'Aye,' said he with a sigh, 'I was his mentor. I'll tell you what he did next, and we shall see how blithe you are when you've heard it. He came to me one day not long after, announcing that he was appointing himself my partner. Henceforward he would be Mr Halfshare – the jest pleased him vastly – and take half my profits. I pitied him. I thought him insane. But before I could send for Haskell to throw him out, he said: "Shall I tell you where Twiss is at this moment? He is holding a blade to your wife's throat and dreaming of the day I'll let him cut it.

258

I've fostered in him a prodigious hatred of you, Durrant, and her presence reminds him of your existence. Nothing keeps her breathing but my influence. And if I should fail to return he'll take even that for his signal" '

He looked expectantly at me, supposing I would be horrified by yet another instance of Heathcliff's depravity. I was not, and said as much. I was merely surprised that Heathcliff had neglected to inform me of my predicament, for it was unlike him to overlook an opportunity to gloat.

'I could do nothing but consent,' continued the weakling. 'Yet I knew half would not satisfy him, and I did not have long to wait before he attempted to seize the rest. He has all but ruined me, Elizabeth. I'm no pauper, but I am not respected as I was formerly, and to me that is ruin. Well, that was his first mistake – a ruined man fears nothing, not even death. And his second was to release you. Now I can replay him, which I intend to do by exchanging my life for his. That's a game he cannot cheat at.'

I reproved him for talking so wildly, arguing that he'd be doing Heathcliff a service if he killed him, the wretch having even less to lose by death than he had. But he was resolved and would not be dissuaded. I believe he wanted my approval, Lockwood. I neither gave it nor withheld it, but watched him load his pistols with a sneer on my lips.

'Who will murder him?' I asked. 'You or Haskell?'

'I'll not involve Haskell,' was his reply. 'Not in open murder.' Then, bidding me wait in the house, he kissed me – a clammy, loathsome kiss full on the mouth – and opened the door. He hesitated in the doorway, and said, without turning: 'I wish you to know that I have always loved you above everything, Elizabeth.'

'Then you should not have,' I rebuked him.

'No, I should not,' he allowed.

'Alex,' I called, as he walked into the hall, 'I do not intend to wait here meekly until you return from the wars.

Or until I'm brought news of your death. I've done with that. If you really are determined to kill Heathcliff, you must permit me to accompany you.'

'You'll not save him this time,' said he.

'I would not wish to,' I answered. 'But I find it difficult to regard your expedition in a serious light and must witness its conclusion for myself if I am to believe in it.'

That was the truth, too. I was in a very odd humour that day, as you must have surmised – perhaps it was the consequence of too great a draught of freedom, taken too quickly. I felt intoxicated. My husband's plan seemed slightly ludicrous, for although I did not entirely doubt that he was capable of fulfilling it, I couldn't imagine Heathcliff conniving at his own murder, however despondent he was.

It took us almost an hour to arrive at Covent Garden. It was an exceedingly hot day and many of the streets were blocked by carriages and by walkers airing themselves after breakfast. Conditions could hardly have been less favourable for a murder, a score of witnesses standing at every corner, but Mr Durrant appeared unperturbed and did not trouble to conceal his weapons as we mounted the steps to Heathcliff's house. Two chairmen, obliged to rest for the heat, glanced curiously at us, then stayed to watch with the air of spectators at a play.

My husband knocked loudly at the door and stood waiting with both his pistols cocked. It was then that I sobered. Such is the nature of a subtle mind that it is often blind to the merits of a simple design: I had not supposed he would dare to be so direct, or that being so, he would encounter no opposition.

'Alex,' I said, 'you cannot intend to shoot him as he opens the door?'

'Depend upon it,' was his disquieting reply. 'It is the way with wild beasts.'

'I forbid it,' I said. 'He is a man, not a beast – more of a man than you are. He would not kill in cold blood. Why do you not challenge him?'

He laughed. 'Because I should doubtless die without first obtaining the satisfaction of killing him. So you still love the wretch, do you? Despite what he has done to you.' He applied himself once more to the knocker, with greater force, then said: 'Perhaps if I'd treated you more harshly – '

I did not permit him to complete his sentence. Seized by a sudden terror at the thought of Heathcliff dead, and fancying that I could hear his step in the hall, I screamed: 'Heathcliff! He intends to murder you! Stay within!'

It was a foolish warning. I realized as soon as I'd uttered it that no other words – save 'Cathy is here' – could have produced him more readily. But it was too late. The door was already opened and Heathcliff stood there, in his shirt and unarmed. He seemed confused, though his glance went immediately to the pistols, but unafraid. I doubt that his facial muscles were capable of expressing fear. My conjecture was that he had been dozing; and, hearing a knocking at the door, had so far forgot caution. in his drowsy state that he answered it without thinking to take up a weapon. His confusion lasted only an instant, however. He smiled wryly, and said: 'So I'm to be executed a second time before half London, am I?'

I had become aware of the crowd gathering in the street behind us, but dared not turn to look. I half believed that the force of my will had prevented my husband from discharging his pistols, though it seemed more likely that he was relishing his moment of power over his enemy. Yet his expression was not triumphant, nor even malevolent, but composed: as if he were the victim rather than the executioner.

'Do not mistake my hesitation for cowardice,' said Mr Durrant calmly. 'I planned to shoot you on sight, as I would a mad dog; as you deserve. But seemingly my wife persists in loving you, and I wish her to be convinced before I kill you that you have never cared for her. She must hear it from your own lips, Heathcliff, or her hatred will pursue me into the grave, and I could not bear it for eternity.'

'Is the fool appealing to my sense of honour?' said Heathcliff with derision. 'He is about to send me to hell, yet he expects that out of pure charity I'll first save *him* from its torments. I'll laugh if you'll give me time. Nay, the truth is that next to another, whom I've lost now, I love Elizabeth better than I love any human being. She has divined my feelings for her, it seems, though I don't show them. Now, dispatch me. We'll continue our quarrel when we meet below.'

Even while he was speaking this last sentence I had interposed myself between the two of them. Oh, don't take me for a complete idiot, Lockwood. Heathcliff's declaration had not deluded me. But I believed that loveless creature when he said that next to Cathy Linton he loved me best in the world. And though it was not worth much, I would not see him killed for saying it.

'I've contrived a dilemma for you, Alex,' I said, vainly attempting to cover Heathcliff's body with my own smaller one. 'You must either kill me or spare Heathcliff. Or do nothing at all.'

'You'll spoil her dress if you shoot her, Durrant,' laughed Heathcliff from behind me. 'For that she would never forgive you. I'd retire if I were you, before that mob yonder begins to pelt you.'

He should have known better than to taunt my husband just then. With a cry of rage the desperate creature flung himself at us. I believed for an instant that he'd elected to kill us both, but his business with me was brief. Pushing me roughly aside with his shoulder, he thrust his pistols towards Heathcliff's head, and would have fired then had his enemy remained there.

But the other had been too quick for him. Having ducked, he now sprang forward and, grasping Mr Durrant by the forearms, used his superior strength to twist the limbs outwards. One of the pistols fell, striking the stone door-step, and exploded harmlessly. The other they grappled for.

In the ordinary way my husband would have been no match for Heathcliff, but his fury and determination had lent him a madman's strength, and he pressed his larger opponent hard. Helpless to assist, I entreated the chairmen to intervene. Their response was to lay wagers – they were enjoying the spectacle too much to desire a premature conclusion.

The struggle was equal for a minute or two, until, with a sudden wrench, Heathcliff brought my husband's wrist into violent contact with the edge of the door-frame. He grunted, but kept his grip on the pistol. Again Heathcliff dashed the wrist against the frame, as if determined to break one or the other. The pistol slipped from Mr Durrant's grasp then, and fell without discharging. Tearing himself free of Heathcliff's grip, the other leapt to retrieve it, and had his fingers closed around its butt when the younger man's kick struck him exactly in the teeth, with force enough to send him half-way down the steps. He groaned and choked, and seemed finished. But he was not finished. I had never ascribed as much spirit to him as he showed next. His mouth was all blood; yet I imagined that I saw him smile as with both hands he raised the weapon – he'd retained his hold of it even in his fall – and managing its weight with difficulty in his dazed and weakened condition, aimed it at Heathcliff. He, to his credit, did not flinch; and when, a moment later, the shot was fired, an expression of moderate surprise was all I perceived in his face.

My husband fell forward, a bullet having entered his back and penetrated to the heart. He died quickly, but I have always believed there must have been a final instant of sensibility when his physical suffering was less intense than his mental anguish; and that I regret, though I cannot say I am sorry he died.

His assassin, you will have surmised, was Twiss. That monster we had all forgot. He'd been out of the house an hour, and, returning, had seized his chance to repay both his old master and his new, one with death and the other with self-sacrifice – for he was subsequently hanged.

'We should be content, you and I,' said Heathcliff, as we watched Twiss taken away by the constables. 'We both have what we wanted from him. I have a good part of his money and you'll find you are far from destitute. Are you happy? Will you buy yourself another Bassett, Elizabeth?'

'Will you buy another Cathy?' I returned. 'You are a worse hypocrite than that man you destroyed.' I indicated my husband's corpse, which still lay on the pavement.

'Nay,' said he, 'but I'll see her face once more, when I can summon the spirit for it. I'm compelled to do that much. You would not understand it, though *he* would – that wretch understood it too well. And I've still a score to settle in Yorkshire. You will not be troubled with me again.'

'When Mrs Linton rejects you,' I said spitefully, 'do not expect to find me at Hill Street. You must come seeking me, Heathcliff, if you wish to win me back. And be sure to do it on your knees.'

He laughed. 'You have my solemn promise, Elizabeth,' was his answer, 'that if ever I come seeking you it will be on my knees.'

He said nothing more to me, but went into the house. I did not see him again. Later that summer I moved here, and here I have lived since, Lockwood. Now you can imagine my feelings yesterday, when you spoke his name to me. I have not heard that name for twenty years.

'How did you know that he returned to Wuthering Heights?' I inquired.

'I did not encounter that name until I read his letter yesterday,' was Mrs Durrant's answer. 'But I assumed he would see *her* once more. I had never known him to conceive a plan which he failed to fulfil. *Did* he steal her away from her lawful husband? I have always supposed that he did.'

'Not exactly,' was my careful reply. 'At first his intentions were those he confided to you, or so the person who told me his history would have me believe – Heathcliff referred to her as Nelly in his letter. But your account has inclined me to a different opinion; namely, that he planned his later life while he was here, in London. At any rate, he waited until the September of 1783 before going back into Yorkshire.' Here I hesitated, then said, rather artfully: 'But it is a long tale, and if you will permit me I will leave it for another day.'

'Unfair, Lockwood,' she laughed. 'You are right, however. It is late. You must tell me one thing now, though, and tomorrow I expect to be supplied with the rest. I will not have it deferred longer.'

'Your servant,' said I.

'Did she tolerate him or did she despise him? I refuse to wait. You will answer that now.'

'Neither,' was my circumspect reply.

'Then she was indifferent to him?'

'If you will allow me to say it,' I remarked, 'your manner suggests a somewhat higher regard for Heathcliff than your words have signified.'

'I think you very impertinent to say it,' she said, 'but since you have already said it I can only reply that women regard such rogues very much as men do whores: they are fun, but it would be unthinkable to marry one.'

I took my leave shortly after, and have been to Grosvenor Square twice since. Like the sultana in Galland's book, I have stretched a tale to serve my own ends, contriving to tell a little each day, and that little much embellished, in the hope that the musician will eventually prove more interesting than his music. I believe I have cause to be hopeful. Though a woman of mature years, Mrs Durrant has all the vigour of youth and a penchant for younger men; I fancy she would welcome an *amour* with the right gentleman, and am resolved to be more forward with her than has hitherto been my practice. She appreciates directness.

Yesterday, employing Mrs Dean's words when I could remember them and my own when I could not, I completed my account of Heathcliff's early life, taking him as far as 1780. I related the events which occasioned his departure from Wuthering Heights, and today I must tread cautiously. It vexes me that she should be so jealous of Catherine Earnshaw (now Catherine Linton), for I can hardly be faithful to Mrs Dean's version of the tale without distressing her with every sentence. Yet it is impossible to falsify and be consistent; and deuced difficult to omit a story's substance and still preserve its integrity.

I curse them upon waking and upon retiring – Lintons and Earnshaws, Heathcliff and Cathy. Confound them all!

Perhaps I'll attempt to distract her with a kiss.

I wish with all my heart I had met Elizabeth in any other capacity than as an editor.

Forgiving
LaVyrle Spencer

A magical new novel in the glorious Spencer tradition.

It is 1876 and young Sarah Merritt is a woman with a mission: to set up the only newspaper in the dusty gold-rush town of Deadwood, Dakota. But determined Sarah hasn't reckoned on the rawness of the town, or of its people, and she soon finds herself at loggerheads with the headstrong and arrogant local sheriff, Noah Campbell.

Enemies can be friends in the face of adversity, and when Noah discovers Sarah is also in Deadwood to find her sister Adelaide, he vows to help her. For Addie is working as an 'upstairs girl' in the bordello of Mrs Hossiter . . .

ISBN 0 586 21324 4

The Homecoming
Mary Lide

A sweeping story of first love and forbidden passion set among the moody wilds of Cornwall.

In the fading years of the last century, young Guinevere Ellis falls heartbreakingly in love with Julian, son of the local gentry. To the fatherless girl, he embodies all the strengths, all the courtesy of a world out of her reach, and brings a hope and a promise which is to change her life.

Her quest for a future leads her into a quest for the past – for a father whom she had never known, and an understanding of a mother whose history foreshadows her own.

A Killing Kindness
Reginald Hill

'One of Mr Hill's best.' *Financial Times*

Who was the Shakespearean strangler?

When Mary Dinwoodie was found choked in a ditch following a night out with her boyfriend, a mysterious night caller phoned the local paper with a quotation from *Hamlet*.

The career of the Yorkshire Choker was underway.

If Detective-Superintendent Dalziel was unimpressed by the literary phone calls, he was downright angry when Sergeant Wield called in a clairvoyant.

Linguists, psychiatrists, mediums – it was all a load of bloody nonsense as far as he was concerned, designed to make fools of him and his department.

And meanwhile the Choker struck again – and again . . .

'Reginald Hill's stories must certainly be among the best now being written, and with each successive book he seems to be widening his range.' *Times Literary Supplement*

'All the fun of the fair and the fizz of the fuzz . . . Spin-drier revolutions before a plausible motive takes shape.' *Observer*

'Hill has the gift of constant surprise.' *The Times*

ISBN 0 586 07251 9

Frost Dancers
A Story of Hares
Garry Kilworth

Amongst the gorse and the heathers of his native highlands, Skelter the mountain hare enjoyed an idyllic life: browsing and gambolling; taking in the superb scenery and making female friends, including the beautiful Rushie. Then one day Skelter's life of ease came to an abrupt end. Netted and captured, he and several other hares are transported hundreds of miles, to the strange lands of the south, destined for the cruel sport of hare coursing. Amidst a hell of shouting men and howling greyhounds, Skelter witnesses a nightmare, before making a miraculous escape.

Alone, stranded in a landscape he does not understand Skelter must learn to survive, despite the hostility and distrust of the local hares and other natural hazards.

By far the most horrifying peril that faces Skelter is the *flogre*: a vast, flying monster which is terrorising the countryside, killing indiscriminately.

Raised in isolation by a man, thousands of miles from his native habitat, Bubba is a killer more terrifying than any natural creature: for he believes himself human. Can one small mountain hare survive against such a monster?

ISBN 0 586 21463 1